FATALE

By

Lewlin Chard

About the Author

Born in London, Lewlin Chard has lived and worked in Great Britain, France, Portugal, USA and the Middle East, and now shares residence between Devon, England, and the Algarve, Portugal.

Other novels by the same author include The Angela Tapes, Taint, Long Con, Relative atonement and Missing Persons.

Acknowledgements

With thanks to Eva Cahill, Elane Harvey, and Megan Ashworth-Jones, without whose assistance and encouragement this publication would not have been possible.

FATALE

By

Lewlin Chard

Chapter One

The woman left the cinema, blinked in the low, late mid October sunlight and sought her sunglasses.

Already people were arriving for the next performance, milling by the entrance. She preferred the earlier programme; it was rarely more than a quarter full. Film, to her, was an art form and the cinema akin to a church and she deplored even the slightest noise from others once the programme had commenced. It had been a good film, French: a country whose cinema industry she considered a bulwark to Hollywood's output of crass rubbish. Not that America didn't make good films, it did, and when they were good they could be very good indeed, and she was ready to concede that half of the films made by the French industry were trivia for home consumption, but in general her opinion was that the bias was on the European side of the Atlantic.

She was a woman who could be passionate about subjects that mattered to her, including some, she was prepared to admit, that were not always logical. Parking was one of the more illogical ones, and if it could possibly be avoided she refused to pay to park her car. It wasn't that she couldn't afford to pay; it was that it just rankled her to do so. To this end she sought out back streets that allowed free parking, even, as on this occasion, it meant a ten-minute walk. The exercise was good for her she reasoned; besides the weather was unseasonably clement and the route took her along part of the city she particularly liked. Three storey Neo-Georgian town houses to one side, the park with its cast iron railings protecting the unwary from the sudden drop to where ancient catacombs lay on the other.

The tight skirt and four inch heels might not be conducive for a half-mile walk but she was in no hurry. The recriminations that awaited her at home offered little incentive.

A car rounded a bend cautiously, from the direction she was walking, and from the way it slowed down as it neared her she anticipated that she was going to be asked the directions to somewhere or the other. The window slid down and the driver leaned across the passenger seat and asked if she knew where the Albion hotel was situated. As she had no recourse to use hotels in the city she had no idea – true they sometimes had visitors to the plant but when that happened she left it up to one of the secretaries to make arrangements. Sorry, she said, then pointing back towards the cinema suggested that he ask someone there.

The man held her eye for a second before thanking her with a smile and driving off.

The woman resumed walking. The man's smile and voice remained with her. He was of an age and had had the type of looks and appearance that attracted her: well dressed, early-thirties, clean-shaven, fair wavy hair. Some sort of businessman she guessed. A few minutes later, as she made to cross the road, the car passed, returning in the direction it had originally come from. It halted at traffic lights and as she passed she couldn't resist the urge to look in. The man looked back at her and lowered the window. "I've found out where the Albion hotel is," he said and smiled his smile again. "Would you like to come and see it?"

It was as blatant a pick-up as one could imagine. Everything in the woman's assessment of the situation and social upbringing told her to ignore the solicitation. Except - as on other occasions, when she had been similarly approached by someone who attracted her - when it came to the point she thought 'Why not?'. And besides it would provide a pleasant interlude to the crises she was facing. So, without any further hesitation, she got into the car.

The man made no effort to introduce himself and the woman felt no compunction to volunteer her name. As they drove he mentioned something about having been guided to a meeting with a colleague that morning but returning on his own couldn't remember exactly what the route had been. The woman wasn't listening that attentively, all she was aware of was the anticipation of what was to come and the racing of her heart. It never failed to excite her. The unknown. The man lapsed into silence.

The hotel was a modern three storey building situated on the edge of the city. They drove to the rear and parked near an entrance with a sign above it proclaiming the legend, Starlight Bar. Was he contemplating a pre-emptive drink, the woman wondered a little disconcerted? Alcohol had not been on her anticipated agenda. But the man escorted her through the glass panelled entrance and instead of proceeding to the heavy plush door that led to the bar he guided her in the direction of a corridor, off which was a stairway leading to the hotel rooms. On the second floor he led her to room 209 and produced the key. She presumed he hadn't handed it in to the reception that morning. He opened the door and they went in. It was a standard international, mid bracket hotel room: double bed, mirrored fitted wardrobe, easy chair, coffee table, dressing table with a stool beneath, and a pair of scenic prints on the wall. Through its open door she could see that the bathroom's decor was to the same intrinsic standard. The man threw his jacket on to the chair and removed his tie. They faced one another. Neither spoke.

When she thought of it afterwards, minutely analysed each moment, her complete abandonment, as opposed to the wanton impetuousness of allowing herself to be casually picked-up, began the moment his fingers touched her bare arms. A simple caress of fingertips that heightened the response of her nerve ends and caused an ecstatic tremble to traverse the whole of her body. A reaction engendered by a heightening of the senses: body language, smell, animal magnetism, a chemical reaction? Something like that she supposed, although what she was experiencing wasn't part of the syllabus when she was studying for her degree. The one thing she was certain of was that if he had asked her there and then to go with him, leave family, home, career and responsibilities, she would have done so without a moment's hesitation.

The same fingertips had brushed against her breasts as he unbuttoned her blouse, against her hips and thighs as her skirt was unzipped and slid to the floor. Half naked she had received his kiss upon the lips. Nothing was hurried. During the prolonged embrace he had removed the remainder of her clothes and then laid her on the bed. She had watched as he took off his own clothes. He smelt of soap and cologne and his body had been hard to the touch. They had blended into a slow, exquisite exploration of one another. The surrender to stimulation had been mutual; his arousal had been as intense as hers, of that she was sure – she was an experienced woman and she knew no man was capable of simulating the responses she had felt and sensed. The languid tempo was maintained after he entered her, allowing each new sensation eclipse the other. When she felt the commencement of her orgasm it was if he had sensed it too. There was an increase in his tempo, he pushed deeper. He filled her. She felt his hands cup her face, and when she opened her eyes she saw that he was looking down on her, his intense stare holding her mesmerized. It couldn't be possible but she could swear he was growing even larger within her. Then the hands were around her neck, but she was lost to an all-encompassing sensation, and was oblivious to the increase of their pressure. Her last recollection was a look of bewildered surprise on his face.

Then the little death and blackness.

Chapter Two

Without opening her eyes she gradually became aware that she was in a hospital: a sequence of sounds and smell unique to a hospital ward. Then, before she could lift her eyelids and confirm the deduction, sleep once again took precedence.

A nurse's voice finally brought her to full consciousness; an precautionary enquiry to ascertain that she was awake, combined with a suggestion that she didn't speak but just moved her head in reply.

"Your throat is quite severely bruised, best to save it until the doctor comes to see you." The woman instinctively moved a hand to her throat and tentatively felt it with her fingers: it was tender to the touch and sore when she swallowed.

She opened her eyes. Although a screen surrounded her bed it wasn't sufficient to block the sunlight that filled the ward. Two nurses were in attendance. She returned a nod of confirmation – something in itself that seemed to satisfy them – and then she was helped to sit up in bed and her temperature and pulse checked. One of the nurses left and the woman mimed to the one that remained that she would like something to drink. She was told that she would have to wait until the doctor had seen her, but the nurse did produce a moist sponge and dampened her lips. The doctor arrived a few minutes later. He examined her throat and then ran through a number of tests to ascertain the state of her reflexes. He was of dark complexion with black tightly curled hair, and although his voice was middle-class English and without the trace of a foreign accent, the woman surmised that his ancestry was Middle Eastern. He also seemed ridiculously young. The attendant nurse poured a glass of water and handed it to him. He held it to her lips, allowing only a small trickle into her mouth, and watched her swallow the liquid. He asked if she wanted more. She nodded and he allowed her hand to accompany his on the glass – she observed the abundance of hair on his hand and wrist and his watch revealed that it was seven minutes past ten o'clock. "Just a little at a time," he warned. When she had swallowed half the contents of the glass he asked if she could tell him her name? "In your own time. If it hurts too much just shake your head."

"Sha .." Her throat constricted. She held up her hand to silence any censure, waited a moment then tried again. "Sharon." It was a bit of a croaky whisper but not unbearably painful. "Sharon Greaves."

"And your date of birth, Sharon?"

"Twelfth September nineteen sixty-six," came the unhesitant whisper.

The doctor nodded his head. "Good," he said and then busied himself adding some notes to her file. When they were completed he returned his attention to her. "Well, Sharon you've been very lucky, the timely discovery by one of the hotel maids makes it look as if you're going to get away with nothing more than a sore throat. There is some damage to your voice box but that will right itself in time, provided you don't do anything silly like screaming or Louis Armstrong impressions, and although there was some initial restriction of oxygen to the brain, due to the skill of the paramedics who answered the emergency call it doesn't appear to have resulted in any permanent damage.

You owe your life to them, together with the maid who found you." Then after a moments hesitation he added, "And presumably an inefficient strangler."

Sharon nodded her head in appreciation. That she didn't make any verbal comment was attributed to the painfulness she still experienced in using her voice.

"Your husband will be relieved, he's waiting to see you." Sharon Greaves expression indicated that she might not wish to see him. The doctor, cognizant of the factors surrounding his patient's admittance into the hospital, added; "However I feel that over use of your voice at this juncture might cause irreparable damage to your vocal cords and my advice would be to wait another twenty-four hours before speaking with him. Would you prefer that?"

Sharon nodded in relieved agreement.

"But there is a detective sergeant waiting to speak with you and I'm not so sure he can be put off until tomorrow. I can ask for the interview to be delayed until later this afternoon."

"Please," Sharon mouthed.

"One other thing," the doctor said as he was about to leave, "Do you like ice-cream?"

Sharon nodded in surprised affirmation.

"That's good, because in my opinion it's still the best remedy for a sore throat."

Eight hours, and three substantial helpings of ice cream later, and after the screen had been once more discretely drawn, Detective Sergeant Andrew Latimer was seated beside Sharon's bed. He was a sturdily built man, beginning to go to fat, with a pleasant face. Sharon gauged his age as being a couple of years senior to her own. A uniformed WPC sat by the door.

DS Latimer said, "I understand that speaking is still a bit painful for you, Mrs Greaves, so I'll tell you what we know already and then we can proceed from there." His voice retained a pleasant Devonian accent. He opened a notebook. "You were found naked and unconscious in room 209 in the Devonshire Hotel. There were signs of sexual intercourse having occurred. Your handbag and purse, containing over sixty pounds, were still there, which indicates that the attack on your person wasn't motivated by robbery. From the contents we were able to ascertain your name and personal details." He extracted a small crocodile-skin handbag from a plastic shopping bag and handed it to Sharon. "Can you examine it and confirm that nothing has been taken?"

Sharon checked through the contents and nodded.

Latimer returned to his notes. "No one was registered as being booked into the room; in fact that whole wing of the hotel is closed for refurbishment."

The detective looked up, Sharon Greaves made no sign of comment so he continued. "I will try and keep my questions as succinct as possible and if you prefer you can answer by a nod or shake of your head. Okay?"

Sharon nodded.

"Is the man who raped and attacked you, known to you?"

Sharon shook her head vigorously and motioned the detective to come closer. "I wasn't raped," she whispered.

"Oh, I see, so the man is known to you?"

"No," Sharon mouthed.

"Did he tell you anything about himself? Did he give a name?"

A negative shake of her head.

DS Latimer looked perplexed. "How long had you known him? Where did you meet?"

Sharon motioned and the detective leaned forward again.

"He picked me up and suggested I go back to his hotel. We didn't really speak much." Her voice had become a little stronger and clearer. It was an educated voice.

"Do you remember what make of car he drove or it's registration number?"

"Neither, just an ordinary car, blue I think, the type of car you hire."

Or peasants like me drive, Andy Latimer thought. He said, "Can you give me a description of the man? Age, height, colouring, voice?"

Sharon Greaves answered, "Caucasian, early thirties, well dressed. He was tallish, attractive with fair wavy hair. There was a slight accent, could have been American."

She stopped to pour and drink a glass of water. "He was in very good physical condition," she added.

Sharon's candour disconcerted Andy Latimer; he didn't know whether to be censorious, or to smile.

"Let me get this clear, you get picked up by a stranger, other than suggesting that you go to a hotel room with him you don't speak, and then you have sex with him?"

"Yes."

Recalling an extract from a book his ex-wife had once read out to him, Latimer said, "Zipless sex in fact."

Sharon nodded, then said, "Erica Jong, Fear of Flying." She smiled in reflection and said, "The most perfect zipless fuck." There was a muted cough of laughter from the WPC, and

Andy Latimer couldn't restrain a smile. Then remembering the gravity of the incident he said soberly,

"Well not quite, I don't recall anyone in Ms Jong's novel succumbing to attempted murder."

He was guessing here, having never actually read the book. Sharon Greaves looked bemused, as if this aspect of the encounter hadn't occurred to her. The doctor had indicated to him that Mrs Greaves hadn't seemed too thrilled at the thought of seeing her husband. Intuitively he asked,

"Are you in the habit of having sex with strange men?"

Sharon returned a candid shrug.

"Only this time it was a bit of rough sex that got more than a little out of hand?"

Sharon's eyebrows shot up and she opened her mouth as if about to vehemently deny the accusation. Then she hesitated, and just as quickly closed her mouth and lowered her eyes.

Latimer took this deflation as a sign of resigned realisation. He said, "As soon as you're discharged, Mrs Greaves, I would like you to come into the station and look at some photographs of faces.

"Also to talk with one of our artists so that an E-fit can be compiled.

"Did he use a condom?"

Sharon nodded.

"Well he had the good sense to take it with him, so it's highly likely that the man who attacked you has done this type of thing before. And he knew about the room being vacant for refurbishment, so he might well have stayed in the hotel recently."

The room had been dusted for fingerprints but what were found hadn't matched any on record, and Latimer suspected that the case wouldn't be given sufficient importance to warrant the manpower necessary to trace and check those of clients and staff who had passed through the room. No one had actually been killed, and all probability the attacker had wiped the room before leaving in any case. But he didn't impart this to Sharon Greaves.

"The sooner you can make yourself available the better, while it's still fresh in your mind. And the hotel staff's for that matter."

"Yes, of course," Sharon Greaves said, abstractedly.

Poor cow, Andy Latimer thought; the address he had for Sharon Greaves was a manor house, which meant money; and there's nothing the press likes more than a scandal involving wealth and sex. They were going to have a field day once this got out.

Soon after DS Latimer's departure Sharon took her mobile phone from the handbag and made a call. Later when a nurse came to check on Sharon and remove the screen, Sharon asked her if she knew where her clothes were?

"They're folded in the bottom of the locker," the nurse replied, and she opened it to show Sharon.

When Jonathan Greaves arrived the following morning to visit his wife he was informed that she discharged herself the previous evening.

Chapter Three

Sharon Lee agreed to marry Jonathan Greaves because he was passable: passably rich, passably affable and passably attractive. She didn't love him, but who needs to be head over heels? She'd been there and come to the conclusion that it wasn't worth the pain and trouble. She met Jonathan when she came to work for him, or rather his father, Thomas Greaves who still ran the business then. The old man was hanging on until his son and heir married and begat another generation of Greaves.

The Greaves family had produced cider for near on a hundred and fifty years: Ulme Valley Cider. The plant was situated on the outskirts of Ulmeford, sitting on the banks of the Devon river that gave the village and valley its name. The family home, Calderham Manor, had progressed from being the lowly farmhouse of Silas Greaves, when cider making was a by-product of the farm, to the present ten-roomed manor house situated within four acres of parkland. Most of the major improvements to the house and grounds had occurred during Thomas Greaves' reign as head of the business. He had brought the company into the twentieth century; extending and up dating the plant, doubling its capacity and investing in a dynamic sales and marketing department. By the time Sharon joined the company it's range of ciders were enjoying nationwide sales. Ulme Valley Cider's name was best known to the public in general for it's strongest brew: Farmer Silas Special. It wasn't their best selling range – it was far outsold by the more prosaic sweet and mild ciders – but the television advertisement had caught the public imagination.

It's target market was males between the age of twenty to thirty; who would endeavour to surpass the capacity expounded by a straw chewing, smock wearing local, when he uttered the warning that had become a household catch-phrase: 'Us'n say two pints is all ee needs fer appy feet'. Like all of Ulme Valley's products it was marketed worldwide: enjoying sales in Europe, Scandinavia, the eastern states of America and, for some unknown reason, South Africa. Jonathan might not have inherited his father's business drive and flare, but he was an intelligent man, who had been amongst the high achievers at the London School of Economics, and the general consensus was that when he took over from Thomas the company would be in safe hands.

Sharon joined the company as an analytical chemist. Not exactly the cutting edge of scientific endeavour, but with her meagre degree it was all she could expect. It was far beneath her capabilities; the degree she had been expected to obtain was a first, more than probably with honours. Love and romance had put a stop to that.

The only child of a Manchester shopkeeper, she was
orphaned at the age of eight and brought up in a series of foster homes. In spite of this traumatic childhood she shone at school and achieved the necessary A-levels to obtain a place at university. Chemistry was her chosen subject, and the trust set up from the insurance policy paid following the motor accident that killed her parents covered her costs. A model student, great things were expected of her, just as she expected great things of herself. Then, at the commencement of her final year, she met Matt.

The university authorities had seen it all before, counsellors made the necessary noises and offered advice, but they knew from bitter experience that it was a lost cause. Sharon didn't have the ammunition to handle it. She was an attractive girl and had had boyfriends, but her romantic encounters had never progressed further than 'heavy petting' – as the jargon of the time would have it. Perhaps if she had been more promiscuous as a teenager, or joined her fellow students in random emotional and sexual encounters, instead of studiously completing assignments, she might have accumulated sufficient experience to see, and deal with, the inevitable. Perhaps? As it was, she was a twenty-two year old virgin when she fell hopelessly in love.

For Sharon, closeted for so long in academic endeavour, it was a physical as well as an emotional awakening. For Matt it was like being a child locked in a chocolate factory. He couldn't believe his luck, a good-looking girl whose sexual capacity appeared to be insatiable. And she adored him, would do anything for him.

Inevitably, for Matt, it became too much of a good thing. A surfeit of chocolate that began to cloy. Unremitting adoration, unless you are prone to basking in self-glory, can engender contempt. Matt had no real faults; he was a young man with normal appetites, the world at his feet, having a good time. He was not an egotist, and he was sufficiently fond of Sharon to recognise the self-destructive element of her infatuation. She was one of a succession of girls he had had affairs with and, like her predecessors, was not in love with, and he envisaged no long-time commitment.

He had a girlfriend, studying at another university in another town, no doubt enjoying the same sexual episodes as himself, and with whom he knew it was preordained that he would finally settle down with. Sharon had to go, if for no other reason that it was his final year and he had to get down to some serious studying. He was also fearfully aware that dumping Sharon was not going to be easy.

When Matt suggested that they should see a little less of one another, what with finals looming ahead, Sharon complied uncomplainingly; after all it was the same for her. She vacated his room and returned to the one in the flat she shared with three other girls. For her, seeing a little less of Matt meant a hiatus of two days, so when she went to see him and was told that he needed his space and that he would call her, she was shaken and confused. It never entered her mind that his love for her wasn't as all embracing as hers for him. Sitting alone in her room, staring unseeingly at textbook pages, she listened for the ringing of the communal telephone for a call that never came. Unable to contain herself she phoned him, successively, only to be informed that he was either out or unable to come to the phone. Finally, when he did deign to speak to her, it was to say that she was to cool it and stop bothering him, and then abruptly put the phone down. Sharon wouldn't believe what she was hearing, he wasn't himself, his mind was unhinged by too much hard work. The same couldn't be said for her, she hadn't attended a lecture or handed anything in for weeks. She began to hang about outside his lodgings, but when he appeared and she made to approach him, he turned abruptly and walked off in the opposite direction. An interval of stalking followed, until after two weeks of it, and unable to bear it any longer, he turned and told her that she had to grow up and face reality. He didn't love her, the affair was over and he never wanted to see her again.

Sharon's breakdown was complete. Since meeting Matt she hadn't contemplated a future without him. She could see no reason to carry on. Friends, and staff, rallied round, sadly aware that their encouragement and advice was falling on deaf ears. Eventually she recovered, inexorably changed and determined never to allow herself to become so vulnerable to heartache and pain again. Finals were perilously close. She was advised to seek a dispensation, on medical grounds, and sit them six months later. But Sharon had had enough of academia; she sat the exams and when they were over left the university and the city. Months later she learned that she had scraped through with a third. She didn't return to collect her degree, and it was mailed to her.

The legacy from her parents insurance was dwindling to an end. The position at Ulme Valley Cider offered a sufficiently low salary for her to contemplate applying, on the grounds that anyone with a passable degree wouldn't bother. And should she be successful, Devon and Ulmeford would be a pleasant change to the suburban Birmingham bed-sit she presently inhabited.

On the day the number of applicants waiting to be interviewed amazed and disconcerted her. Surely they couldn't all have as meagre degree as hers, she wondered? When she spoke with some of them she learned that they did in fact have good degrees, but the job market was so inundated with graduates that they were prepared to take anything.

Fortunately for Sharon, Mr Thomas Greaves was amongst the trio that interviewed her. He was sufficiently intuitive to recognise that the intelligence behind this young woman's face was far keener than her degree intimated.

After she left the room he announced that, "This is the one," convinced they would be getting a first class brain for half the rate she was really worth. There was, of course, no argument.

Two weeks later Sharon was informed that the position was hers.

Six months later she was promoted to head of department. This meteoric advancement had to be tempered with the fact that her predecessor was retiring, and that amongst the other members of staff within the department she was the only one with a degree; the remainder being laboratory technicians. All the same it was a meritorious promotion, earned from her immediate impact on the department and her fresh approach to its duties; culminating in the implementation of an improved system for quality control: all achieved without rancour or treading on any toes. The outgoing head had no reservations in recommending her for the post. Her staff liked her. She was popular.

Sharon soon realised that the job under utilised her abilities and that what was required was well within her capabilities; just as she was aware that she was receiving nowhere near the salary of the previous department head. It was of no bother. The situation suited her. Happy would have been too strong an adjective to describe her state of mind; contentment would be closer.

As a village, Ulmeford's charm lay in its ability to have absorbed incomers – mainly the recently retired from the affluent Midlands and Southeast – without succumbing to picturesqueness. Its location couldn't be faulted; nestling in a valley surrounded by pasture and wooded hills. On the debit side it was a bit lacking in amenities - a pub and village shop comprising the sum total – but two miles along a narrow winding lane led to an arterial road to the M5, and hence into Exeter. There was a bus service, so it was feasible to get to the city by public transport, except it only ran twice a day and took up to two hours each way. To overcome this problem Sharon purchased a course of driving lessons and a flamboyant, if somewhat ancient and unreliable, Triumph Spitfire. It could be guaranteed to get her to the city and back, but not always on the same day. With her promotion came a company car, a more prosaic small Nissan: not so exotic as the Spitfire but a damn site more reliable.

Exeter, at first, had presented Sharon with a problem; it was a university city, with all the mental garbage that carried with it. It was a mental block she knew she had to overcome. In the eventuality, after almost turning back, she discovered that her trepidation was quickly lost in the lure of the shops. Even more so now that she had money to spend. She soon grew to love the city, with its restaurants, theatres and quayside. And it had an independent cinema. Film, as an enjoyment and an art form, was one of the few things Matt had introduced her to that she still retained. That and a broken heart. Now and again she would see a couple together and experience the knife turning in her stomach, but she learned to live with it. In time, when seeing similar couples, her thoughts would turn more to the type and quality of sex they might be having, rather then their emotional feelings towards one another.

Initially, when she moved to Ulmeford, she had rented a room. After becoming established in the company she looked around for something more permanent. There wasn't a lot on offer, and whet there was did little to inspire: anything half way decent was way out of her price range, and those within it were rural slums. Eventually she settled on a one-bedroom garden flat situated on the outskirts of a neighbouring village. It was more than she had budgeted for but it was superior to anything else she had viewed. She took it there and then, got the bank to agree to a larger mortgage, and asked Ulme Valley Cider for a raise. Their fairly unequivocal assent to this request made her wish she had asked for more.

When Jonathan, the son and heir, asked her out for a date Sharon was somewhat taken aback. In the nine months she had been with the company he had hardly spoken to her more than half a dozen times. As head of sales and marketing their paths rarely crossed, other than at the monthly heads of department meeting. At the three of these meetings she had attended he was polite and affable but at no time did she get the feeling that he was hitting on her: unlike his father, whose reputation had gone before him and whose every sentence to her was loaded with innuendo.

She said yes; mainly because Jonathan's request took her so much by surprise that she couldn't think of a ready reason to say no. He took her to his golf club for dinner, and Sharon found herself enjoying both the food and the company. Jonathan was an urbane man and he maintained a stream of amusing conversation throughout the evening. Not trivia, he was well read and intelligent; fully abreast with the latest developments in current affairs and the arts. Sharon was stimulated. To his credit he barely mentioned golf. Two further dates followed: a concert and the theatre: always accompanied by a bunch of flowers when he collected her.

The first evening together, when he dropped her off at her flat, was concluded with a handshake: the second by a chaste kiss: and the third by a longer kiss. On the forth occasion, parked outside her flat, he endeavoured to take his advances a step further; and Sharon discovered that his sophistication did not extend to his sexual technique. Following a lunge, grapple, and a sharp rebuff on her part, Sharon made it quite clear that she had no intention of having casual sex in the front seat of a sports car, or anywhere else for that matter. She'd been down that road before, and the only way he was ever going to get into her bed was with a ring on her finger, on her wedding night. With that she stormed out of the car, or as close as one can storm out from the bucket seat of a Lotus.

She slammed the door of her flat and waited behind it for the repercussion. Had she actually said that – ring on her finger – wedding night? The concept of marriage must have been in her mind, subconsciously, but it had come as a surprise to actually hear herself declaring the notion. Then, with the sound of the Lotus burbling into life, she realised that there was little chance now of it actually materialising. One didn't rebuff the likes of Jonathan Greaves and get a second chance. He was sufficient a catch to ensure that there'd be only too many candidates prepared to put up with his inadequate technique in the hope of landing him. Maybe herself included, if she hadn't known better: Matt had spoiled her.

The silence and apparent ostracism that accompanied the following days confirmed her diagnosis. Then, one week exactly from the night she had left him sitting alone in his sports car, she received a letter from Jonathan. It was short and to the point: he apologised for his behaviour and declared that he was in love with her; his intentions were honourable, and would she marry him? Fully cognizant that love was an emotion she wouldn't be able to reciprocate, Sharon returned a one-word reply:

Yes.

She didn't love him, but as she had so painfully learned,

love is for the birds. However, although Jonathan might not hold any overwhelming physical attraction for her, for the main part he was courteous and intelligent, and could be passably good company. Plus, now that the concept had been considered, becoming the wife of a rich man, and all that it entailed, rather appealed to her. To this end she was prepared to declare her love vocally, if not with her heart.

A rather old-fashioned courtship followed, with an engagement ring, announcements in The Times and Country Life, and visits to members of the Greaves family and other County notables. Not the top echelon - the Greaves were still considered as 'Trade' and too nouveau to enter into that rarefied society - but all the same it was a world of formal afternoon teas and dinner parties that Sharon hadn't realised still existed.

During this period she continued to maintain the principle of remaining chaste until her wedding night, to which Jonathan complied with equanimity. He made no secret of his own motive for wanting to marry her. Thomas, his father, had made it patently clear that the only way he would release the reins of Ulme Valley Cider was when he died or when Jonathan presented him with an heir: preferably a son. Sharon, it appeared, was acceptable to Thomas as a daughter-in-law, provided there was no impediment preventing her having children. A subsequent medical examination, proving this fact, was a mandatory formality Sharon knew she had no choice other than to accept, not with her pedigree: if the Greaves were considered nouveau, where did that place her?

All very feudal

Meeting Celia Greaves, wife and mother of Thomas and Jonathan respectively, was a trial Sharon viewed with some trepidation. She had only seen the woman once; at a meeting held at the manor when remedial work was being undertaken on the boardroom. A tall elegant, ethereal presence, that glided unknowingly into the room, and out again once the mistake was realised. All that Jonathan had told Sharon about her was that she was American, and that she spent most of her time in London, and always had done, even when he was a child. Sharon got the impression that he new little more about the woman than she did. Celia had sent a note, asking Sharon to meet her in London, for lunch at the Savoy Grill, saying that she could catch a train to Paddington station and take a taxi from there. Sharon surmised that she would be expected to return from this imperious summons, later in the afternoon, by the same method and route.

They were expecting her at the Savoy; the moment she mentioned Celia's name at the reception a waiter was summoned to escort Sharon to where she was already seated. The previous day Sharon had agonised for hours over what to wear, and had spent the afternoon in the hairdressers. As Celia rose to meet her and proffer a small, manicured hand, she realised that it had all been in vain, and that compared with this vision of couture elegance she felt like a country bumpkin.

·

"Sharon."

"Mrs Greaves."

"Celia, please." The two women took their seats and the waiter offered them menus. Celia gave her order without consulting it, and Sharon said she would have the same.

"So, you're to be my daughter-in-law." The voice was low and the American accent cultured.

"How is Jonathan?" she asked before Sharon could make any comment.

"He's fine," Sharon replied with a smile.

"Do you love him?"

Sharon was aware that she had instinctively hesitated for a second before answering, "Yes, of course."

The wine waiter materialised, and it was decided that they would share half a bottle of Moselle, together with a bottle of mineral water.

The waiter departed.

Celia said, "Don't take it personally, I felt it was something I was supposed to ask. I'm as new to this as you are. It's fairly irrelevant anyway."

Sharon was at a loss as to what to say.

"I was in love with Tommy," Celia continued, "head over heels, the whole works." She didn't elaborate, and what she didn't say spoke volumes.

Sharon's knowing nod and wry expression intimated that she too had been there.

The hors d'oeuvres arrived.

"I believe you're some kind of scientist?"

"A chemist actually," Sharon replied. "I'm head of the department."

"Will you continue to work after you're married, or perhaps I should say, after you give birth? After all that's what this is really all about."

"Yes." Sharon had never contemplated not continuing, and she had answered with none of the previous hesitation.

"Good girl," Celia said, and she laughed. It was a very pleasant, infectious laugh.

"It's extremely important to retain one's independence, and sense of humour. I have, although I don't possess your brains, but I do have my money."

Sharon guessed she had passed some kind of test, and found herself warming to Celia. The conversation continued amicably through the meal, with Celia doing most of the talking. Reading between the lines, together with the snippets of gossip she had already heard, Sharon gleaned that although it had been Thomas Greaves acumen that had brought the company into the twentieth century, it was Celia's money that made it possible. Fortunately she had inherited her father's business prudence, as well as his estate, and tied up the money she gave Thomas in such a way that (a) he did not have carte blanch to squander it, and (b) that she became a stockholder in the company. "Gave me my independence." Early in the marriage Celia came to realise that "Tommy wasn't the kind of hound dog to stay on the porch." Sharon could appreciate the hurt and betrayal her husband infidelities must have caused the young bride. Celia just said, "It was a fact I grew to accept, but not one I was prepared to live with. Don't get me wrong, Tommy's a dear and I wouldn't be without him, just not all the time." Which meant that she spent nine months of the year between London, Florida and New York.

"I don't see a lot of Jonathan these days, and when I do he doesn't tell me very much; so I've no way of knowing if he's inherited any of his father's traits."

Sharon said "Some of his business sense, but nothing else to give me any cause for concern."

Celia grinned. "You'll do," she said.

A mutual respect had been formed: their worlds were too far apart to allow them to be friends, but they liked one another. Sharon was only to see Celia in England on three other occasions: her wedding, Leon's christening, and Thomas's funeral – after which she decamped for Palm Beach and, as far as Sharon was aware, never returned.

Sharon conceived during the honeymoon. The birth was complicated and Sharon was informed that it was unlikely that she would ever be able to conceive again. Which suited her, as she had no wish to go through the process again.

The promise Thomas made, that he would step down

once Jonathan presented him with an heir, was never put to the test: a stroke, sufficiently serious to incapacitate him, pre-empted the decision. He did not relinquish the reins gracefully, initially insisting that the privately hired nurse wheeled him into his office each morning. Jonathan connived in maintaining the illusion, by directing inconsequential documentation for the Old Man's comment and signature, whilst effectively taking over the day-to-day running of the business. But there was nothing wrong with the Old Man's mind and he quickly became aware of what was happening. Once he would have reacted in a way that would have had the rafters of the plant ringing with his anger, but now he found he tired too easily and hadn't the energy to make an issue out of the deception. Rather than continue, with what he considered a humiliating pretence, he stopped coming in altogether. With nothing to fill the vacuum he developed into an irascible and uncooperative patient – Celia only visited him the once – and took to drowning his frustration in a variety of beverages far stronger than any produced by Ulme Valley.

He outlasted his doctor's prediction, that he'd be dead within the year, by two days.

After Leon was borne Jonathan's sexual interest in Sharon waned; as if having done what was required, and sired a son and heir, he didn't have to bother any more - except on the odd occasion – birthdays, anniversaries, or when the rare urge took him. There was nothing to indicate to Sharon that he was redirecting his passion towards anybody else; rather it confirmed her suspicion that he wasn't really all that interested in sex in the first place. Now golf, that was another matter entirely, that was where his real passion lay: and he was very good at it, playing for the county and entering for the British Amateur Open. He was careful never to allow it to interfere with the running of the company, except when it was beneficial in entertaining clients, but outside of business it swallowed up most of his spare time and interest. If Sharon had been in love with him, she would have viewed the relinquishing of her sexual allure to a pastime that consisted of hitting a small ball with a variety of sticks as constituting an act of mental cruelty. As it was it suited her just fine.

For as much as Jonathan's libido had decreased hers had increased, or rather returned to its former state, with the honeymoon as the catalyst. Not that Jonathan's never-mind-the-foreplay-let's-get-to-the-missionary technique was much of a turn on, but it was sufficient to awaken Sharon's more than healthy appetite. Once past pregnancy and post-natal blues - which put it on hold for a while - and the necessity of regaining her figure, she was ready to resume where she had left off after Matt. Except this time she wasn't going to get her heart broken. There had to be rules: Jonathan must never be compromised: no partners amongst people they knew: no involved affairs: and, unless she was one hundred percent sure of her partner, safe sex at all times.

Her son, Leon, was to become the one unconditional love of her life, but as a baby he held little attraction, and as soon as it was feasibly possible a nanny was employed to look after him. Sharon was then free to return to work. As chief chemist she received numerous invites to conferences and seminars, and she began to take advantage of the ones that were of interest to her. The advantages were twofold: it kept her abreast of developments: and provided an environment for meeting suitable partners – either from attendees, or guests at whatever hotel she was staying. Over the ensuing years she became adept at vetting suitable candidates – early on she discovered that although most men, when free of constraints, are willing to indulge in casual sex, not all are any better at it than Jonathan. She also became a member of an extremely discreet club that provided a venue for like-minded people to enjoy sex, in all its forms, free of entanglement.

It would have been impossible for Jonathan not to suspect that his wife was finding sexual gratification elsewhere, and so an unspoken acceptance developed between them: provided it never affected him personally, or Leon, he was prepared to go along with the deception. Sharon would inform him that she was going to be away for a brief period – sometimes citing a particular conference, sometimes giving no information – and as long as it didn't interfere with a particular business or social function he would prefer her to be present at, he would make no objection. It was a compromise that suited them both. Basically theirs was a happy marriage, and there was much they enjoyed together.

Had the crises not come along it might have been a situation that would have continued indefinitely.

Chapter Four

The tail end of the final decade of the twentieth century saw a steady decline in the profitability of Ulme Valley Cider. Changes in society mirrored its drinking habits; it was becoming a youth centred market, one within which cider wasn't considered to be a part. It wasn't cool.

Jonathan and Sharon discussed the matter in some depth and concluded that if Ulme Valley Cider were to survive it would have to choose one of three options:

Find a niche market with the present products.

Produce a new product(s).

Look for someone to merge with or be taken over by.

The first option, they decided, would be the least suitable; their competitors were already there, and as divisions of multinationals they had the advertising budget to match.

Merger or takeover would be the easiest way out if it was not for two stumbling blocks: Finding someone interested in an ailing company in an already shrinking market: and if they did it would be unlikely that they would retain the present plant; with the resulting affect on the local community. Plus it was part of Jonathan's life, a family tradition, and to loose it would create a void he would find difficult to fill.

Which left the new product. Sharon was already sure she knew exactly what was required, the type of drink and the market it was aimed at. In fact it was something she had been on to Jonathan about for some time, but as it entailed a complete change from their traditional market, plus the installation of a different production technique, he had been loath to give it consideration.

Now he had to concede that it might be the only viable alternative to a rapid decline in sales, reduction in personnel and even the possible closure of the plant.

It was decided that they would break the news to the heads of departments; after all their cooperation would be paramount if it was going to succeed. A special meeting was convened.

Apart from Sharon's department three others were represented: Sales and Marketing, Production and engineering, and Finance. Jonathan opened the meeting by reiterating the disturbing sales and profit figures for the past few years, a fact they were already only to well acquainted with, then went on to present the three options left open to them if they were to survive. He asked for their ideas and/or comments. Predictably, apart from Sharon, they were negative on all three.

Sharon addressed the meeting.

"The largest percentage of money spent on the consumption of alcoholic beverages is by people between the age of eighteen and thirty. And within this group the fastest growing section is young women below the age of twenty-four. I know some of you have daughters, nieces, within this age group, and if you were to ask them the type of drink they prefer they would come up with one word: Alcopop."

Sharon paused to let the word sink in.

"A soft drink containing alcohol," she continued. "A beverage I would have thought ideal for Ulme Valley Cider to enter into producing. We already make a sweet cider whose alcoholic content is so low that it is all but a soft drink, all we would have to do is mix it with something a bit stronger."

"You make it sound very easy, Sharon," Production commented. "Is it really as simple as that?"

"Well no, not quite. You have to choose which spirit you're going to add, and the necessary percentage, plus the flavour of the finished product. It's got to be sufficiently different to the others to capture the markets imagination."

"Are you advocating the employment of a specialist firm to develop this drink?"

"No, I feel that my department is fully able to come up with something, with assistance of Blending."

None of the three felt sufficiently confident to question Sharon's credibility in this assumption: they were equally in awe of her quick intelligence and the fact of her being the boss's wife. Instead, almost simultaneously, Sales and Marketing asked how long it would take to develop, and Finance how much it would cost.

Sharon had no idea but as she was trying to sell confidence she stated, "I would guess six months, a year at the outside. Development costs would be minimal, and actual production costs shouldn't be any greater than for the present output. The major cost would be in the redevelopment of the plant to accommodate the new procedure; and that will have to be worked out when we're ready to go. After all we know what the bottom line is, a price on the shelf that's competitive, if not better, than the opposition's."

"Are we to assume that this will result in the closure of some of the existing lines?" Production asked.

It was Jonathan who answered.

"I think you can safely assume that it will supersede at least half of current production, if not more."

The inference being that one way or another the current output of Ulme Valley cider was going to be halved, with the new product the only candidate for taking up the redundant manufacturing capacity.

End of the meeting.

As Sharon saw it the mix had to be a combination of extremes, a sweet cider with a dry spirit, or the reverse. Vodka with one of the sweet ciders was the obvious first choice. The result was a more alcoholic, slightly less sweet tasting cider. Subsequently they tried gin, rum, whisky and tequila: then brandy, followed by various sweet liqueurs with dry cider. Of them all only the brandy-based mix resulted in anything like an acceptable drink; and then only half of the people they tried it on said it was something they would buy.

Sharon wasn't totally dissatisfied for it allowed her to try an additive whose unique flavour she had thought all along might work, but one with a reputation that had engendered sufficient caution for her to leave it as a last resort. Wormwood, the bitter aromatic oil used in absinthe: the French drink associated with the likes of Monet, Picasso, Wilde, Hemingway and van Gogh – said to be drinking absinthe when he cut off his ear: a drink so addictive that it was universally banned for a period.

Because of its addictive properties Sharon and her team tried a mix using a minimal amount with one of the drier, more alcoholic, ciders. It didn't work, the result was too bitter – but there was something about the combination that remained on the taste buds, which made the members of the team who tried it, ask for a second helping, 'just to make sure'. Sufficient inducement to continue with further experimentation. Flavour requirements indicated a move to the sweeter ciders. Various combinations of the liqueur content versus sweetness were tried until it was narrowed down to three possibilities. An invite was placed on the company notice board for members of the workforce to apply to go on a tasting panel. The response was enthusiastic, which allowed the team to select applicants who represented a cross-section of the drinking public, but with the emphasis being towards the younger end of the market.

The outcome was predictable. Older and predominantly male gravitated towards the drier mix: younger and female preferring the sweeter drink. Encouragingly a great percentage thought it had a unique taste that wasn't unpleasant – a high number of 'try it again, just to be sure'. Discouragingly most thought there was just a certain something missing. It was confirmation of Sharon's own conclusion. Concerned that her taste buds might become jaded she had participated frugally during the trials, not until the mixes were completed did she try them, and had found herself agreeing with the team that they had got it right, while at the same time feeling slightly disappointed.

She gathered the younger female tasters together and asked if they could explain: amongst the – "It's difficult to say exactly," – one of the came up with an answer that supplied Sharon with the indication she required. The girl said, "It's like when you try a supermarket's version of Coca-Cola, it just doesn't have that something that the real thing has."

That was it.

Sharon and two of the most trusted members of her team isolated themselves in the laboratory to find the missing ingredient. In the end it wasn't one ingredient but a combination of three: two flavouring additives, and what Sharon preferred to call the 'Y Factor'. In actuality 'Y' was a commonly used domestic product, which had been added into the 'missing ingredient' blend by mistake. The pseudonym 'Y' was given because of the hazardous nature associated with it, even though the amount being used was so infinitesimal as to be of any danger. Assailed from all sides by experts telling them what was and wasn't good for them, the public had grown susceptible to scare-mongering, and Sharon was only too well aware that just a hint of 'Factor Y' would be sufficient to scupper the product irretrievably.

And 'Y' was imperative.

The girls from the original tasting were asked to try one mix containing 'Y' and one without. Their choice for the blend containing 'Y' was unanimous. After drowning her second glass, Clare, the girl who had come up with the Coca-Cola analogy, put it in a nutshell.

"You've got a winner there, Mrs Greaves."

The ensuing months were spent making sure the drink had no problematic side effects: in essence feeding measured doses of it, at regular intervals to laboratory rats. Once completed and found to be innocuous, she presented the package to Jonathan, and only then revealed the identity of factor Y. Assured of its safety, but in agreement with Sharon that it should remain a secret, he gave the go-ahead for the beverage to be tried at selective venues throughout the south west of England.

One final thing remained to be resolved, what they were going to call it? From the outset, when the idea of using wormwood occurred to her, Sharon had thought of a name.

"Think of French association," she said, "absinthe, the artistic climate of sophisticated decadence of fin de siecle, the early nineteen hundreds, Toulouse-Lautrec, Oscar Wilde, Picasso, Hemingway. Think of Mata Hari. Think of the market we are targeting: impressionable young women."

Jonathan laughed. "Okay, I'm thinking about all of them. So what should I arrive at, what's the name that it is all supposed to evoke?"

"Fatale."

After a predictable slow start repeat orders began to materialise, which increased with a momentum that caught the plant off guard. The engineering department had to work nights and weekends to convert the production lines.

Fatale went national, then international: including the USA where thujone (wormwood) is technically still banned, but nobody seemed to be pursuing the point. An advertising company was employed. A new bottle, representing a corseted hourglass female figure, was introduced and dominated billboards. There was global television, radio and cinema advertising, some more risqué than others, depending on the country.

A separate company was formed, UVC Ltd, with Jonathan holding fifty-one percent of the shares and Sharon forty-five. Linda Cotton and Nicolas Fairweather, Sharon's two assistants and the only ones apart from her and Jonathan who knew the secret formula of Fatale, and the identity of Factor Y, equally held the remaining four percent. The price of their continuing loyalty.

A sealed copy of the formula was lodged with a firm of solicitors and held in their safe, and another was held by Jonathan and interred in a safe deposit box.

The Fatale phenomena.

Chapter Five

Sharon was a diligent scientist and she continued to monitor her product. Laboratory rats were subjected to a constant intake of diluted Fatale dosage and their reactions logged. It wasn't the inclusion of Factor Y that gave her any trepidation – the amount was so small that a person would have to be imbibing a gallon a day for it to be a problem, and the alcohol content would kill them way before that happened. No, it was the wormwood, thujone, which gave her some cause for concern.

The amount legally permitted in absinthe is ten milligrams of thujone per kilogram. In the 1850 's chronic use of absinthe was believed to cause addiction, hyper excitability, and hallucinations. Termed absinthism, there was also widely held the belief in the Lamarckian theory of heredity; that these traits could be passed on by absinthists to their children. It led to absinthe being banned in many countries in the beginning of the 1900's. Subsequent investigation revealed that the detrimental effects were not due to thujone alone, but by the balance of the various herbs that were added to it.

The amount of thujone in Fatale was far less than that in absinthe. It was combined with cider, albeit an extremely mild cider, which brought its alcohol content up to five percent, but that was also much lower than in absinth. It was the flavouring additives, one of which contained herbs and Factor Y, and the effect the combination of these additives might possibly have with thujone, over a prolonged period of regular consumption, which prompted Sharon's continued monitoring.

Market analysis already revealed a brand loyalty to Fatale, a factor on its own that could suggest that the theory of absinthism was not totally without foundation. It was not something she was prepared to leave to chance.

All the same, when no particular adverse affects had materialised after thirteen months she was prepared to call it a day. So complacent had she become that the abnormal behaviour of one female rat – later to be named April, after the month within which the effect occurred – almost went unnoticed. Sharon was looking into the cage with unseeing eyes, her thoughts far away on other matters, and it wasn't until the commotion of two other rats attacking April drew her attention to what was happening. Although April was larger than her adversaries she appeared to be completely unable to coordinate her movements and defend herself.

Examination of April revealed that there was nothing physically wrong with her limbs, only the nervous system that moved them. Consulting April's chart Sharon saw that she had been receiving a steady intake of Fatale dosage for a month, and that her last dose had been six hours earlier. A sample of blood was taken and analysed: there was no trace of thujone or alcohol, it having passed through the rat's system. After two hours the effect disappeared and she regained coordination. When Sharon resumed dosing April the affect returned a week later, again six hours after the last intake, and vanishing a couple of hours later. However, on subsequent trials the loss of coordination effect did not occur.

Sharon wrote a detailed record of April's reactions and showed them to Jonathan.

"So, a rat-arsed rat," he said with a laugh.

"No, not really," Sharon said, soberly. "If the lack of coordination had been caused by intoxication it would have occurred while the alcohol was still in its blood stream, but it didn't happen until well after the dose had passed through the rat's system."

"I'm not sure what you're trying to tell me, Sharon?"

"The rat's nervous system ceased to function for a period on two occasions after receiving a measure of Fatale dosage. The strength and frequency of the dosage is diluted to accommodate a rat's body weight, but it would be equivalent to an adult human weighing sixty kilograms, drinking four litres of Fatale concentrated in a period equivalent to one day within a weekly interval."

"Or a young woman drinking six bottles of Fatale on a Saturday night binge," Jonathan concluded."

"Thereabouts. Using the same rat to human comparison the affect on the nervous system would occur two to three days later, when the alcohol had passed through the blood stream, when the person might well be driving a car or operating a machine. The result could be catastrophic."

"Hold on, you're jumping the gun a bit aren't you? This phenomenon has occurred in one isolated rat, in what, a thousand?"

"Something like that."

"And it only happened twice, then never again, with no factual evidence connecting it to the Fatale dosage. All a bit nebulous don't you think? I mean it could well be some genetic fault in the rat, or something similar. I think far more research is necessary before you start making the type of statement you've just come out with."

Sharon gave Jonathan a withering look.

"I was simply acquainting you with the result of my tests, and ensuring that you are aware of the possible consequences. The worst-case scenario. I'm not prone to scare mongering but it is my considered opinion that there is cause for concern. However, I like to think that I'm a competent scientist, and I would never consider making a public statement on my work without first having sufficient data and conclusive evidence to support my findings."

"Thank God for that."

Jonathan's comment was more heartfelt than his flippant delivery gave reason to suspect. Unknown to Sharon, or any other board member or employee, he was engaged in preliminary talks with a multinational distilling company regarding the takeover of UVC.

Lucidel was a Swiss company, based in Lucerne, and with holdings worldwide. For a while, following the success of Fatale, it had been a competitor of UVC, producing their own version called Pigalle. But it lacked the zing of the original and died on the shelves.

Through an intermediary Lucidel's CEO, Luc Barr, arranged to meet secretly with Jonathan in London. The opening figure Barr mentioned for the acquisition of UVC was quite breathtaking: £60 million.

Jonathan had asked for reassurances regarding the tenure of present staff and the Ulmeford works, which included Sharon and the two other board members – the custodians of the Fatale Formula. Barr said he would look into these matters, and as Jonathan spoke with Sharon he was waiting to hear Barr's response. If they were able to come to some agreement the next step would be to put the takeover proposal before the board. He anticipated that any scepticism the other three might have regarding Lucidel's promises as to the future of the plant and staff, would be overlooked when they realised what their personal stake would be: Nick and Linda's minority holding alone would put each in the millionaire category, and make Sharon a very wealthy woman. Jonathan had made up his mind to sell his fifty-one percent holding, so whatever the outcome of the board meeting, whether Sharon, Linda and Nick decided to keep or sell their shares, Lucidel would gain controlling interest. Once their proposal was accepted, Lucidal would send in a team, or more likely a specialist firm, to check CVC out. Due Diligence it was termed, examining the company to ensure there were no financial problems or shenanigans, that sales and asset values were genuine, and that nothing untoward was likely to creep out of the woodwork.

Now would definitely be the wrong time for Sharon to publicize her rat-arsed, or otherwise, rodent.

It was not Jonathan's convoluted pleadings that prevented Sharon from voicing the findings of her tests, but the fact that she had insufficient data and evidence to sustain or prove any theory. It was to take a further three years before she had concrete proof.

During this intervening period the takeover took place. As Jonathan had predicted the sum being offered was sufficient to sway the other three board members: for Nick and Linda it was more money that they had ever thought possible for them to own: for Sharon, already, as Jonathan's wife, a comparatively rich woman, it wasn't so much the money as the independence it would give her. The terms and conditions of Lucidel's acquisition of UVC Ltd were:

That it would include Ulme Valley Cider Ltd (of which Jonathan held 98% and Sharon 2%), worldwide ownership of the Fatale trade name and the Fatale formula.

Ten percent of the agreed purchase sum would be retained for two years in lieu of any detrimental incidences occurring within that period.

Payment to be paid in the form of 45% cash and 55% in shares to the corresponding value – not disposable for a period of two years.

Jonathan was retained as Managing Director of UVC UK Ltd, and UK consumption of Fatale continued to be produced from the Ulmeford plant.

Likewise, Sharon stayed on as Chief Chemist.

Linda and Nick resigned to pursue other interests: market gardening and sailing respectively. Jonathan retained his Lucidel shares, whilst the other three sold theirs – extremely profitably - shortly after termination of the two-year retention period.

The popularity of Fatale continued to grow and represented 8% of Lucidel's global profits.

Sharon continued with her singular practice of dosing and monitoring laboratory rats. Visiting Lucidel chemists accepted this as a commendable, if perhaps slightly excessive practice, and as it did not compromise the efficiency of the department, one they were prepared to countenance, requesting only to be kept regularly abreast of the test results.

Which Sharon did, resolutely sending them copies of her monthly procedures and findings.

Nine months after April's display of uncoordinated body movement another laboratory rat, Christened Noelle, showed identical symptoms. This time Sharon was better prepared. It was obvious to her that as there were no records of any of the constituents causing the symptoms on their own – not even the much maligned wormwood – that the effect materialised from a reaction of one of them upon the others. She needed to isolate the guilty constituent. Unknown was how long Noelle would display the symptoms: once, twice - as had April – or more? Recalling that various herbs were reported as having a contributory effect in absinthism, Sharon's inclination was to initially go with the additive to Fatale containing herbs.

Noelle's dosage was changed to one without the herbal additive, and a week later she once again lost her sense of coordination: demonstrating that the herbs were not the problem.

Acting on a hunch Sharon tried a mixture with Factor Y omitted, and Noelle had no further attacks. However, as she never displayed the symptoms again when returned to the full Fatale dosage, and as her predecessor, April, had only succumbed to two attacks before the condition disappeared for good, it wasn't conclusive proof. The tests, experiments, and results were logged on to the department computer.

A copy, without comment, was included in Sharon's monthly report.

There was no reaction, which endorsed Sharon's suspicion that the reports were shelved, unread. All the same, in anticipation of a negative or hostile reaction she had made another copy for herself, which was secreted in a bank safe deposit box.

It took a further twenty-two months before sufficient tests were completed to confirm Sharon's theory: that in certain cases Fatale had a detrimental affect on the nervous system as to impede the coordination between brain and limbs in rats, and that the constituent in Fatale responsible for this condition was the additive Factor Y.

And another five months to assert that it was applicable to humans.

If it hadn't happened locally she might well have missed the connection.

A report in the West Country Gazette regarding the death of a student, Emily Farrow; who apparently detached herself from the group of friends she was with and stepped into the road in front of an oncoming lorry. In particular it was the words of one of these friends that caught Sharon's attention:

"Emily's legs seemed to be uncoordinated with the rest of her body".

Sharon attended the inquest and listened to the evidence.

Emily's parents, tutors, and friends stated that she was a normal, happy nineteen year-old woman, a good student, with no pressing personal or academic problems.

A pathologist said his examination revealed that there were no traces of alcohol or drugs in the blood stream, nor any obvious evidence of a physical disorder that could be attributed to Miss Farrow's reported behaviour.

He went on to say that sudden malfunction of the limbs can be as the result of various causes, both physical and psychological, and often a combination of both, but that the complexity of the nervous system of the human body is such that without details of a prior similar malfunction of the deceased's legs there was no way of pinpointing an area within which to concentrate a thorough examination, and that it had been impossible to determine the exact cause of the problem.

However, he confirmed that he was unable to find any obvious damage neither to Miss Farrow's brain, nor to the muscles and nerve ends relative to her limbs.

The Farrow's family doctor confirmed that Emily never reported a similar incident of limb malfunction – a fact endorsed by family and friends - and that she had no history of any psychological disorder.

Summing up the Coroner said that Emily's tragic death

appeared the result of some sudden, undeterminable, malfunction, sufficient to cause a lack of coordination between her brain and legs. A seemingly momentary, uncharacteristic act of behaviour that had it occurred on any other occasion would have led to medical examination and diagnosis, but which in this instance led to a tragic accident.

The verdict was death by misadventure, attributed to causes undetermined.

Outside the court Sharon approached a group of young people, amongst which were three of Emily's friends who had given evidence. She introduced herself as a scientific journalist, and proffered the identification card she had been issued at a recent seminar - headed Biochem Foundation - stating that she was Sharon Greaves BSc.

"I'm researching instances of unaccountable behaviour patterns amongst young people possessing higher than average IQ's. It would appear that cases similar to Emily's have been reported in other European countries, the USA, and Scandinavia: countries that enjoy a high standard of living. There is a theory that it could be due to diet, and or eating and drinking habits. I appreciate that this is a very distressing time for you, but I wondered if you might be up to answering a few questions? Perhaps we could have a coffee somewhere near by?"

The group looked at one another. One of them, a tall thin young man, asked what would be the outcome of her research?

"Provided there is sufficient evidence of some particular contributing factor, I will then write an article for publication in one or more of the reputable scientific journals."

"What happens then? Does it mean people, companies, can be sued?"

"Oh, give it a rest, Kieran," one of the girls said.

"I'm just thinking of Emily's family, that's all." Kieran said, indignantly.

Sharon said, "If it becomes obvious that there is a link between an unusual behaviour pattern that can be attributed to diet or eating or drinking habits – be it due to a certain proprietary item or consumption habits in general, then steps can be instigated to correct the problem. Perhaps even save lives. On the other hand there might not be any connection at all, and the other reported incidents similar to Emily's simply a statistical coincidence."

"Lies, damned lies and statistics," Kieran intoned.

Whether it was in defiance to Kieran's scepticism or as a result of Sharon's appeal that perhaps lives might be saved, the two girls agreed to accompany Sharon to a near-by coffee shop.

Treading a careful path Sharon asked a series of questions regarding Emily's diet and social habits before raising the topic of her drinking. The answer confirmed Sharon's worst fears: as a rule Emily did not drink on a regular basis except for a

Saturday night, when she would have four to six bottles of Fatale.

She drank nothing else.

Over the years Sharon and Jonathan had grown closer and spent a great deal of time in one another's company.

Each of their individual passions – sex and golf - was tolerated; with the exception that although Sharon occasionally accompanied her husband to his, Jonathan never joined Sharon in hers.

This apart they pursued a number of mutual pastimes and enjoyed empathy within a caring and affectionate relationship. Like most couples they had had, and continued to have, differences of opinions – at the time Sharon felt that Jonathan was somewhat underhanded in his handling of the takeover, although in hindsight she conceded that he had probably had little other choice – but in general theirs was a tolerant coexistence.

They were more than sufficiently rich to indulge themselves; and if Jonathan's lifestyle entailed a higher expenditure than her own Sharon made no censure to curtail it. With the sale of her shares, which Jonathan did nothing to dissuade, she was an independently wealthy woman.

All in all they enjoyed a good life.

It was natural for Sharon to discuss with Jonathan the revelation of Emily Farrow's death and the Fatale connection, and it's bearing in regard to her laboratory experiments.

What she was unsure of was how he would react.

They were seated in the library, Jonathan's favourite room and where they tended to take coffee after dinner. With the proceeds of their increased wealth Sharon had transformed and modernised most of the manor house. Jonathan had agreed to give her a free rein with the exception of his bedroom and dressing room, and the library: they remained unchanged – dark oak panelling and floors, leather chairs and ancient Persian rugs.

From past experience Sharon knew that the library was the most advantageous environment within which to broach 'difficult' topics with her husband.

She gave Jonathan a brief synopsis before handing him her report to read. When he finished she said,

"I've been sending detailed reports to Lucerne every month but from their lack of response I get the impression that they've been filing them unread. As I had no concrete evidence to prove a possible detrimental affect on humans I didn't bother to say anything, but now with the death of this unfortunate girl it puts a different complexion on the matter. Perhaps I should bring it to the attention of Luc Barr? You've read my report, what do you think?"

"Well yes, I've read it, and I understood it up to the part where you connect the death of the girl with Fatale, but when you go into the actual reason why the lack of coordination occurs I'm afraid you lost me. Is it possible to put in laymen's language?"

Sharon gathered her thoughts before replying,

"A general, and fairly good, analogy is to compare the nervous system with a telephone network or computer, with the brain generating its own electric power. However the contact between nerve and the muscle or other organ it is controlling is chemical. So when an electrical impulse arrives at the end of the nerve fibre a chemical is released into the gap between it and the organ, and it is this chemical that carries the stimulus forward. What occurred with the two affected rats, and I believe Emily Farrow, is that an agent within Fatale causes a chemical reaction to take place that is sufficient to disturb the stimulus."

"And that agent is Factor Y?"

"Precisely. This reaction is rare and only affects a tiny percentage, and even then only occurs intermittently. The trigger might be physical or psychological, I don't know, it's not really the determining factor. What I believe is that the present Fatale formula can cause unnecessary deaths and should therefore be withdrawn from sale and replaced by a substitute that does not contain Factor Y."

"And this is what you propose to tell Luc Barr?"
"Yes."

Jonathan rose from his chair and walked to the window. He stood and looked out at the row of cedars that lined that side of the house: his father had planted them a young man. After a moment he turned, and motioned to the brandy decanter.

Sharon nodded and he poured two glasses.

"Then I think you should," he said and handed Sharon her glass.

"Thank you, darling, I was hoping you would say that."

Jonathan's motive for agreeing with Sharon was far less altruistic than hers. Golf, his love of and skill at the game, had been the impetus to his present life style. He had donated a cup, then a foundation to help fund young up-and-coming professionals. Invitations arrived to play in pro-am advents, nationally and then internationally. He played and socialised with the worlds leading players, who in turn introduced him to other rich aficionados. He was invited to join foursomes that included top tour players, and discovered that professional sportsman never play just for the love of the game: bets and side-bets, the complexity of which often had him confused, were made on every hole. And whereas professionals are used to holing putts that have large sums of money riding on them, Jonathan was not, and he missed more than he sunk. Because this high living social life had to be integrated with his duties as managing director of CVC UK Ltd a private jet, with accompanying aircrew, became de rigueur.

All very nice, all very expensive: which was okay because his wealth funded it and the income from his shareholding serviced the costs.

Shares that would plummet should Fatale be withdrawn

from sale.

At any other time that in itself wouldn't be the end of the world for Jonathan, he would still have his fortune, and the jet and jet-set life could be let go. That was if there had not been amongst the other 'aficionados' investment specialists, with records of changing small fortunes into large ones. Except in Jonathan's case it worked the other way round.

In a nutshell he was strapped for cash.

He wasn't an uncaring man, the moral principles he was raised with demanded that there was no alternative to the removal of Fatale. Only right now would not be the most advantageous time for the major source of his income to dry up.

The few minutes he had spent gazing out of the window at the cedars, had allowed Jonathan sufficient time to evaluate his situation and realise that Sharon was, unintentionally, solving the dilemma for him. For from what Jonathan knew of Lucidel's Chief Executive Officer he very much doubted that the man would share any similar moral reservations.

There was no way Luc Barr would withdraw Fatale.

Luc Barr's response to Sharon's letter and report was swift, and two pronged, and it did not come directly from him but from the head of research, who was technically Sharon's boss. He arrived in person, along with a team of four technicians and two large vans. Sharon was thanked for bringing the situation to his attention, and then requested to hand over all her data to his team: the matter would now be handled from Lucerne.

While he discussed the nature of her work with the rats and her findings from the death of Emily Farrow, the technicians removed Sharon's desk, four filling cabinets and two computers from her office and laboratory, and loaded them into one of the vans: any personal items found would be returned to her, she was informed. All her rats were loaded into the other van. Four hours from their arrival, the group departed with the total content of Sharon's research.

Before the month was out Sharon was informed that it had been decided that her department was surplus to requirements, and apart from retaining two junior technicians – who would come under the auspices of Production and Engineering – to carry out routine quality control, it was to be closed down. Sharon and the remains of her staff were now redundant.

Jonathan said he was prepared to be indignant on her behalf, but Sharon told him not to bother, other than to ensure that her staff received well over and above the statuary redundancy package.

She said her work had become repetitive and boring and that she would have probably resigned in any case, and of course her personal financial status negated any necessity for redundancy. Her apparent equanimity allowed Jonathan a sigh of relief: he had feared a far more bitter reception to the Lucidel decision.

In the aftermath Sharon accompanied her husband to America: initially to Georgia, as guests of the Augusta Golf Club for the Masters golf tournament, then to   Florida and   Palm Beach, and finally up to New York.

On their return she busied herself with further refurbishment of the manor house, together with certain weekends away: the nature of which she did not volunteer, and Jonathan did not ask.

Fatale remained on sale, worldwide.

Four months and ten days from the date of Sharon's letter to Luc Barr, informing him of her trepidations in regard to the possible side affect of Fatale on certain people at certain times, Wendy Lister, a twenty-seven year old, third generation West Indian dental hygienist, crashed her car on the M4 motorway.

Of the three passengers, her boyfriend, sister and her boyfriend, only Wendy and her sister's boyfriend survived.

At the inquest Wendy stated that they were travelling at around seventy miles per hour along the motorway when they saw the traffic ahead had come to a halt, but when she went to change gear to slow down, and then to brake, she couldn't get her limbs to coordinate.

Her sister's boyfriend, giving evidence, said that Wendy's arms were waving about, and that the last thing he heard her say, before the car careered into the rear of a stationary lorry, was that she couldn't make her arms and legs do what she wanted them to do.

Chapter Six

The door clicked shut behind the secretary. Luc Barr indicated to the four men gathered in his office to serve themselves from the coffee paraphernalia she had just deposited. It was a sparsely furnished room – his desk and chair, and a table and four chairs, two of which had been brought in for the occasion – and far smaller than those of his immediate underlings, but Luc Barr had no need for office space to prove his pre-eminence. Besides, he was rarely there, preferring to be constantly on the move from one Lucidel branch to the other. It was also different from the other offices in that it was entered through double doors and was completely sound proof. The environment fitted the man; Luc Barr, at fifty-two, was spare in build, clean-shaven, with only a dusting of grey in his close-cropped dark hair giving evidence of his years. He was habitually dressed in a dark-blue suit, matching tie, and white shirt. And while the four men in his office were seated,

Luc Barr remained standing and constantly paced about the room.

Three of the men were Lucidel employees:

Otto Klee, head of research: Dmitry Balakireff, head of finance: and Charles 'Chuck' McCoskey, head of security. Like Barr, Klee was Swiss; Balakireff and McCoskey, Russian and American respectively.

The fourth man was Ruben Nadleson, the lawyer the company used for matters pertaining to British law.

The language spoken was English.

Barr was the last to avail himself of the coffee, as he poured a cup he said, "Tell me, Otto, in your opinion just how accurate is the Sharon Greaves testimony these people are basing their case on?"

Klee placed his coffee cup to one side and opened a folder, the contents of which he knew intimately and had little need to consult. "After we removed the data and records from Frau Greaves laboratory. ."

"Which she had taken the precaution of copying?" Luc Barr interrupted."

"Apparently," Klee said.

He continued, "We examined her research on the rats and then conducted our own series of experiments, plus clinical examination of the Factor Y affect on the stimulus forwarding chemical. All of which confirmed her diagnosis."

"What exactly is Factor Y?" Burr asked.

The answer Klee gave was a five-syllable word that even he had difficulty in getting his tongue around.

"Basically it is a toxic cleaning agent," he clarified, "used extensively in industrial dry cleaning. Also many laboratories use it for cleaning, that's how initially it got to be added when Sharon Greaves was concocting Fatale, she added it by accident. Her reason for giving it the misnomer Factor Y was that five years earlier, when it was readily available under a proprietary brand name, there was a high profile case in England when a child was blinded by accidentally getting some in her eyes. However it is not the toxicity of Y that is the problem here - the amount used is too small to cause any toxic harm - but the chemical affect it has when mixed with the additives to the basic Fatale ingredients. The other problem is that it is Y that gives Fatale its unique taste, that something extra that gets people hooked. Right at the very start Sharon Greaves tried, unsuccessfully, various combinations without Y."

"Without Y there's no Fatale," Barr said. It was a statement, not a question, and was for the benefit of the others.

Klee said, "That is correct. As you know we have been trying to find a replacement, but up to now it has been unsuccessful."

"What are the chances of this reaction occurring?"

"Impossible to say because we don't know what triggers it. There might be another case tomorrow, or next year, or in five years time, or it might never happen again."

Barr curbed his impatience; he had never been able to get a definitive answer from scientists, or technical people. He tried again.

"One in a thousand? One in ten thousand? One in a million?"

Klee, equally impatient, made no attempt to hide his frustration at the question.

"When you pressed me for an answer initially, after we had received Sharon Greaves first report, I said that as she had only encountered one case, and as, at a guess, there had been over ten million bottles of Fatale sold, then statistically the chances were one in a million. Using the same basis it is now two in as many bottles sold."

Ruben Nadleson said, "If I might interject, Mr Barr, the question of probability is irrelevant. Two cases have been identified in England; the second occurring after Sharon Greaves had sent you a report advising that Fatale be withdrawn from sale. That is the real crux of the matter."

Barr nodded in acquiescence. In a worst-case scenario, what would be the sort of damages they could expect to face?

"At a guess, between one and three million pounds," the lawyer replied.

Barr then asked Dmitry Balakireff what the financial effect to Lucidel would be should the case go against them.

The Russian listed the options.

"At best Fatale is withdrawn from sale, meaning a loss in

revenue equal to eight percent of Lucidel's total turnover, and the write-off of the sixty million pound investment. In regard to the affect on Lucidel shares; at best they could be halved in value; at worst they could be devalued sufficiently for it to take decades to recover from.

"At best we are talking in hundreds of million euros, and at worst thousands of millions."

An ominous silence followed.

All of those present held shares in Lucidel, and each stood to lose a considerable amount, not in the least for the three Lucidel employees being the possibility of also losing a well remunerated position. For Luc Barr it would be a certainty, his dismissal would be instantaneous.

Ruben Nadleson was the first to speak, and he directed his question to Otto Klee.

"Would I be correct in assuming that although you could present a counter claim repudiating Mrs Greaves accusation, and have well qualified experts stand up in court and confirm that this was the case, the opposition could also do the same in support of Mrs Greaves?"

"Yes, you would be correct. Although I suppose we could question the validity of the videos."

"Ah, yes, I'd forgotten about them. Just how crucial are they to the oppositions case?"

"Sharon Greaves managed to film two of her rats during the period they were in a state of un-coordination. When this film was shown to Wendy Lister she is reported as saying that their movements resembled her own. The friends who were with Emily Farrow when she walked under a lorry have confirmed the same thing."

"Emm, pretty damning," Nadleson mused.

"Yes, but couldn't we counter by saying that the video film is manufactured?" Barr suggested, hopefully.

Nadleson didn't answer Barr directly; instead he said to Otto Klee, "Would I be correct in assuming that Sharon Greaves is a competent scientist, and one not given to emotionally motivated conclusions?"

"Extremely competent, in my opinion, Klee answered. "Her case-notes, experiments and results are exemplary in their presentation, and her conclusions are based solely on the evidence gathered. And, I might add, articulately and convincingly argued."

Turning to Barr, Nadleson said, "Then my answer to your suggestion is that by all means we can try it, but I would have to warn that it could be counter-productive. Under cross-examination Sharon Greaves would probably say that she had no motive for forging evidence. She stands to make no personal gain, on the contrary in fact: her husband, as MD of CVC UK and a major shareholder, stands to loose a great deal."

"She could be said to be vindictive after loosing her job," Barr retaliated.

"I think that the fact that you had her removed directly

after she wrote to you would be best not mentioned," Nadleson replied, then added, "Besides, I'm sure that was the reaction she expected the moment she decided to write to you."

Barr's expression mirrored his displeasure at being censured in front of his staff. Nadleson only got away with it because they needed him. As if to re-establish his pre-eminence he said, "Aren't we forgetting that the data Sharon Greaves is presenting was gathered while she was an employee of UVC UK, and as such is company property. Surely the Court Injunction we obtained when she was threatening to publish her findings in that scientific journal still stands."

Aware that he had overstepped the mark earlier, Nadleson was careful to temper his reply with a hint of humility. "You're right, of course, and it will be our first move. However, I would be failing in my capacity as your lawyer if I were not to warn that this could be over-ruled. In my experience, from similar cases - so unfortunately there are precedents - the judge may well rule that it is in the public interest for the evidence to be heard."

Luc Barr's reaction was of one syllable, and from the heart.

"Fuck."

"Sorry, but it had to be said."

The effect of the lawyer's apology on Barr's temperament was negligible.

"Do you have any positive suggestions?" he said, icily.

Nadleson said. "You are a multinational company being sued in a British court for negligence leading to the death of two innocent young people. In these types of cases the court is biased in favour towards the plaintiff. With no positive counter argument to the proof being presented my initial advice is to try and reach a settlement with the plaintiff out of court. Failing that I would suggest that you endeavour to get Sharon Greaves to withdraw her support."

Barr considered what Nadleson had said for a moment, and then asked, "This lawyer who's acting for Wendy Lister, how good is he?"

"She," Nadleson corrected. "Leigh Murray. She specialises in civil law, and her record for taking on the establishment, and winning, is impressive. Unlawful death, wrongful arrest, unfair dismissal, medical negligence: and in a number of them she's obtained sizable damages. Also Wendy Lister and her family trust her, she's from the same background: second/third generation West Indian middle-class."

"Would she be in possession of Sharon Greaves testimony; the reports and the video?"

"I think you can take that as fact."

"So if Sharon Greaves withdrew, this woman could still present her testimony?"

"That's correct. But – and I think Otto will support me on this – with technical evidence a lot depends on the originator presenting it. Even if Leigh Murray was to use another scientist to present Sharon Greaves evidence, because that scientist hadn't been intimately involved in the research, he or she wouldn't necessarily be able to answer cross questioning convincingly."

"Otto?" Barr asked Klee for confirmation.

"Yes, that is quite probable. In that circumstance I would be able to provide Mr Nadleson with sufficient questions, regarding the nature of Mrs Greaves work and how the results were obtained, that the person presenting the evidence would be at a disadvantage in answering."

"Interesting," Barr said.

"However," Nadleson countered, "it shouldn't be overlooked that Murray might well be able to subpoena Sharon Greaves for cross questioning."

With no further suggestions being presented, Barr brought the meeting to an end, but he asked Chuck McCoskey to remain.

The big, ex-CIA man, had a pretty good idea as to the reason and pre-empted what he expected Barr was going to ask by saying, "You can discount Wendy Lister agreeing to an out of court settlement. She and her family are staunch Presbyterians and her reason for bringing the case in not monetary gain. She lost a boyfriend and sister, and she's after public denunciation of Lucidel as a means of expunging her own sense of guilt."

"She told you all that, did she? Did you offer her the total amount I told you to go to?"

The American moved his sizable girth in the chair. "Mr Barr, I've been negotiating deals, both legally and illegally, for more years than I care to remember, and if I haven't learnt to read people and their reactions during that time I wouldn't be of much use to you or anyone else. And I've also been around long enough not to become personally involved, nor to mention figures and leave myself open to accusations of bribery. Miss Lister was approached by a third party, and the cost to Lucidel of defending the case plus the adverse publicity intimated rather than spelt out. She's a clever girl she was able to work it out."

"Offer, or intimate, double the amount."

"Won't do any good."

"Maybe, but try it all the same. Now, what have you found out about Sharon Greaves? How's her marriage? One would have thought Jonathan's finances, and the damage a collapse in his shares would do to him, might have been sufficient incentive for her to have pulled out by now."

"Well now," McCoskey drawled, "according to Jonathan the atmosphere between them is pretty tense, but neither of them is talking about separation, so in that respect the marriage is still sound. We had quite a heart-to-heart, and he said that he had explained the consequences to Sharon, that he could lose everything, but her reply was that she was sufficiently wealthy to ensure that he would still enjoy a comfortable life style, and that he would be far better off than the Ulme Valley workers. She told him that she had weighed up the effect the withdrawal of

Fatale would have on the workforce against the future deaths she sees arising from allowing it to remain on sale, and had come to the conclusion that there was no contest; people can always find other jobs."

"And Jonathan goes along with this? When I spoke with him, when this thing first broke, the impression I got was that he was pretty pissed off with his wife, and that he was going to do everything to talk her out of it."

"As I see it she's got him so he's between the devil and the deep blue sea. That deep down part of him agrees with her, and admires her conviction. But he's also become used to the life style Fatale's money has given him, and he's convinced that his present money problems are temporary, or would be if the Fatale money keeps rolling in. So, yes, in that respect he'll keep trying to talk her out of it, but I can't see it doing much good. At best he'll keep us posted on her movements and anything he thinks we should know, except, as Sharon is fully aware of his stand on the matter, I can't see her telling him very much from now on."

Barr ceased his pacing and perched his rear against the desk. "I agree," he said, "I don't think we can rely on Jonathan for much input. In the back of his mind will be the fact that if Lucidel loses he'll be reliant on his wife for the future."

McCoskey smiled. "Which in one way is a little surprising, seeing that it has been what they call an 'open' marriage, and for quite some time, or so I gather."

"Oh yes?" Barr leaned forward, his interest aroused. "I

never saw Jonathan as that type," he said, and laughed. "I always thought it was only golf that stirred his passion."

McCoskey said, "I didn't say it was Jonathan," and it was his turn to smile, at wrong-footing Barr, a rare occurrence. "Fucks like the proverbial rabbit."

"Well, well, Mrs holier than thou Sharon Greaves. Your little chat with Jonathan really was a heart-to-heart."

"Oh, it wasn't Jonathan who told me, it's all done tres discreet, and I guess they've come to some sort of agreement, no it was one of my people who dug it up. If you pay enough you'll always find someone who'll talk. It appears that she doesn't have affairs rather than one-night stands. She goes to a number of conferences, seminars, that sort of thing, and it's there where she tends to meet her partners. She also belongs to one of those secret groups that have orgies at regular intervals."

Barr grinned maliciously. "Can we use it to discredit her? There's nothing the British public, and the establishment, likes more that a bit of sex scandal: murder, rape and pillage they can forgive, but give them a Mother Teresa bitch on heat, who's whoring her wares to all and sundry, and they'll crucify her. It could be the difference between us being found responsible or given the benefit of the doubt."

It wasn't often that Barr let his prejudice show, like Sharon Greaves he was careful to keep his particular foible discreet, but from the odd lapse McCoskey had gleaned his boss's misogyny early on. And one had only to look at the company structure for confirmation: there were no women amongst the senior management, and only a token few at the middle level. Barr wasn't, and never had been married.

McCoskey said, "Providing it's true, at the moment all we have is someone's word for it. We'll need at least two other people willing to publicly confirm the fact, plus documented and photographic proof. Relying solely on innuendo can result in totally the opposite result. But it's certainly something we can look into."

Barr nodded. He pushed himself from off the side of his desk and walked round to the other side. For the first time in the meeting he sat down. The following five minutes were spent in thought; then he took a key from his pocket, opened a desk drawer, removed a slip of paper and pushed it across the desktop to McCoskey.

He said, "That's the number of a bank account I've opened for you to use. The fund should be more than sufficient for the purpose but it can be topped up if necessary. If, as you predict, the Lister girl turns an increased out of court settlement down, then use the fund to ensure that Sharon Greaves doesn't appear in court. By all means try to use the whoring to discredit her, but the most important thing is that she doesn't present her evidence; neither voluntarily nor by being subpoenaed. Use any method necessary to obtain this result. Do I make myself clear?"

McCoskey heaved himself up from the chair and pocketed the slip of paper. "As the day is long, Mr Barr," he answered.

"You have carte blanche, do whatever you have to," Barr reiterated, "but I don't want to know the details. If anything goes wrong it can't be traced back to here."

"That goes without saying, Mr Barr."

Chapter Seven

Alan Swift removed the folded fifty-pound note from the top pocket of his tuxedo jacket and handed it back to the man who had just deposited it there.

"Thanks, but no thanks," he said.

The young woman, clinging to the man's arm said, "Tell him you're a personal friend of Mandy." From the look on the man's face it was obvious to Alan that he was wishing he had never made the boast.

"Sorry, sir, madam, but no exceptions," Alan said. "I'm afraid you'll have to join the queue."

The man attempted a nonchalant shrug and guided his reluctant companion towards the end of the line of other hopefuls. Alan heard her say "Why don't you give Mandy a call, I've got my mobile," and smiled inwardly. It was coming up to midnight, the club was packed, and looking at the number of people waiting Alan not only doubted that the man had the owner's number but also, unless they were prepared to hang about for the next two hours, that they would ever gain admittance.

Then, not for the first time since he had taken the job, he wondered if this was what it had all come to: doorman cum bouncer at a nightclub. Even if the club was Mandy's, for the moment London's most needed to be seen at nightspot.

The mobile phone in his inside pocket trilled – he had refused to wear the ear and mouth set the other bouncers, along with wraparound shades, considered de rigueur. He took a step back into the doorway and took the call.

"Yes?"

"I've had word that Lady Fiona Dudley-Howard is on her way. Don't let in; I'm not having her in here, dealing; she'll get me closed down."

Alan liked Mandy Constantine but her smoky rasp grated. Her surname, and money, came from a Greek husband, now long departed. She was of a certain age, stick thin and elegant, and on everyone's 'A' list: but she rarely appeared. Mrs Constantine kept her private life exactly that.

Alan passed the message to the other bouncer sharing doorman duty with him. Sean smiled, "Be a pleasure." He had never concealed his dislike of the privileged classes and welcomed any opportunity to humiliate them.

"But discreetly," Alan added.

"What ever you say, Sarge."

The nickname, Sarge, originated from Alan's rank when he was a serving marine, and also his unofficial but generally recognised leadership of the security staff.

Ten minutes later the lady in question, wearing a dress that missed being obscene by a hairs breath and which probably carried a price tag of four figures, marched past the queue, fully aware of being instantly recognized. Alan barred her entrance and said, "Sorry, your ladyship, Mrs Constantine says you're not to be let in tonight." He spoke softly in order that their conversation should not be overheard by the crowed still waiting in line.

Lady Fiona, however, had no intention of being quiet about the matter. "Don't be stupid, Mellors," she proclaimed, which brought a ripple of laughter from those in earshot, and stepped round Alan. Sean barred her way. Alan said, again softly, "Don't make a scene, Fiona, you're not coming in." Her face took on a petulant pout but Alan saw the confusion in her eyes, and something else: fear? Unused to not having her own way, she resorted to elitism disdain and said, "Don't be so fucking familiar." Then she turned on her heel and marched back down the street.

Sean looked at Alan. Alan shrugged; neither had expected such an easy capitulation.

Half a dozen people came through the door, and there was an expectant surge from the line of waiting hopefuls. One of those at the front grinned at his three companions and said to

Alan, "Going to let us in now, Mellors?" The laughter this remark imbued quickly petered out as Alan stared at the man with unblinking eyes. Then he pointed at the people standing behind the perpetrator and his audience and said to Sean, "Let six of them through."

"You can't do that," the man at the front said.

"Yes I can," Alan replied, then added, "Goodnight." The implication was clear, the man and his friends could wait all night but they were never going to be let in. The angry group reluctantly left the queue; their ire directed more to the big-mouthed cause of their disbarment than the two bouncers. Sean's murmured but audible, "Wanker", summed up their opinion.

Alan thought, 'What the hell am I doing here?'

The excitement over the queuing crowd settled back to resigned waiting. Over the next half hour a few more gained entrance, and some, tired of waiting, left of their own accord. Taking advantage of the lull, Sean left Alan to use the staff toilet situated at the rear of the club.

An open topped Maserati pulled up outside the club and Alan recognised Lady Fiona wedged in the rear seat. Ignoring the double yellow line two men got out of the car, with Lady Fiona in tow. The driver was a tall man in his late twenties, wearing a dinner jacket over jeans and an open necked white shirt. Alan noticed that the tie, pulled down to half- mast, was that of the household cavalry. His companion was shorter, dressed in a black roll neck sweater and jeans, and wore a belligerent expression: a fellow officer, Alan surmised. The pair strode across the pavement and faced Alan, with Lady Fiona hovering in the background. There was a bruise on her arm that hadn't been there earlier.

"Could you please inform your employer that Thomas Yeoward would like a word with her."

Alan took out his mobile and pressed the coded number. Mandy answered on the second ring, and Alan passed on Thomas Yeoward's request. "Tell him to go fuck himself," Mandy said and the line went dead. Before taking the mobile from his ear Alan assessed the situation: the right hon. Thomas Yeoward was probably Lady Fiona's supplier, augmenting his allowance and guards officer salary to pay for expensive Italian hardware. Mandy's terse reply indicated that maybe his appearance was not unexpected, and that she had set the confrontation up: Yoeward was a nuisance who needed nipping in the bud. He looked in good shape and had the manner and confidence of a man used to getting what he wanted, and Alan wondered if he had seen action: Northern Ireland, the Middle East?

The tall guards officer watched Alan replace the mobile in his pocket. "Well?" he asked.

"Mrs Constantine advises that you leave and sexually abuse yourself."

The queue was enjoying the scene, and the laughter that

greeted Alan's reply rippled down the line as what he had said was relayed back.

Although not a small man, compared with the pumped muscle and bulk of Sean and the other bouncers Alan was made to seem almost diminutive. Yoeward's expression indicated that this was the impression he had formed, and that he wasn't going to meekly accept being ridiculed in public by someone so insignificant. Alan wondered what form Yoeward's attack would take, and how he was going to handle it. Mandy did not encourage her security staff to get into brawls, either in the club or outside; expecting any disturbance to be swiftly defused with the minimum of fuss. Not so easy when you are on your own and the opposition is two handed. What the hell was taking Sean so long?

As it was, Yoeward made it easy for him: when he made to grab Alan's lapels, in preparation of delivering a head butt. Alan's hands intercepted those of his adversary, and then they began to apply pressure. His father had possessed strong hands and Alan had inherited the trait, and then some. Their strength bordered on the phenomenal, and had in no small way been responsible for his promotion during a certain covert kafuffle. Yoeward's mouth opened in a silent exclamation, the excruciating pain preventing any sound from coming out, and his legs began to collapse beneath him. It took the fellow officer a moment or two to realise what was happening, when he did he stepped forward to intercept.

"Stay where you are," Alan snapped, and the barked order had sufficient impact to momentarily halt the friend's offensive. But Alan knew it would only be momentary and then, against Mandy's strict instruction, he would be left with no other option than to severely hurt both men. In public, and it wouldn't be pretty. Fortunately, at that moment the intimidating bulk of Sean reappeared.

"Problems, Sarge?" he asked, assessing the situation and placing himself directly in front of Yoeward's fellow officer. Alan saw the sound of his nickname register in Yoeward's eyes: the guards officer probably had been in one of the trouble spots at some time, and he may or may not have distinguished himself, but he had been in command of someone like Alan and seen him in action and he was afraid. A command bought by position rather than earned, Alan thought contemptuously. Then stopped himself: never make it personal, he reminded himself, it leads to mistakes.

"Nothing I can't handle," he answered Sean, "but you could escort those two back to the car. Call for reinforcements if necessary. One of them had better take the wheel."

Sean's contemptuous sneer and the threat of reinforcement was enough to ensure the fellow officer's compliance. Lady Fiona, who had observed the whole scene with a look of spaced out detachment, meekly followed suit. She had probably been sampling some of her own wares Alan thought, not unkindly recalling the bruise on her arm. Thank God, if she had been a screamer the whole thing could have been a damn sight messier.

Alan still held Yoeward on his knees, although he had lessened the pressure on the man's hands slightly. After Sean had seen the other two into the Maserati, Alan asked him to go through Yoeward's pockets. Amongst the usual paraphernalia the search revealed a switchblade knife. "Not what you would associate with an officer and a gentleman," Alan commented, "but I suppose it's a little less conspicuous than a sabre." Sean pocketed the knife then prepared to go through Yoeward's wallet. "Just give me his driving licence then put the stuff back in his pockets," Alan ordered.

The grip on Yoeward's hand was then released. Alan and Sean lifted him to his feet and helped him into the car. "Give me your driving licence," Alan said to the fellow officer, then quietly, out of earshot of the spectators, he opened both of the driving licences and said, "I know who you both are and where to find you. If either of your names comes within my hearing again I'll come looking for you."

The car drove off amongst a buzz of appreciation from the queue. All were in agreement that they where happy not to have gained admittance: nothing in the club that night would have matched the entertainment outside.

Alan made his way back into the club to report the details of the incident to Mandy.

He had to get out of this life.

Until he was eighteen Alan Swift had lived in America and had held dual nationality. His father, Ronald 'Ron' Swift, was a Sergeant Major in the British Army, who met and married Stella Wingate when he was stationed in Belize. Stella, a nurse, was working in the American hospital there. The marriage didn't last, once the passion had abated they discovered that they weren't really compatible, besides which Stella couldn't settle to the constant move from base to base that is the life of a British NCO who trains others. After two years Stella returned to her home base of San Diego, taking seven months old Alan with her.

Stella remarried twice, the first time to Stan, when Alan was three – which lasted five years – and the second time to Eugene, by whom she had a daughter, Kelly, when he was nine. Alan quite liked his first stepfather, detested the second and was indifferent to his stepsister. Between the ages of ten to seventeen the high spot of his year – and that of his stepfather and sister - was when he spent the summer vacation with Ron, who by this time was permanently stationed at the British Army training centre, situated in the Hampshire town of Aldershot. Alan was his father's son, and felt comfortably at home within the military establishment.

The life Stella had planned for her son was for him to graduate from High School, study Business Administration at college, join Gene's real estate business, marry a nice American girl and provide her with grandchildren. To Alan it sounded like pure hell. On his eighteenth birthday he caught a flight to England and stayed long enough with his father to exercise his right and adopt British nationality, and then enlist in the Royal Marines.

Stella was heartbroken, Gene and Kelly over the moon. In the distance of time Alan became reconciled with all three.

By the age of twenty-three he was a corporal, and eligible to apply for a post in the Special Boat Service, SBS. His strength and fitness were more than adequate – he boxed successfully for the regiment, with few of his bouts going the distance – and the sessions with psychiatrist confirmed that he possessed the correct mental attitude for guerrilla and covert operations. He was accepted, and trained in the art of reconnaissance, sabotage and commando techniques. It was during training that his innate strength became apparent to the instructors, and in a particular session, for unarmed combat, the extraordinary power of his hands. Alan had been picked at random from the rest of the trainees and told by the instructor that he was going to come at him with a knife. What usually happened was that the trainee would side step, try and grab the knife hand and endeavour to wrestle it from the instructor, to which the instructor would make a counter move which resulted in the trainee finding himself with an arm around his neck and the knife at his throat. Then the instructor would show them the right way to go about disarming a knife-wielding assailant. In Alan's case, instead of sidestepping he simply wrapped one of his large hands over the instructor's knife carrying hand and applied pressure. It wasn't sufficient to disarm the instructor, he was too experienced for that to happen, but it did necessitate a more contrived manoeuvre to arrive with the knife against Alan's throat. Afterwards, ruefully rubbing his wrist, the instructor passed on the fact of Corporal Swift's special gift to the other instructors. In future sessions, especially where pressure to the neck was used as a method of disarming, special observation was kept on Alan to ensure he didn't, unintentionally, go too far. But Alan had been aware of his talent for some time and had learned to control it.

On completion of training he graduated amongst the top half dozen.

He saw action on three occasions within his eighteen months service with the unit. On one mission, where the SBS was seconded to a 'friendly' African country – a former colony – to help counter an insurgent force gathering in a bordering country, it was necessary to 'take out' two sentries, and Alan was assigned to the task. It was imperative that the sentries be 'retired' silently and swiftly, and was doubly dangerous, as it had to be carried out in early morning daylight. Alan strangled both of the sentries with his bare hands; rising up suddenly in front of each, clasping the startled man's neck and watching the life go out of his eyes before he was able to utter a sound. The removal of the sentries played no small part in the success of the operation, in which there were no SBS casualties, and earned Alan a promotion to sergeant and the Distinguished Service Medal – undisclosed as the British Army was not officially at war with the bordering country.

In the post action debriefing Alan stated that he had disposed of the sentries by the standard textbook method – from behind, placing an arm around the throat and administering sufficient pressure as to make the man inoperable. He gave the psychiatrist the same story. As the unit hadn't hung around there was no one to contradict his account - not that any one wanted to. All the same if he had given the correct version he would have undoubtedly been suspended from further action, and most probably given an honourable discharge.

At the conclusion of his term in the unit Alan's personal body count was four.

The return to his regiment felt like an anticlimax. Post service counselling and analysis was mandatory, the Army being only too well aware of the void left after the high-octane intoxication of special services, a way of life and state of mind it was too easy to become accustomed. It was the main reason for only allowing a person one term in the unit, and then only for eighteen months. That and burn out.

Two years later, when his term of enlistment in the Marines expired, Alan did not re-enlist. Instead he joined what was termed a private security company, a synonym for private army, mercenaries.

Except the number of conflicts requiring highly trained and disciplined, and expensive, private armies was diminishing. With the fall of the Soviet empire there was a plethora of inexpensive ex-professionals and an abundance of cut-price hardware available, sufficient to flood what had already started to become a diminishing market. Tin-pot dictators were now able to arm their forces with an endless supply of weaponry and ammunition. These armed forces that might be ill disciplined and untrained but with enough guns and bullets to indiscriminately blast away with, they were able, by the law of averages, to defeat or contain any invasion or insurrection. There was also an added bonus: Despots realised that armies manned by an over armed, undisciplined, often drunk, members of an opposing, and mutually hated, tribe or clan were a far more terrifying proposition for subjecting a populace than a force of unbiased, disciplined and relatively civilised professionals.

To survive, companies like the one Alan had joined, Paladin Security, had to seek alternative employment. Tycoons, whose wealth from oil, minerals, armaments, computer technology, drugs (legal and illegal) and consumables in general was often greater than the gross product of their native country, were the new employers. Concerned for the personal safety of themselves and their families, they were willing to pay top dollar for the best n security. The path from protection to aggression to elimination is a fine one. As a means of protection a case can be made for hitting your opponent before he hits you: nipping the problem in the bud, as it were. However, sometime during such a skirmish, if it was to be successful, the leader of the opposing faction has to be positively eliminated: which means someone, on a one-to-one basis, has to fire the bullet or put the knife in. Subsequently it is a logical path to argue for the assassination of the enemy leader, thus removing the necessity of a full scale armed confrontation. Alan discovered that he was able to fulfil this task without the loss of appetite or sleep. He became an assassin, a hit man.

Once again this was an overcrowded market, so to be able to command top price an assassin needed to be, versatile, invisible, and dependable: one hundred percent dependable. Alan was all of these.

He was expert with firearms, an above average shot, was familiar with explosives, and had been taught how to kill with knife, garrotte and bare hands.

His physique, although muscular, was not a distinguishing feature: he possessed a pleasant countenance, without being noticeably handsome or ugly: his transatlantic accent was classless and could be broadened or anglicised to suit: and he was as equally comfortable in a business suit, tuxedo or jeans. He possessed a quick, retentive and versatile brain - the teenage choice to enlist in the marines, instead of going on to higher education, had been from inclination rather than any lack of intelligence necessary for college entrance. In the field his commando training enabled him to be self-sufficient and to be able to blend into the terrain, while at the same time his unpretentious appearance and manners allowed concealment within an urban environment - similar to a waiter, airline steward, shop assistant, with demeanour and features that were unassuming and unthreatening and, therefore, immediately forgettable. Ostensibly he was an employee of Paladin Security, had a National Insurance number and paid income tax.

As an assassin he had killed six times: twice in the Balkans and once in Hong Kong, Brazil, America and Ireland. Five men and one woman, two of them, including the woman, strangled using his bare hands. Only in America and Ireland had his presence been noted, but when questioned the witnesses were able to give the police only the sketchiest of descriptions, none of them corroborative.

Alan took a pride in his work: his kills were quick and clean with no innocent bystanders involved. On the one occasion he had used an explosive device, attached to the chassis of a car, he had not detonated the device until the car was in an unpopulated area, so only the driver – the target – had been killed. In Brazil he had been forced to kill someone in addition to the target, but as he was the target's bodyguard Alan did not consider him an innocent victim.

Each contract was meticulously planned from start to finish, and always with at least two contingency plans in case of hiccups. False paper, passports and driving licences were destroyed after the operation, and never duplicated. Every item of his clothing was devoid of maker's name and, also, destroyed afterwards. Nothing was left to chance. Carl Peterson, the owner of Paladin Security and the person who arranged the contracts, was his sole contact. Earnings from each contract were paid into an offshore numbered account.

Privately, Alan considered his greatest asset was his ability to know and understand himself. He was aware that his capability to murder without conscience was abnormal, yet he did not consider himself as being insane or a psychopath. There were no sudden urges to kill when the moon was full, he didn't hear voices, nor did he get a sexual kick from killing. It was purely business, and apart from the satisfaction of a job well done there was no enjoyment.

That wasn't completely true: during the act of strangulation, when he was looking into the victim's eyes watching the life ebb away, he had to admit to an adrenalin rush: but he rationalised it as being akin to a boxer knocking-out an opponent, or a tennis player hitting a winning forehand to take a Wimbledon final. Unlike a winning athlete it didn't make him want to go out and do it again – unless he was being paid to.

Money was the sole motivation, as Alan saw it he was cashing in on a talent. And it was extremely lucrative, five more years and he should have sufficient funds stowed away to enable him to live a comfortable life without ever needing to work again.

Perhaps he would buy a boat.

He could not recall ever hating any one – even his teenage dislike for his step father and sister was never actually hatred – and although he had never experienced overwhelming love he did not consider himself to be without feelings. The grief of a mother mourning the death of a child had moved him, and he had felt compassion for fellow servicemen when they received letters from wives or girlfriends saying that they had met someone else and it was all over. He could understand that at some time, with the death of his father, and perhaps his mother, he might feel grief, but he couldn't imagine himself ever being in a position to suffer the pangs of desertion or unrequited love.

The concept of consuming hatred or love - being in love – was outside of his emotional scope, because as he had never been emotionally involved with any one person, he lacked experience of either.

Sexual gratification was within his realm of sensual responses. He enjoyed sex and, partly because he feared the consequences of his abnormal strength should he loose control during the throes of the act, and partly because he had discovered that you had to give enjoyment to receive it, he was considered a tender and considerate lover.

Although he liked being with women he did not seek or encourage the forming of relationships, and the majority of his encounters were of the casual variety. Pick-ups and one-night stands when he sought female company and sex, bar girls or prostitutes when it was simply sex. Because he had a number of male acquaintances he was thought of among them, and their wives and girlfriends, to be gregarious, but should they have been questioned at any time few would have known his history or where he lived.

He possessed no actual friends.

The self-knowledge that he was different to other people, that he lacked certain emotions, he accepted without regret. He wasn't unhappy because of it. Early on in his career he had realised that it was a positive advantage.

"Will he need to go to hospital?" Mandy Constantine asked after Alan related what had occurred with Thomas Yeoward.

"He will if he has any sense."

"Could the police become involved?"

"Yeoward and his friend won't say anything."

"You seem positive of that."

"I am, believe me."

Mandy Constantine looked at him quizzically.

Alan stared back blandly.

After a moment Mandy said, "How about Lady Fiona Dudley-Howard?"

Alan recalled the frightened little girl with the bruised arm that lurked beneath the brash, sophisticated veneer.

Yeoward, or someone like him would be the death of her. He said, "I think she had imbibed sufficient nose-candy, or what ever it is she's on, to ensure complete amnesia."

Mandy smiled. "It sounds as if you've handled the matter very nicely, Alan."

She rose from behind the desk and moved to one of the two sofas that resided in her office. "I think you can take the rest of the night off." She sank down into the sofa and crossed her legs, the skirt of her dress parting to reveal the fabled legs.

"Why don't you pour us both a drink?"

Alan's face remained a blank. Fucking the boss was definitely not on; the complications that would follow didn't bear thinking about.

Not that he wasn't tempted.

"If you don't mind, Mrs Constantine, I think I'll just have an early night."

It was two o'clock in the morning.

Mandy burst out laughing. "Okay. Alan," she said with a wave. When he reached the door she said,

"Ask Sean to come up would you?"

That was it, he was going to phone Carl Peterson the next morning and tell him that he had had enough.

Two days later, after reconsidering his position – if he quit Mandy's he'd only end up doing the same thing somewhere else – Carl Peterson telephoned

"I've got a contract that's just up your street."

Chapter Eight

Parked across the street, Alan watched the woman emerge from the cinema, take a pair of sunglasses from her bag, don them and then walk off. He watched until she rounded the corner and was lost from sight. She walked well, like a model strolling on a catwalk, back straight, her hips undulating beneath the tight skirt. He started the car and drove away in the opposite direction, taking a circulatory route that brought him back round to the path he knew she would be taking. Catching sight of her he slowed down, and then stopped when he reached her. Lowering the window he asked her for directions - to a fictitious hotel. She answered that she didn't know and suggested he ask at the cinema, where people were arriving for the next performance. She had a pleasant voice, cultured without being forced. For a moment their eyes locked, then he thanked her, smiled, and she smiled back.

He drove to the cinema, did a U turn and retraced his route, giving her a wave as he passed, but she didn't see it. Then, as luck would have it, he caught an immediate set of traffic lights. She looked in when she reached him. He quickly lowered the window. "I've found out where the Albion hotel is," he said and smiled. She also smiled: there was something there, he was sure of it, taking a chance he added, "Would you like to come and see it?" Immediately he regretted asking her, it was too soon, it could jeopardise the whole operation. Fuck!

But she opened the door and got in.

It wasn't meant to happen like this, his original plan was to take it more slowly, stage a few chance meetings and go from there. The client, or someone, had been keeping tabs on her for some weeks and had provided a comprehensive dossier, so Alan was fully acquainted with her life style. As well as visiting the cinema regularly, she attended a chess club on a Tuesday evening and a bridge club Thursday evenings. She was a member of a Sports Centre, where she swam, worked-out, and did an aerobic session.

The dossier on the woman, Sharon Greaves, had also included her predilection for promiscuous sex, and her preference for partners: she portrayed no apparent prejudices in regard to race creed or colour, but showed a tendency for men between the age of thirty to sixty, and of a similar social and intellectual background as herself. She usually met them at seminars and conferences, either at the venue or hotel she was staying at. There was no trawling pubs and dives for 'a bit of rough'. The selective sex club she belonged to did not meet on a regular basis but advised members of the date and venue for the next meeting through a coded advert in one of the daily newspapers.

Mrs Greaves was discreet but, apparently, not discreet enough; and when you have sufficient money to spend there is always someone ready to 'kiss and tell': and the comprehensiveness of the dossier certainly confirmed that the client had the necessary funds. Alan surmised that this was Jonathan Greaves, the target's husband.

Sharon Greaves was thirty-eight years of age. There was one child, a son, Leon, who attended a public school as a border. The photographs supplied showed a slim attractive dark haired woman.

Alan had been given a time limit of three months to complete the assignment, with a stipulation that Sharon Greaves' death should, preferably, not look like an obvious hit. There was an added incentive of a twenty percent bonus if it was completed within one month.

Sharon's sexual tendencies interested Alan, the casual encounters with no emotional ties or recriminations; in many ways they mirrored his own. The more he thought of it, using them as a means to undertake the contract, the more it seemed like an obvious method to achieve the required, stipulated result

- an over vigorous sexual encounter culminating in an unpremeditated death. He fell within the scope of her preferences, being more or less in the right age group and felt himself sufficiently able to comply with necessary intellectual requirements. The idea appealed to Alan, thinking through the mechanics of the enterprise he found, somewhat to his fascination, that it also excited him, which in turn disturbed him.

First he had to devise a method to meet with Sharon. One of the conferences she liked to attend would have been ideal, but when he checked he found that there were only two scheduled, one in Sunderland and the other in Birmingham, and Sharon Greaves was not registered to attend either. The sex club, because of its anonymity and selectiveness, was out, but the fitness centre could prove to be an ideal venue. Checking it out, and then familiarising himself with the streets and environs of Exeter, he conceived a strategy. Initially, asking the way after she left the cinema, followed by a couple of chance encounters at the fitness centre. By then he should be able to ascertain if she found him attractive; if she didn't then it would have to be something a little more prosaic: hit and run, a fatal fall, or perhaps an abduction to a lonely spot - except that would have to look like a sex killing and rape was something Alan was incapable of. An unwilling sex partner was a turn off for him, not a turn on. He would think of something, hopefully it wouldn't come to that.

Next he had to find a hotel, sufficiently large so as there would be unused rooms. Peterson could supply him with a bunch of keys or a selection of master plastic cards that would open any hotel room. After he had selected half a dozen he checked them out: hanging about the foyer between five and six o'clock in the evening on a week day, when it was at its busiest, and then making his way to the least desirable section of the hotel – where people were only put when nothing else was available – and waiting to see if the rooms there were being used.

The Devonshire Hotel was perfect, better than he could have hoped. A section was closed off for refurbishment, when he inspected it Alan discovered the work had not yet commenced and that the rooms were still made up. And there was access for patrons to the bar cum nightclub at the rear of the hotel. Posing as the representative of a firm of interior decorators, Alan telephoned the hotel manager, saying that he had heard of the refurbishment and asking if his company could bid for it.

The manager informed him that the contract had already been awarded. Alan then called the successful company, asking for details of the scope of the contract and to ascertain if there was anything his company could bid for as a sub-contactor. He learned that the contract included completely stripping and disposing of the present furnishings and fittings, and then doing a complete makeover, but he was a little late in the day, as work was scheduled to begin in four weeks time. Alan concluded the call by saying that he would send them a selection of brochures, just in case there was something. He had learned all he needed to know. Four weeks would fit nicely into the period for earning the twenty percent bonus.

As a precaution, a false name for his designated hotel was easily obtained by searching through the relevant section of Yellow Pages – there was no Albion hotel listed.

Alan attempted a few words of conversation during the drive, relating the excuse he had made up earlier for not knowing the route to the hotel, but she didn't seem interested in it, or conversation. Her excitement was palpable. It stimulated his own mounting arousal.

No one saw them arrive. In the room she barely glanced at the décor, just stood there, waiting, as she watched him take off his jacket and tie: shrugging off her own jacket. He went to her and removed her blouse and skirt, feeling a tremble beneath her skin, and the nipples hardening as the back of his fingers brushed against her breasts.

They kissed tentatively, her arms entwining about his neck as the kiss deepened.   Her clothes, he noticed, were expensive: the linen jacket and skirt cut to minimise the intrinsic creasing of the material: and her underwear, though minimal, fitted as if tailored - when he removed the bra and thong there was no tell tale lines or welts. Her pubis had been waxed and was totally devoid of hair, and was soft and smooth to the touch of his lips.

She responded to the caresses of his hands, fingers and

mouth, reciprocated in like; to an intensity he had never experienced or thought possible.

Their bodies moved to a gradually accelerating rhythm. He held himself back, waiting until her undulating body announced the commencement of her orgasm. He cupped her face in his hands. She opened her eyes. As his hands moved to her throat his excitement intensified, and his temples throbbed as the blood coursed through his veins. Her mouth parted in a small, startled sigh, as if the blood was pumping into her. She stared up at him. The words, I love you, I love you, echoed in his head.

She climaxed as he increased the pressure of his hand around her throat. His own followed as she went limp beneath him.

He dressed quickly, putting the used condom in a plastic bag, and using a handkerchief to wipe all surfaces he thought his hands might have come into contact with. The same handkerchief was used to open and close the door to the room. He vacated the hotel and car park with the same anonymity as his arrival.

The hire car, also suitably wiped of fingerprints, was returned and the bill paid in cash. He caught a bus to the outskirts of the city, deposited the plastic bag containing the used condom in a trash bin, and then walked the remainder of the way to the field that housed his solitary caravan.

The adrenalin was still pumping. Changing into jeans and walking boots he tramped the surrounding fields and hills until exhausted.

When the trilling of his mobile woke him the next morning and a none too pleased Carl Peterson told him that Sharon Greaves was still alive, Alan was surprised to experience a sensation of relief.

Chapter Nine

Ed, the hire car driver who worked for Leigh Murray almost exclusively, was waiting for Sharon outside the hospital. He opened the rear door of the ubiquitous grey Mondeo as she approached, taking the over-night bag from her hand and depositing it in the boot. "'Evening, Mrs Greaves," were the only words the usually loquacious Ed uttered; Leigh having cautioned him against engaging Sharon in conversation and endangering her tender vocal cords. The motorway was quiet and it took a little under three hours to reach London and Leigh Murray's Islington flat.

In appearance, the lawyer favoured her stern lipped Jamaican, schoolteacher, grandmother; whose photograph sat on a small occasional table. Next to it was one of Leigh's mother, a contrast of beautiful smiling face surrounded by an abundance of thick black curls. Leigh, like her grandmother, opted to wear her hair cropped to within a quarter of an inch of her scalp. Sharon had never seen her dressed in any other colour than black: this particular evening consisting of cashmere sweater and jeans.

In the brief telephone call from the hospital, Sharon had simply said that a man had left her for dead in a hotel room, and Leigh's reaction had been to arrange for Ed to collect her straight away. Now, with Sharon sat in an armchair, provided with a large tumbler of whisky, lemon and honey in hot water, Leigh requested a more detailed account of what had happened.

Sharon had initially come in to contact with the lawyer after Lucidel slapped the court injunction preventing the publication of her article. The editor of the particular scientific journal had mentioned Leigh Murray's name in connection with the success she had had in representing individuals seeking redress from the establishment and large corporations, and winning. Sharon made contact with her, they met and, after she had had Sharon's work and results independently scrutinised, agreed to contact Wendy Lister.

Gathered with Wendy and her parents in the living room of their Hammersmith house, Sharon explained the history of connection with Fatale, the nature of her experiments, the results and Lucidel's reaction. Leigh Murray then detailed the legal position and, should Wendy wish to take the matter further, that she would act for them on a no win no fee basis. Sharon added that she would meet all the other costs, including those of the barrister.

Wendy and her parents asked for time to discuss the matter between themselves, and with the parents of Wendy's late boyfriend.

The following day Wendy telephoned Leigh to say she wanted to go ahead with the action. Notice was subsequently served on Lucidel, informing that they were being sued for negligence.

Leigh Murray's reaction, after Sharon had completed her story, was similar to the detective who had interviewed her in the hospital: "You've done this before, you make a habit of going with strange men," etc. She then added, "I think you had better appraise me with the full account of this," hesitating for a moment, "side of your life."

"So," Leigh said, after Sharon regaled her with the details of 'that side of her life', including the arrangement she had with her husband, and she had contemplated the possible consequences arising from the incident, "why didn't you acquaint me with all of this before?"

"Because I didn't think it was relevant. Also because I gauged what your reaction would be."

"Oh, and what was that?"

"Disapproval."

"Whether I approve or disapprove is immaterial. Didn't it occur to you how vulnerable it might make you?"

"No, I didn't. I still don't, for that matter."

Leigh raised her eyes to heaven. "Your recent escapade is a reported police incident, which means there's a chance the press will get wind of it, if they get the full details they will have a field day – Wife of multi-millionaire in casual pick-up, rough sex romp – and this is before the case with Lucidel has even begun."

"It has nothing to do with the scientific evidence I'm presenting."

"Oh come on, you can't be that naïve. There is nothing the British public like more than hearing about someone having a bit of sex on the side – and in your case it's a whole lot more than a little bit. Look at politicians; theft, murder and rape they can commit with almost impunity to public disdain, but let them be found to be a little bit of nooky on the side and their resignation is mandatory. And even in these enlightened times there are still a few members of the British judiciary who maintain a rather moralistic outlook: a prejudiced judge could be extremely detrimental to the outcome of the case."

Sharon looked suitably reproached. "I'm sorry," she said, "It honestly didn't occur to me."

Leigh accepted the apology with the merest hint of a forgiving smile and an upward tilt of the chin.

"Another aspect we have to consider is the motive of the man who nearly killed you. When you telephoned my immediate reaction was that you had been the victim of a hired killer, and it is by no means a theory I've totally abandoned."

"What! You don't actually think Lucidel hired someone

to kill me?" Sharon said, the sentence ending in a croak, a result of the extended talking she had been subjecting herself to over the past half hour.

"Isn't that . ." Leigh held up her hand as an indication for her to cease talking and conserve her vocal cords, but Sharon insisted in completing what she had been about to say. "Isn't that being a little far fetched?"

Leigh intuited that part of Sharon didn't want to believe it.

She said, "Once the case goes to court the sales of Fatale are going to be hit, which will have a detrimental effect on the value of Lucidel's shares. If the case goes against them their losses will be catastrophic – they've already indicated to Wendy that they would be ready to go to a six-figure sum should she be prepared to settle out of court. Your presence in court, presenting your evidence, is pivotal to our case, as Lucidel is fully aware. No one knows Fatale like you do, you invented it, you've been involved with it all along. People have been killed for far, far less."

The image of those mesmeric eyes gazing down at her, as his hands tightened about her neck, came back to Sharon. Leigh said, "Of course I might be wrong and you were simply the victim of some serial sex maniac, and your near strangulation was just a bit of sex play that went too far," but Sharon knew in her heart that that wasn't the case, and that her fantastic zipless lover had meant to kill her all along. She thought of Wendy Lister, and asked Leigh, that if the man was a professional killer, wasn't there a chance that Wendy might also be a potential victim?

Leigh considered the suggestion, then answered,

"Unlikely, because her family and church are behind her on this and would continue with the case. He'd have to commit genocide."

For someone who had spent most of her life satisfying her own desires and ambitions, the selflessness of Wendy Lister – who was prepared to turn down a six figure inducement – came as something of a jolt to Sharon. She could afford to refuse Lucidel's bribery because she was already a wealthy woman, but for Wendy it literally was a fortune. It was belittling, and made Sharon feel that, even if it was her life that an attempt had been made on, and the urge to capitulate extremely tempting, it would be morally cowardly to let Wendy and her family down.

"Whatever the reason or motive," Leigh continued, "the harm has been done, and I think it is imperative that we move you into hiding until the case comes to trial. Somewhere that neither the press or hitman can get to you."

"But that's not for another three months!"

"I know. Personally I think it's for the best but I can't make you do it, it has to be your decision. Stay here tonight – I've made a bed up for you in the spare bedroom – and sleep on it. See how you think about it in the morning."

Sharon agreed to the suggestion, if for no other reason than she didn't feel like making a three-hour journey back to

Devon and facing Jonathan's questions. Although she had said she would think about whether or not she was going to go into hiding, she had already made up her mind that she would go.

Because she was afraid and in fear for her life.

The next morning Sharon accompanied Leigh to her office. From there she telephoned a distraught Jonathan – "Where are you? The police told me you were attacked by some man" – and told him where she was. She then handed the telephone to Leigh.

"Hello, Mr Greaves, this is Leigh Murray, I'm the solicitor acting for Wendy Lister and my offices are in Wembley. In order that you are assured I am who I say I am, you can get my number from Directory Enquires and then call me back." She put the phone down. Six minutes later Jonathan was reconnected to her. Sharon took the receiver. "I'm going into a private clinic. For reasons I don't want to go into now, it's best that you don't know where. I'll be home in a few days, two weeks at the outside, and then I'll explain everything to you. Sorry to be so mysterious, darling, but it is for the best. Oh, and if the press contact you say nothing. Talk with you soon. Bye."

Immediately Sharon and Leigh left the building by the rear exit, where Ted was waiting with the engine running. At the same time a car containing two cars turned into the street outside Leigh's office. One of them pulled into the curb while the other drove round to the back to cover the rear exit, but by the time it got there Ed's Mondeo was long gone; driving Sharon to the clinic and dropping Leigh off at a tube station; from where she made her way to Covent Garden.

Graham Foreman was waiting for her in a coffee shop, seated at an alcove table. They both ordered large espressos, and chatted about nothing in particular until after their order was placed on the table and the waitress had departed. Then Leigh came to the point.

"I need to put someone into hiding."

"For how long?"

"Three months."

"Man or woman?"

"Woman. Does it matter?"

"Maybe yes, maybe no. Is it to keep her from the press or is she in some sort of danger?"

"Both."

"How quickly?"

"Like now, two weeks max."

Foreman emptied two sachets of sugar into his coffee and stirred it pensively. "Let me make some calls."

Chapter Ten

The bar cum club was heaving. Minutes after entering it Graham could feel his clothes begin to stick to his body in the stifling heat. Even in tee shirt and chinos he felt overdressed, with the majority of the clientele appearing to be wearing next to nothing above the waist, and the female element in precious little else below. He also felt old, the only person there over the age of twenty-five – in his case by double that. Except, that was, for the band: four middle-aged rockers, belting out earthy rhythm and blues. Graham considered himself something of an aficionado of rock and R&B, and to his ear these guys were pretty good. The lead and rhythm guitarists, sharing vocals - beer-bellies and receding hair giving evidence of their advanced years - certainly knew what they were about, but it was the power-house, solid beat from the drummer and bass guitarist - who in contrast to the front guitarist's expanding waistlines looked positively emaciated – who had the writhing throng bouncing on their feet. Good stuff.

Graham stood by the bar and looked around for Gayle. He couldn't imagine what had possessed her to decide on this place to meet. It couldn't be for the sake of secrecy. What would she be now, mid fifties? Recalling the be-spectacled bookish figure, Graham thought that in this youth orientated environment she would be even more conspicuous than him. Anyway, there was no need for secrecy now, not after all these years: anyone who might have been interested in her would either be dead or in politics by this time. He ordered a beer and leaned against the bar, deciding to let her find him, and in the meantime to enjoy the band.

The session came to an end, the lead guitarist announcing in passable, but Dutch accented Spanish, that the band was taking a break for half an hour. Graham looked at his watch, Gayle had said midnight and it was now twenty-to-one. She wasn't going to show. He laid a ten-euro note against the receipt for his beers and entrance fee and prepared to leave. There was a tap on his shoulder, and Graham turned to see a skinny figure in vest and jeans, wearing dark glasses and a bandana round his head, whom in the flashing strobe lighting he recognised as the base guitarist. A finger was crooked, indicating him to follow. Lifting a flap on the bar, the base player crooked a finger and ducked under it. Graham followed suit and allowed himself to be led down a narrow corridor and into a storeroom. It was empty save for empty beer crates and excess tables and chairs. No sign of Gayle.

"Hello, Graham."

Some things change but the voice remains the same. The Roedean educated accent. The base player unwound the bandana, freeing fair hair from behind the ears. A pair of recognisable wire framed glasses, produced from a shoulder bag, replaced the shades.

"Jesus! Gayle. What . ."

"What's a nice respectable middle-aged lady doing playing rock and roll in a Costa del Sol nightclub? For the same reason that a dog licks his balls, because I can."

Graham laughed; in contrast to her genteel upbringing, or perhaps because of it, Gayle always did have a ribald turn of phrase.

"H said you had a job for me, but you know that although I'm still on the payroll, officially I'm retired."

"So am I, but this is in the private sector. But you would have known that, or guessed it, otherwise you wouldn't have agreed to see me."

Gayle smiled and said, " Perhaps I should have played a bit harder to get." Then added, "Not that you've got me."

Graham said, "It will pay well."

Gayle gave a shrug, that Graham interpreted money wasn't the issue. But then you never really knew with Gayle, there had always been a side, sides, of her life that she kept to herself, like playing in a rock band.

"How long have you been playing bass guitar?" he asked.

"Since I was at school, we had an all girl group, middle of the road pop stuff. Then, while I was at university, I got into rock and blues, and I've been playing on and off ever since."

"I never knew, and I can't recall anyone else ever mentioning anything about it."

"Yes, but you didn't know me until I joined the unit. Before that I was playing pretty regularly. Of course certain people, security, were aware of it - you don't have any secrets in the department – but none of my colleagues had any idea. It was my separate life. But once I was in the unit having any sort of separate life wasn't on. It was the longest I went without playing, that and afterwards. Then, when I finally surfaced here, I saw a billboard with the names of a couple of guys I used to play with. I went to the gig, we got to chatting, I jammed a couple of times with them, then I was back in the scene."

"You're pretty good.

"Yeah, not bad. There are enough old rockers out here, musicians and fans, to create a scene, but it's mainly kids who come to places like this. They seem to like us."

"You're not so old."

"So, what's this job? No details, just a bare outline."

The subject of conversation had been turned so abruptly that Graham had to pause a second to re-gather his thoughts. "A, err, woman, key witness, has to disappear. She's vulnerable to the press, and there may have been an attempt on her life, so she has to cease to exist until she'd required in court."

"And how long is that?"

"Three months. Nobody can spirit someone away quite like you, Gayle."

"How soon?"

"Like yesterday, but in the next ten days. I know it wouldn't give you long but I thought that you might be able to use something from one of your past assignments."

"Did you. Do you have full details with you?"

"At my hotel, the Marriott."

"My, they are paying well. Okay, I'll think about it, if I'm interested I'll meet you there at twelve tomorrow."

Graham knew then that she was hooked; subconsciously she probably had been from the moment H had told her about him. For half a dozen years, while she was with the unit, and then later when she was on the run, Gayle Meredith had led a high-octane existence, an existence from which, as he knew only to well, it was hard to adjust back to normality. Even a rock and roll normality.

"And you can take that self-satisfied look off your face, saying that I'll think about it doesn't mean I will."

"I was thinking nothing of the kind," Graham pleaded.

"Bollocks, it's written all over your face – she's bored, she misses the life. Well maybe I do, but I had the shit scared out of me, Graham, and I'm not so sure I could face something like that again."

"This is entirely different."

"Didn't I hear you say that an attempt had been made on her life?"

"It was a perhaps."

There was a tap on the door and a voice called, "We're due back on, Della."

"Okay," Gayle called back.

Graham looked at Gayle and said, "Della?"

"Separate life, separate name," Gayle replied. She retied the bandana and exchanged the glasses for the shades. "There's an exit at the back, if you don't want to fight your way through the crowd. Or you can stay for the second set, but if you do, don't wait for me."

Before closing the behind her she said, "I'll think about it."

They gathered in Sharon's room at the clinic: Graham, Leigh, Gayle, and Sharon.

It had taken Graham three days to get Gayle to commit herself. She had sat in his hotel room, spent an hour scrutinising the dossier on Sharon Greaves and asking him questions, and had then said that she had to leave to make a long distance telephone call. "You can use this phone," he had offered. "I'll leave you to it while you make the call." To which she had returned a look that said – I might have been out of the game for some time but I'm not that rusty – and had left the room. Following her was too risky, if she had spotted him he would never had seen her again. Of course he could have found where she lived and pulled some strings to have her telephone calls checked, except it would have been a waste of time: an old hand like Gayle would have used a public call box.

He didn't see her at all the next day, and when he went to the club that evening and saw that someone else had taken her place in the band's line-up he surmised that she had decided to give his offer a miss. He checked out of the hotel the following morning, only to find her waiting at the airport, in well cut jeans and jacket – unrecognisable from the androgynous base player of three nights earlier - with a ticket on the same flight to London. "Does this mean you're in?" he asked. "All the way," she replied, a smile creasing her café au lait tanned face.

Allowing for the trauma that had necessitated her flight from the unit, Graham thought that the intervening years hadn't been too unkind to Gayle. She looked well, too thin but then she always had been, and her skin bore a healthy glow. And it was not only her health that had weathered the storm. He knew nothing about clothes, other than the label on her raincoat said Burberry, but he had noticed the understated quality of her luggage when they landed, and that she wore a Rado wristwatch, of which he had sufficient knowledge to know that it wasn't a fake. The Department would have made sure she was provided for when she had to disappear: sufficient rather than generous, and that was some time ago. And okay, she was still on salary, but that would be at the same level he had been, so he knew the figures. Somewhere along the line, he concluded, Ms Meredith had augmented her income.

During the journey to the clinic Gayle had intimated to Graham that she might well require him and Leigh to leave her alone with Sharon, so that she could question and get to know her. In the outcome it didn't happen, in fact she said remarkably little to Sharon, only a couple of questions about her past-times and some general chitchat. The two women seemed to get along well enough, and when she spelt out her requirements to the assembled group, Graham assumed that Gayle hadn't experienced any sense of incompatibility that she felt might jeopardise the project.

Gayle said, "My instructions will have to be followed unconditionally, any deviation from them and I walk. Are we agreed on that?"

Graham and Leigh nodded their assent, and then turned their eyes towards Sharon. She said, "What do you mean by unconditionally, can you give me an example?"

"No. Your agreement to this demand has to be unequivocal, otherwise we finish here and now."

Sharon looked at Leigh, who returned an encouraging nod, then said, "Okay, I agree."

"Sharon and I will be completely incommunicado for the three months prior to the date of the trial," Gayle continued. "That means that not only will you," she gestured towards Leigh and Graham, "not know where we are, neither will you be able to contact us. Nor, for that matter, will we be able to contact you. Are we agreed on this point?"

"What if the trial is rescheduled for a nearer date?" Leigh asked "Then it would be up to you to return it to the original date, or, if necessary, a later one."

"But won't that be just as bad? If it goes to a later date, and Sharon turns up at my office on the original date, her cover will have been broken and she'll be as vulnerable as she was before. Or hadn't that occurred to you?"

Gayle sighed. "Ms Murray, please don't take me for a fool, or worse still, an amateur, I have allowed for every eventuality. Contingency plans are in place. Your client would disappear again."

Sharon said, "What if something happened to my son, if he were taken ill, how would I know?"

"You wouldn't," Gayle answered. "You have to be completely incommunicado, it's the only way." Sharon, because it involved the person most dearest to her, looked unconvinced. Gayle said, not unkindly, "Listen, Sharon, the people we are trying to protect you from have unlimited funds. Everyone you know is being watched, their homes bugged and phones tapped. Personnel at their offices will have been offered incentives to pass on anything they hear – bribes of such proportions that even the most loyal employee would have trouble refusing. In coming here each of us has had to take a tortuous route to ensure we were not followed, and that they haven't yet found this place only means that it's discovery is imminent. You must never underestimate their resources, or their ruthlessness." She looked at Graham for support.

"What Gayle says is true, you have to trust her, the only way she can protect you is by you doing what she says." And herself, he thought; in the worse scenario, if Sharon went down so did she, and as she had been there before he guessed her demands were as much to minimise the chance of it happening again as they were to protect her charge.

Gayle said, "It's the only positive way to ensure the non-involvement of your son in this whole business. By not knowing where you are he is of no use to any of them; the press or Lucidel's agents."

"You mean ensure his safety," Sharon stated.

"If you wish."

It was the concluding argument, the one certain subject to obtain Sharon's acquiescence, and ensure her complicity with Gayle's requirements. Gayle then outlined her immediate plan, and gave specific instructions to each of them.

At the conclusion of the meeting Sharon telephoned Jonathan, after which she packed the few items she had brought with her and settled the bill for the clinic. Then she accompanied Leigh back to London and booked into a cheap hotel, remaining in her room and snacking off of the sandwiches provided by the clinic's catering staff. The next morning - after a restless night of being kept awake by the slamming of doors and the noises issuing through the paper thin walls, some of which she surmised emanated from ladies of the night and their clients – she dressed in the change of clothes she had brought with her, pulled her hair back into a severe ponytail, paid the hotel bill (in cash) and made her way to Leigh's offices.

Leigh was waiting in the reception, with croissants and coffee, and told her that Jonathan had already arrived and was waiting in her office. They had half an hour to talk privately. Before going in Sharon wolfed down the croissants, and then used the reception telephone to call Leon's school, only to be informed that her son was away on an orienteering field trip and wasn't expected back until later that afternoon. And no, she was told in a tone of barely concealed exasperation, there was no way he, nor the master in charge, could be contacted, that was why it was called orienteering. Dejected, Sharon put the phone down and went up the stairs to Leigh's office.

Jonathan jumped up from Leigh's chair as Sharon entered the room. She kissed him on the cheek and then, before he could say anything, spoke quickly to him. "We have always respected each others private life, and I think because of that we have established a stable and caring relationship. Without going into details, I went with a man to a hotel room and was strangled by him, and if I hadn't been found in time by a chambermaid I would be dead. It could have been accidental, but at this juncture we have to assume that it was a premeditated attempt on my life.

Whatever, we can be pretty sure it will have been brought to the attention of the press."

"They've already telephoned me," Jonathan interjected.

"I told them nothing, as you instructed, not that I knew anything in the first place."

"That's why I want to ensure it remains that way. You and Leon are the two people closest to my heart, and I don't want you involved."

"I'm already involved, Sharon; that is if you are inferring that it's Lucidel who was behind the hotel room incident?"

"They have a lot to lose if the case goes against them, even before then, just from the accusation of negligence. Desperate measures and all that."

"Then why put us all through it, why not stand down now, before it goes any further?"

"That would be the easy way but would I be able to live with myself? Would you be able to live with it? I know your finances are in jeopardy, but if the worst happens and you go bankrupt, it won't be the end of the world, I've got more that enough to keep us in luxury. Wendy Lister has turned down a six-figure bribe, more money that she could ever hope to see. How could I possibly let her down with all that I have? And what of all the other Wendys and Emilys who might be stricken by the Fatale curse? I have to go through with it, you do see that, don't you?"

"Yes," Jonathan said, softly.

Sharon gently caressed his face with her hand. "Leigh thinks it's best if I go away for a while, until any possibility of scandal blows over."

"Where will you go?"

"Abroad somewhere."

"When do you plan to leave?"

Leigh answered the question for Sharon. She tapped on the door and said, "Whenever you're ready."

"Just a minute," Sharon called back. Then to Jonathan, "I have to leave now. That's why I had to talk to you; it will make things a lot easier if I know I have your support. Do I, Jonathan?"

He gave her a small smile. "Yes, okay, do what you think you have to."

"Thank you."

She kissed his cheek, and then left the room. He could hear the conversation of muffled voices, leaving the outer office and descending to the floor below. Looking out of the window he saw a car draw up on the opposite side of the road, and Sharon, wearing a white raincoat, a Louis Vuitton overnight bag hanging from her shoulder, walk over to it. She looked up, saw him and waved, then got into the car.

Jonathan returned the wave and watched the car turn on to the main road and disappear round the corner. He sat down onto the lawyer's chair to gather his thoughts, and then realised that there wasn't much to think about, that he hadn't really any other feasible choice. The various other options he had been musing over, since Sharon had first informed him of what she was going to do, were, he realised, ultimately, unacceptable. It was the right thing to do, but would he be able to go through with it? Maybe some sort of compromise? He began to format a possible plan of action.

His mobile rang.

"Hello?"

The American accent at the other end of the line was all too familiar. "We've just seen you wave your wife good bye. Did she say where she was going?"

Any doubts Jonathan might have been entertaining were terminated by this blatant invasion of his privacy, the fact that his every movements were being monitored. Besides, he didn't like McCoskey. "No," he replied brusquely, and terminated the call. Time to commence remedial action, set in motion measures to extricate him from some of the mess he was in, or at least minimise the final outcome. He placed a call to his broker and instructed him to sell his Lucidel holdings: surreptitiously, so as not to cause any waves, but as quickly as possible.

"Do you have some insider knowledge I should know about?" the broker asked, cautiously.

"Let's just say more a difference of opinion. Do you have a problem with that?"

"No," the broker replied, mentally calculating his commission on the sale. All the same, the answer was ambiguous and he would keep his ear to the ground. "Do you want the proceeds spread over the usual accounts?"

Jonathan thought for a moment then said, "I'll have my accountant contact you with instructions."

Next he called the accountant and advised her of what was happening, adding that he wanted her to sell off all his assets, save the Manor House, extricate him from all commitments he was pledged to and pay the necessary cancellation penalties. The balance to be split into two, one half to be spread over his various accounts, the other half to be used to set up a trust fund for his son. The accountant was non-committal; it was a plan of action she had been advising for some time. She said she would get on with it right away.

This settled, Jonathan turned his mind to Leon. The boy should be told about his mother going away, or at least some of it. Had Sharon spoken to him? Perhaps it would be a good idea to go and see him, he could do it today, drive directly to the school from here.

The mobile rang again. It was McCoskey.

"Look, Jonathan, she must have given. ." Jonathan cut the call off. Immediately he tapped in the number of Leon's school, and was given the same information as Sharon had received less than an hour earlier. Jonathan said he would call back later in the day or tomorrow. Then he turned off the cell phone. He wanted no more interruptions from McCoskey. Right now he was going home, to write his resignation from the board of CVC.

The car following Sharon contained two of McCoskey's operatives, a man, the driver, and a woman, whose mobile telephone was on open line to McCoskey. "The car is a grey Mondeo," she told her employer, and repeated it's registration number.

"Yeah, we know it," McCoskey said, "belongs to an Edward Morrison, self employed car hire driver who works primarily for Leigh Murray."

"We're turning on to the Hammersmith flyover, could be they're making for Heathrow."

"Her husband's fucking me about, just said he didn't know where she's going, and now he's turned his phone off. But she could very well be leaving the country."

As predicted, the Mondeo took the Heathrow turnoff. The pursuit car trailed it to terminal two, where it drew up outside the departures entrance. "Sharon Greaves is getting out, she still has the shoulder bag and is making for the entrance. The Mondeo is leaving."

McCoskey said, "Marie, you follow Sharon Greaves. Michael you stay with the Mondeo."

Marie jumped out of the car and ran to the terminal entrance. It took a moment or so for her to locate the black haired ponytail and white raincoat. She followed Sharon Greaves to the British Airways First Class check-in desk and watched her present a ticket and passport. Apparently the Louis Vuitton overnight bag was deemed to be considered as cabin luggage, as once the checking procedure was completed she made her way through the departure gate with it over her shoulder. Marie checked the flight destination above the check-in desk: Rome. Then she reported back to McCoskey.

"See if you can get a seat on the same flight."

He didn't have to ask Marie if she had her passport with her, she had worked for him long enough never to be without it. She made her way across the concourse to the BA desk and waited in line until she was able to buy a ticket – economy only. Then it was back to the check-in desk, through passport control, security, and into the departure lounge. Sharon Greaves, of course, was in the executive lounge, and Marie did not catch sight of her until they were all in the boarding area, and then only for a moment as economy seats were called first for boarding. She quickly advised McCoskey of her position, before switching her mobile off and entering the aircraft.

McCoskey had telephoned ahead and arranged for the local Lucidel representative to have someone at Rome airport, holding a placard with Marie's name on it, waiting for her at the arrival's gate. Once the aircraft had landed and come to a halt, Marie had pushed and badgered her way through the disembarking passengers so as not to loose sight of Sharon

Greaves. There was a momentary hiccup when her lack of luggage was questioned by customs – explained as a last minute business trip, and giving the name of the Lucidel representative.

"I need to follow that woman," she explained to the young woman who had been designated to meet Marie, and pointed at the departing figure of Sharon Greaves making for the exit. They tore after her, but instead of going through the exit Sharon Greaves veered off to the bureau de change and changed a large wad of sterling into euros. Then she proceeded to the shopping area where she went from one designer name to the other, taking over forty minutes in deciding to purchase two sets of bras and thongs from La Perla, a Prada hand bag and pair of boots, and a bottle of Chanel No.5. She kept the boots on, placing her shoes and the other purchases in the overnight bag. Marie had to admire her taste, all classics that would stand the test of time, and which she calculated had cost around £1,000, and then some.

Then Sharon Greaves walked through to departures and stood in line behind two couples waiting at the First Class BA check-in for Heathrow, ticket and passport at the ready. Marie and her companion looked at one another in utter amazement.

Marie had never actually seen Sharon Greaves prior to this assignment but she had a photograph of her. Taking it out she walked over to the queue, stood in front of Sharon Greaves and compared her to the photo. The woman was heavily made-up and the likeness superficial.

"You're not Sharon Greaves."

"I'm not Sharon Stone either. What's it to you?" the accent was London, but not Knightsbridge.

"Then why are you impersonating her?"

"Who, Sharon Stone?"

"Don't get clever with me." Marie grabbed the woman's hand and twisted it so as she could read the name on the ticket and passport: Hanna Winstone. Marie said quietly, in the woman's ear, out of the range of the people queuing in front, "I suppose you know that it's an offence to aid and abet a suspect who has jumped bail, Ms Winstone?"

It had the desired effect. "You the law?"

"Marie took out her Lucidel Security pass, flicked it open for as long as it took the woman to think it was a police warrant card, then took her arm and guided her over to a couple of vacant seats.

"I thought you were the private eye the husband hired," the woman said.

Marie said, "Who hired you? Sharon Greaves?"

"I guess so. I got a call from my agent yesterday morning, saying he had a last minute job for me. A thousand quid for one days work. I was a bit leery at first, but Denny, my agent, explained it was just to create a false trail for some woman whose husband was having her followed. I was given the same photo as you've got and told to make-up like it, and given these clothes to wear. I had to sit on the floor in the back of the hire car when she got in, then change places when we got to the airport."

"Did Sharon Greaves say anything to you?"

"Only to give me another thousand quid to spend in the airport shops, and to say that I could keep the bag and the clothes in it – all good stuff."

"She didn't give you any idea where she was going?"

"No."

"Not the slightest hint. Think carefully."

"No, she didn't say a word for the rest of the journey; honestly."

Hanna Winstone nervously watched the policewoman move out of earshot and call someone on her cell phone. Her stomach was churning, what had started a fun, lucrative caper was now turning pear shaped. The policewoman finished her call and returned, and noted down Hanna's name, address and passport number. Hanna waited to hear the worst.

The policewoman said, "I'm going to let you go, Hanna, and you can keep all your ill-gotten gains. However, this case is still under investigation and I'm officially cautioning you not to say a word about what has happened. If it should come to our attention that you have not complied with this request you will be arrested and charged not only with aiding and abetting but also with contravening the Sub Judice Act of 1976. Do you understand?"

139

Oh yes, oh most definitely yes.

A disgruntled Marie returned to London on the same flight as a relieved and delighted Hanna. Once again she had to take an economy seat while Hanna travelled first class.

There were only two places the switch could have been made, and it wasn't from the rear of Murray's office because he had had a car covering it. Which left only one possibility.

McCoskey grilled Michael: "Tell me again what happened when you followed the car from Heathrow?"

"Morrison went back the same way he had come until coming off at the Hammersmith flyover, then he took a short cut through the back streets to his base in Shepard's Bush."

"And what's there?"

"He uses a shop in a parade. It's got Morrison Car Hire as a sign. He parked outside and went in; I double-parked, ran over and checked the car to see if anyone was still in it. It was empty."

"Now think clearly, was there any time when Morrison's car was out of your sight?"

"Well yes, a couple of times, round the back streets, when he turned a corner, I would lose sight of him for a few moments until I turned into the street."

McCoskey dismissed Michael, he had told him all that he needed to know. The switch had occurred in one of the back streets. Whoever Murray was using was good; which was more than could be said for his lot so far: a hit man who only half strangles his victim, and a surveillance team that loses their quarry and doesn't realise it until four hours later. And now he had no idea where Sharon Greaves was or where she was going? Fuck knows how he was going to explain this to Luc Barr if he asked for a progress report? Fortunately they had blanket cover on all the contact systems: telephones, mobiles, computers, mail, homes, offices, and even the son's school. Everyone connected to Sharon Greaves and involved with her in the case.

She would have to make contact at some time.

Chapter Eleven

Sharon and Gayle sat each side of a table, at one end of an almost deserted railway carriage. The table was scattered with the remains of sandwiches and plastic coffee cups. They were dressed in jeans, sweaters, parkas and hiking boots, and carrying commodious backpacks. There was an uneasy silence between them. A few minutes earlier an unbelieving Gayle had watched Sharon extract a mobile telephone from her backpack.

"What the fuck do you think you are doing?" Gayle had hissed.

"I'm just going to make one last call, to my son," Sharon replied, and went on to explain, "I tried to reach him earlier, from Leigh's office, but the school told me he was away on some course until this afternoon."

In a swift movement, that took Sharon completely by surprise, Gayle grabbed the mobile from her hand. "Didn't you listen to what I said from the start, no calls, no mobiles?" She looked round to ensure no one was looking, then slide open the top widow sufficiently to drop the offending item from the moving train.

Sharon glared at Gayle, then slumped back in her seat and stared morosely out of the window. It had almost been fun when it started, an adventure: hiding in the car, swapping places with her double at the airport, turning her raincoat inside-out and jumping from the car when Ed slowed down. Gayle had been waiting in the doorway – the rear entrance to a small Woolworth. They had walked through it to the front, and then to the nearest underground station, from where they made their way to Euston railway station. Gayle already had the tickets. They went and retrieved the backpacks from left luggage, and there was just time for her to go into the toilets and change into the clothes she was now wearing before boarding the north bound train. Gayle hadn't said where   the ultimate destination was.

Gayle was trembling from her head to her toes, not from anger but from fear. This was not a good start, she should have handled it a bit more subtly, not let her paranoia get the better of her. She had woken up that morning feeling sick, and to the realisation that talking herself into taking the job had been a mistake. All the old fears had returned: someone had already tried to kill Sharon, and he could well try again. But it was too late by then; the plan was already in action. While it was all happening, meeting Sharon in the shop doorway as she leaped from the car, getting to Euston and boarding the train, she had been able to keep the nausea and fear under control. Then Sharon had produced the mobile, and the thought of what could happen as a result had brought it all back. She took a couple of deep breaths and tried to get the trembling under control. It was important not to let Sharon – who was in just as much danger – see her fear. She willed her mind to concentrate on the details of the next phase of the plan. The nausea began to subside, and the sandwiches and coffee, her first meal of the day – she hadn't been able to face breakfast – remained in her stomach.

Sharon said, "I'm sorry, Gayle, what I did was stupid and unnecessary, I let my concern for my son over-ride my common sense".

Sharon's words of contrition did more to dispel Gayle's misgivings than all her own attempts put together.

"I'm sorry too. I might have over-reacted. My knowledge of modern information technology is from what I read in novels and see in films, but from them it seems that it's possible to track down the source of any communication. I just don't think we can take the chance."

"You're right, of course." Sharon gave a conciliatory smile.

Gayle smiled back, extended her little finger across the table and said, "Pax." It was a word from her childhood, a gesture of appeasement. Sharon's childhood hadn't contained

144

such niceties, let alone Latin, but she recognised the gesture for what it was and proffered her own little finger. "Pax."

They both giggled.

For Gayle this demonstration of camaraderie acted as an affect of instant gratification, and for a while mollified her trepidations. But while she gushingly went on to give Sharon some indication of their ultimate destination, and what it would entail – a remote part of Scotland, tranquillity, reading, walking and, of course, chess - a tiny part of her remained sceptical and she drew back from revealing exactly where. Why was that? As the two women sat back in their respective seats, conversation lapsing into contemplative silence, Gayle examined this reticence. It wasn't that she mistrusted Sharon, more that she didn't trust herself, frightened what she might reveal of herself. She glanced across the table, Sharon was leaning against the window with her eyes closed, and Gayle caught sight of herself in the reflection and saw that she was smiling. She had seen that smile before, in her dressing table mirror when she had been thinking, expectantly, of meeting with Roland. No, it couldn't be! She couldn't be developing feelings for Sharon. She had never experienced homosexual desires, apart from the usual early teen crushes, pashes, on older girls and teachers, and all her past relationships were heterosexual, and her passion for Roland had been overwhelming. Yet there was something, something more than just wanting Sharon's friendship, something from the moment of their first meeting – which at the time she had attributed to a feeling of empathy. And there was an urge to touch her, to put her arms around Sharon, hug her. Gayle turned her head to look out of the window, and in the reflection saw that she was smiling again.

Oh good God!

Gayle's immediate reaction was that Sharon must never have any inclination of how she felt. From all that she knew of her it was apparent that Sharon was demonstratively heterosexual, and although Gayle had read of men who had been notorious womanisers in an effort to hide their homosexuality, she doubted the same was the case with Sharon. If Sharon had felt attracted to a woman she would have gone ahead and had an affair with her. A sudden mental image of Sharon rejecting an advance made Gayle blush with embarrassment.

Sharon too was thinking about her companion for the next three months, but in an entirely different form. Her thoughts were directed at what she saw as Gayle's paranoia regarding calling Leon. Over-reacting was an understatement, the sort of scenario she was imagining – the monitoring of all communication systems – was straight from the films she had had to sit through with her son. Virtual reality nonsense from the Hollywood hype factory. Okay, the CIA with a superpower's budget and satellite surveillance might have something close to it, but Lucidel wasn't in that league.

She could appreciate Gayle's concern so she had kept her opinions to herself. Besides, she liked the woman – Gayle's constant gaze hadn't really registered, as an attractive woman Sharon was used to being looked at, by people of both sexes, and would only be likely to think something was amiss with a person if he, or she, didn't pay her attention - and as they were going to be keeping one another company for some time she didn't want to create an atmosphere. All the same, she felt an overwhelming need to speak with Leon, give him some sort of explanation as to why she wasn't going to be around for the next three months. Also to prepare him for what might be said about her – God only knew what Lucidel might put the way of the tabloid rags to print? As soon as an opportunity arose she was going to call him, and that most probably would mean a public call box now she no longer had the mobile. Another problem would be the time frame: as a general rule the school frowned upon parents making calls to their offspring, so times were restricted to the evening between five and nine o'clock, and even then they had to go through the house master first. Pupil's mobiles were strictly banned. If she couldn't get through to Leon then she would call Jonathan, and tell him what she wanted to say to Leon and get him to pass it on. It would be a poor substitute, but if needs must.

The train journey took them to Glasgow, via a couple of rail company changes, arriving there at seven o'clock in the evening. Gayle had made a reservation for a twin bedded room at one of the airport hotels, under the names of Susan and Clare

Buchan – apparently sisters. Gayle (Susan) informed the desk clerk that they would be paying by cash, and gave him, on request, £150 deposit, the difference to be added or subtracted when they checked out. The first thing Sharon (Clare) looked at when they entered the room was the telephone, noting the message printed beneath the press buttons informing that outside calls could only be made through the switchboard, that there would be a surcharge, and that any calls would be detailed on the bill. So that was out. Later, on the way to the hotel restaurant, when they passed through the foyer, Sharon looked to see if there were any public telephones, but none were in evidence. On the way to the hotel she had seen that it was situated on a peripheral road around the airport, containing, as far as she had been able to make out, an assortment of other hotels, petrol stations and small factory units, but no housing; so not a great chance of there being any public call boxes in the immediate vicinity. All the same she decided that she would wait until Gayle was asleep and then sneak out and try and find one. Except that when they retired for the night Gayle sat up in her bed reading with the bedside light on, and although Sharon endeavoured to stay awake, the day began to catch up with her, so that the next thing she was aware of was daylight streaming in through the opened curtains, and Gayle up, showered and dressed.

The next leg of the journey was on a Highlands and

Islands flight from Glasgow to the Western isle of Lewis, landing at Stornaway. On a bright clear day, Sharon could appreciate the views of the coastline and islands would be exhilarating, but not on a misty, drizzly, windy late November day. For most of the flight the aircraft stayed above the clouds, with the only sight of land being the wet and bumpy decent to the various airstrips on the way, and finally Stornaway.

They stayed the night in a guesthouse. Down the street, fifty yards from where it was situated, was a public telephone box. Sharon stole out while Gayle was in the bath.

"Hello, darling, it's me. I can't talk for long. I wanted to speak with Leon, explain why I have to be away for so long, and tell him not to believe all that certain newspapers might have to say about me. But it's too late in the evening to call the school and I don't think I'll the opportunity again, so can you explain everything to him, darling?

"I'm missing you."

Chapter Twelve

Alan did not argue the point when Carl informed him that the client no longer desired his participation in the demise of Sharon Greaves. Carl said, "I appreciate that from a professional standing you would like to finish the job, but the client feels that it would be too risky, she's seen your face and probably given the police a description."

"I guess," was all that Alan said.

Carl, whose nervousness had been obvious from the start – letting fall aspects of the contract that he probably shouldn't have – and who had expected a tougher reaction, looked relieved.

"You'd better lie low for a while," he said. "Understandably the client has declined to pay the balance of the contract." Carl extracted an envelope from his desk drawer. "Only the deposit is left." The envelope was slid across the desk.

"I've deducted my commission." He stroked his beard in anticipation.

Alan was fully aware of Carl's terms, fifty percent with the contract, with the balance on completion, but he couldn't be bothered to argue the blatant lie. Instead he opened the package, counted the six fifty-pound notes inside it, nodded and pocked the envelope. "I'll be on my way then."

"Give me a call when you get back, I'm sure I'll be able to find you something."

Alan, half way out of the door, raised his hand in an acknowledging salute without turning round.

Carl let out a long sigh, you never knew with Alan. An automatic pistol, the safety catch off, lay in the still open desk drawer. Carl Peterson was a hard, compact man, in his early fifties and still in good shape, but even in his prime he would have been wary of Alan – hence the insurance of the automatic. Alan's capitulation hadn't come as a total surprise; he had seen similar reactions from men like Alan before - men whose apparent indifference to killing had originated from battle hardness, the witnessing of too much unnecessary bloodshed, often innocent, in un-winnable wars, rather than a psychopathic need. The excitement wanes and they simply become weary of all the killing. Some came back, most didn't, not to the killing. Carl doubted that he would ever see Alan Swift again.

Alan's flat was situated above a convenience store, and

he had lived there rent free ever since helping the owner out when a bunch of local tearaways had tried demanding protection money. He lived quietly and simply, and there were no possessions in the flat that he would miss should he leave and not return. In that advent, Pandit would simply put Alan's effects in store; he would never grass on him.

Alan had no exact plans, only an agenda: to find Sharon Greaves. And this agenda was in no way motivated by any intent of completing the contract he had been hired to do. On the contrary, if anything it was to save her from it; for Alan had no reason to doubt that Carl, rather than lose the second fifty percent payment, would have already negotiated with the client to supply a replacement to finish the contract.

The feelings he had experienced, at hearing that Sharon Greaves, Sharon, was still alive, had developed over the following days from a kind of relief that he hadn't killed her into a desire to see her again; which was now an obsession that monopolised his every thought. The reason for this, he rationalised, was that during the brief time spent in her company she had reached him in a way no one else ever had. That they had reached each other. And the more he dwelt on this revelation, the more he knew that they had to see one another again.

Accompanying this revelation was the extent of the period within which this knowledge of their unique togetherness, albeit in his subconscious at the time, had developed. In his mind, it increased from the less than fifteen minutes of ecstatic copulation to encompass the complete hour or so of their total involvement: beginning from the moment of his first seeing her leave the cinema, until leaving her comatose body in the hotel room. He constantly dwelt on their initial meeting, when he asked her about the hotel, those seconds frozen in time when their eyes met. And then, when he stopped at the traffic lights, her immediate acquiescence to go with him. The journey in the car, when he could feel her mounting excitement. Fate had intervened and they had achieved a oneness.

Never for a moment did it occur to him that his passion might not be requited.

Having an agenda to be a knight in shining armour was one thing, how to locate his damsel in distress was something else entirely. Sitting in one of the two armchairs that consisted the total of his living room seating, Alan concentrated his mind to the few clues he had to Sharon's whereabouts.

From what Carl had let slip, Sharon had evaded the client's people and disappeared. She wasn't at the family house in Devon, or at any of those of her friends and acquaintances. Even her mobile was completely dead. The belief was that the husband (thus disproving Alan's earlier assumption that he was the client) knew where she was but wasn't saying, and that she would remain in hiding for up to three months.

Also that it would be difficult for the client (which from

what Carl implied, was a group or agency rather than one person) to use intimidation to persuade the husband to reveal Sharon's hiding place without incriminating themselves (some lawyer was also involved).

Alan considered this aspect. He wasn't bound by such restraints, but, by the same token, neither was his replacement as Carl's hired killer. Wouldn't it make sense for him to meet with Jonathan Greaves, explain to him the danger he and Sharon were in, and how he could save them? Alan decided to see Jonathan immediately, in person: get to him before his replacement.

The dossier that he had been given on Sharon included the fact that Jonathan Greaves still worked from his office at Ulme Valley Cider, which he was aware was close to the Greaves family manor house. Either way he knew where he could locate the man, although it would be late evening by the time he got there, so it would have to be the house; which was probably preferable, when no one else was about.

Alan collected his car from the lock-up, which he also rented from Pandit, and drove west out of London and on to the M4. It took three and a half hours to reach the manor house, the situation of which he already knew from his earlier stalking of Sharon. As he had known the details of Sharon's life-style, he had concentrated on following her movements in the less noticeable confines of Exeter, and hadn't bothered with the house. But the dossier had been fairly comprehensive, so he knew that it lay within four acres of walled parkland, and that there was a married couple – housekeeper and gardener – living in a flat at the rear.

The wrought iron gates guarding the entrance were firmly shut, which was not unexpected. There was a push button bell and speaker with which to announce ones self, but Alan didn't somehow think he would be made welcome. During the drive down Alan had considered what would be his best approach, and concluded that ringing the bell and trying to explain the reason for his call at this late hour would be unlikely to gain him admittance. In fact a more likely response would be for Jonathan to call the police. The circumstances called for something of a guileful approach. Fist thing was to leave his car where it wouldn't attract attention. After ascertaining that there was nowhere in the immediate vicinity, he drove down into the village and left his car in a side street that already contained a number of other vehicles, and walked back to the house.

There were no obvious surveillance cameras mounted on or about the surrounding wall, and it was easily climbed. Once over the wall Alan remained motionless for a while and listened for any telltale sound of dogs or anyone out walking the grounds, then made towards the house. The grounds consisted of surrounding trees and shrubs bordering on to more formal gardens at the front, with a vegetable garden and greenhouses at the rear. Alan did a circuit of the house. A light was on in one of the upstairs rooms but those on the ground floor were in darkness. He peered in through windows where possible and assessing the probable interior layout - drawing and dining rooms, library – before lights in each were switched on as a woman went from one room to the other drawing the curtains. He moved to the rear of the house. He noticed that that a transom window was open, and when he peered in through the main window he could just make out shelves full of tins and packets in the darkness, and assumed it to be a pantry. Alan was pretty sure that there would be an alarm system in the house, but he didn't expect it would be activated until the household had retired for the night. A light went on in the kitchen, then the door opened and Alan heard a voice say, "Out you go then," and saw the form of a large Alsatian being pushed out. Alan reached into his pocket and tightened his hand around the can of mace, waiting for the dog to catch his scent and come bounding over. "Poor old bugger," the voice said from the kitchen, "seems a shame to make him stay out." The dog shuffled to a sheltered spot and lay down. Moving in closer Alan saw that the dog was very old. His head didn't move until Alan was almost up to him; a bleary eye was opened, and then closed with indifference and the head returned to its recumbent position on the paws. "You know Mister Jonathan won't have him in the house," a woman's voice said. "You coming up then?" The man didn't bother to answer, only close the kitchen door, turn the key in the lock and shoot a bolt. A few moments later the lights of the couple's flat went on.

Alan returned to the side of the house. The pantry transom was still open; if there were an alarm system this would indicate that it either didn't cover all the windows or it wasn't switched on. He put on a pair of thin leather gloves, clambered up onto the windowsill, put his arm through the transom, released the catch on the main window, jumped down, held his breath and opened the window. No alarm sounded. Using the beam of his pocket torch to identify and move any object that could hinder his progress, he climbed in. The pantry door opened into a short passage, which led to the larger passage that ran between the kitchen and the main hall. The door to the room Alan had earlier identified as the library was open, and a soft light emanated from it. He approached it stealthily and looked in. A man was sitting at a desk, writing. Alan assumed that he must be Sharon's husband. He tapped on the door and entered the room.

Without looking up Jonathan Greaves said,

"What is it, Mrs Boldry? I thought you had finished for the night."

Alan said, "I'm not Mrs Boldry."

Jonathan swivelled round on his chair. "What the -? "I never heard you at the door."

"I kind of let myself in. Look I'm sorry to intrude like this but I had to see you." Alan observed Jonathan Greaves, who had risen to his feet, and saw that he was pretty average, of about the same height as himself but of a lighter build, with light, thinning sandy hair and a tanned skin. So this was the man who, to put it crudely, couldn't give Sharon what she needed. "You don't know me but . ."

"I know exactly who you are."

The sickening reality had hit Jonathan the moment he heard the man speak. He recalled the words of the detective who came to interview him after Sharon disappeared from the hospital – "We believe the man who attacked your wife had an American accent. Does that ring any bells with you?" He also knew, with the certainty of anyone who has known that their partner has been with somebody else, that the person confronting them was the 'other' man or woman. It was a new experience for Jonathan; Sharon's lovers (if one could call them that) had always been anonymous, men she herself hardy knew; although it had been a nagging fear that some day one of them might take the liaison more seriously than Sharon. For a moment he wondered if that was all this was, then he remembered that this was the man who had left his wife for dead.

"And I can guess what you want," he continued, with a bravado he didn't really feel. "Well you're out of luck because my wife has gone away, for an indefinite period, and I've no idea where she is."

It wasn't exactly the truth; there was the message on his mobile that Sharon had left less than an hour ago, while he was in the bath. He had checked the number, it wasn't her mobile but a call box, and he hadn't wanted to erase the message. A simple press of a button had revealed from where she had called.

"And now I would like you to leave."

Before I call the police, he had almost added and then had thought better of, in case of aggravating the situation.

Alan ignored the invitation. This wasn't going how he intended; he could see the fear in Jonathan's eyes. He tried again.

"You have to believe me, I'm not trying to find Sharon to do her any harm, the exact opposite in fact, I'm trying to save her."

The words died on his lips, the expression on Jonathan's face was one of complete scepticism.

"I've told you, I have no idea where she is."

This was going nowhere. Alan's SBS training had included interrogation, and he knew from this, plus experience in the field, that Jonathan was lying. Besides, Carl had said that the client was sure Jonathan Greaves knew where his wife was. Added to which his patience was beginning to run out. Alan decided to shake the tree, see what might fall out.

"You'll excuse me if I say that I don't altogether accept that. She may not have said where she was going but I can't believe she wouldn't leave a telephone number or contact address in case something happened, an illness or death in the family."

Jonathan shook his head. There was nothing to indicate that he was lying.

"How about her packing, the type of clothes she took?

Did they indicate the sort of climate she was going to?"

Again Jonathan shook his head, saying, "It was all done without my knowledge, I was presented with a fait accompli at Leigh Murray's office the morning she left."

Jonathan had relaxed, was too relaxed, as if relieved because the questioning was going in the wrong direction.

"Your wife has disappeared, to where or for how long you don't know, yet you appear unconcerned, as if she's already contacted you to say she's all right." Jonathan's body language gave him away. Alan pressed the point home. "Maybe if I was to check the recent incoming calls on your phone?"

Jonathan attempted a nonchalant shrug, "Be my guest," he said but he no longer retained the ease of a few moments earlier.

Alan watched his eyes, and saw them flick in the direction of a side table, and the mobile telephone sitting on it.

Jonathan saw that Alan had seen the mobile and made a movement in its direction, with the sole aim of deleting Sharon's message. It was a futile attempt; he was in the presence of a professional, one whose reactions were younger and better trained. Jonathan was pushed into the chair he had been sitting on when Alan first arrived, by the desk.

Alan then stepped over to the small table and picked up the mobile. "What have we here?" He returned to the desk, pushed Jonathan, who was about to regain his feet, back into the chair and perched on the edge of the desk. "Similar model to mine," he said, studying the buttons.

"You have no right," Jonathan said, and he reached up to snatch away the mobile, only to be restrained by one of Alan's large hands grabbing him by the throat. Using the thumb of his other hand, Alan pressed out the message play code; while Jonathan pulled at the hand around his throat in a futile attempt to release himself from the grip, but it was immovable, and the intense pressure restricted his breathing. After a while he stopped trying.

Alan put the mobile to his ear and listened to Sharon's message. He replayed it over and over again, listening only to four words: darling, I'm missing you.

Darling.

Missing you.

Darling.

Then he became conscious that his other hand was aching. He released the grip and Jonathan slid down into the chair. This time there was no mistake, unlike his wife on the previous occasion, Jonathan was no longer breathing.

Alan had little recollection of retracing his footsteps through the house, returning to his car and driving out of the village; only that he had not seen anyone. Shortly before joining the M5 motorway he pulled into a deserted lay-by and let his mind clear. He felt the bulk of Jonathan's mobile in his pocket and took it out. He listened to the message again; only instead of playing it through again he took a notebook and biro from the glove compartment, and then pressed the button for reply to sender. The number flashed up and he noted it down, listening to the ringing tone at the other end. It rang and rang with no reply. Alan was about to terminate the call when there was a click of someone removing a receiver and a man's voice saying,

"Hello?"

"Can I speak to Sharon Greaves, please?"

"I think you've got the wrong number, laddie."

"What number have I got?"

The man, who had a pronounced Scottish accent, gave the number Alan had dialled, and then added,

"It's a public telephone box, I heard it ringing as I passed. Curiosity always was one of my failings."

"Whereabouts are you? Are you in Scotland?"

"Aye, man, Stornaway, on the Isle of Lewis."

Alan returned to London. From the lock-up he collected a large backpack, which he loaded with camping gear and a package, innocuously made to appear like a first-aid kit, that contained the tools of his trade: probably unnecessary but he never went on a mission without it. On the way to the flat he made an overseas telephone call. It seemed like hours before he finally succumbed to sleep, the adrenalin still pumping: engendered primarily by jealous rage, a passion he had never encountered before.

The next morning he stowed what he thought would be necessary into the backpack, went to his bank, and then took a tube to Euston station. Two trains and a ferry later he landed on the Isle of Lewis: three days after Sharon.

Alan purchased a detailed map of the island and a book of hotels, guesthouses and people doing B&B. There was a daunting number of them, on the other hand it was November, hardly the peak of the tourist season. He hired a car and drove into the town; stopping at the first guesthouse he saw displaying a vacancy sign. After booking in he gave the proprietor a description and showed her a photograph of Sharon, and asked if she had possibly stayed there. The proprietor, a pleasant woman, shook her head.

"But you could ask Mrs Harris, at the Glengarry guesthouse," she said.

"Would my friend be likely to be staying there?"

"I've no idea, but there's not a lot that happens in Stornaway that Mary Harris doesn't know about. Her telephone bill would settle the national dept of many a third-world country. Mind, you'd better be prepared to cross her palm with silver, if you know what I mean."

After locking his backpack in his room, and following the instructions he had been given, Alan made his way to the Glengarry guesthouse and the notorious Mary Harris. The lady in question bore a striking resemblance to the wire-haired terrier that snapped around at Alan's feet, or so it seemed to him.

"No, your friend didn't stay here," she answered Alan's enquiry, "but there was something that rings a bell, now what was it? Sandy, you naughty dog, stop annoying the gentleman." The dog ignored her and continued to snuffle around Alan's feet. "Let me think, what might jog my memory?" Alan slid a folded twenty- pound note across the reception desk, which Mary Harris deftly palmed and slid into her cardigan pocket. "Now I know what it was, there was another gentleman asking after her."

"When was this?"

"Yesterday evening."

"Carl," Alan said, more to himself, referring to his late employer, and meaning that the man would have been one of his operatives.

"He was foreign," the sharp-eared Mary Harris said, "but he sounded French to me, not German, and I got the impression that I wasn't the first person he had asked."

"Of course, the Frenchman," Alan improvised. "We are all supposed to meet up here but the details seem to have gone astray. Where you able to help him?"

"I told him what I've told you, that she hadn't been here. He didn't pursue the matter."

Meaning he hadn't offered an incentive, Alan surmised. "I don't suppose you could help me find out where both of them are, my friend and the Frenchman?"

"I might. It depends on how keen you are to find them."

Alan slid two more twenty-pound notes across the desk top, which were as deftly conveyed to the cardigan pocket as the first one. "It might take a little time. Why don't you pop across the road to my daughter-in-law's tearoom while you're waiting, try some of her shortbread?"

Alan, who disliked tea, was on his second pot of coffee, and plate of shortbread, when Mrs Harris entered the tearoom. "Good morning to you, Janet," she said to the woman who had served Alan, and then sat herself across the table from him. There were no other customers, and after placing a cup of tea in front of her mother-in-law, Janet disappeared into a room behind the counter. Mary Harris said, "Two women, one of them resembling the description of your friend, stayed in Stornaway three nights ago. They registered under the names of Susan and Clare Buchan.

"A Belgium gentleman, Mr Jean Mortier, is registered at a hotel here."

"Do you have addresses for both?"

"Well, I've been thinking, neither woman or the man answer to the names you mentioned and, being a law abiding citizen, I'm wondering if they, or the police, would be interested to know you are looking for them."

Alan took out his wallet and extracted a further two twenty-pound notes and a fifty-pound note. Looking Mary Harris in the eye he said, "That makes a total of a hundred and fifty pounds, is that sufficient to secure the information, together with your silence?" He held her eyes until he saw the fear enter them. Mary Harris took a slip of paper from her pocket and handed it across the table. Alan opened it, read the contents and then gave her the money. He stood up. "I'll leave you to settle up with your daughter-in-law, I think you can just about afford it now"

Mary Harris returned a nervous smile. Alan leaned down, his face inches from hers. "Don't make me have to come looking for you," he whispered.

"Mrs Harris told me that a couple of friends of mine, Susan and Clare Buchan, stayed here a couple of nights ago. I was supposed to meet up with them in Glasgow but I got held up. I don't suppose they left a message for me, or said where they were going?"

"Neither. They left two days ago," the proprietor of the Bernera guesthouse informed Alan. "But I did see them making their way to the bus station."

"Yes, that was one of them," the booking clerk said, looking at the photograph Alan showed him. Two ladies, last Wednesday, they got the bus to Castleway. I remember because they were the only two on it. But I can't recall any Frenchman asking about the bus."

"The Misses Buchan, that's right, nice ladies, they stayed

here two nights ago, but I'm afraid you'll be too late to meet up with them now."

"How do you mean?"

"They caught the last boat to Howth Island, there won't be another until the beginning of February.

"What's there?"

"Only a monastery and half a dozen monks. They take people to stay, a retreat, get away from it all. And you can't get much further away than Howth Island."

"Twenty-miles out, inhospitable, no natural harbours only a single jetty, No telephones, no radio contact, when the ferry stops running it's completely cut off," the harbour master informed Alan.

"What if one of them has an accident or illness?"

The harbour master shrugged. "It's never happened. The monastery has a sick bay, and I believe one of the monks has some medical knowledge, other than that I suppose they'd say they are in the hands of God."

"Would it be possible for me to charter someone to take me there?"

"I shouldn't think so, the season's finished. Anyway it's a tricky bit of water at the best of times let alone when it's like this." The harbour master gestured through the window at the sleeting rain coming in almost horizontally from the Atlantic. "Brian Gray, the skipper of the ferry, is the only one who really knows Howth, and he left yesterday to stay with his daughter in Canada for a couple of months."

"Looks like I'm out of luck."

"I'd say so."

Chapter Thirteen

Sharon said, "I take it that this isn't the first time you've been here?"

"You take it right," Gayle replied, without amplification, a habit Sharon found a little irritating.

They were making their way back to the cabin, a walk of about a hundred yards from the monastery. There, in a reception area, they had met the Abbot, father Cecil, and one of the monks, Brother Adrian. From the way she was greeted it was clear that Gayle was not a complete stranger to either of them. Not that there was a great deal of conversation with the abbot. Gayle had introduced him to Sharon, and he had shaken her hand, "Mrs Greaves," before turning to Gayle and saying, "Good to see you again, Miss Meredith. Everything is much the same since you were last here, but I'm sure Brother Adrian will bring you abreast with the few changes that have occurred." And with that he had given Sharon a brief nod and left them.

The monk was less formal. "You're looking well, Gayle."

In contrast to the abbot's strident Scottish accent, the Brother spoke with a soft Irish brogue

"And you, Adrian," Gayle replied. "You're still here so I gather the life is still suiting you?"

"It is," he said to Gayle, then to Sharon, "Welcome to Howth Island, Mrs Greaves."

"Sharon, please."

"Sharon. The climate can be a little harsh but we are not completely without amenities. There is running water and electricity, although to conserve our limited supply of fuel for the generator at this time of year it is only available between six and ten in the evening and seven to nine in the morning."

Brother Adrian accompanied Sharon and Gayle to the main entrance. "There is a plentiful supply of peat in the barn, so you need never be cold," he said, pointing to a building between the cluster of cabins. "In the event of illness or an accident we have a medical wing in the main building, presided over by Brother Neil." He gestured in the direction of a porch enclosed door on the side of the main building. "The laundry is run by Brother Stephen – still in the same place, Gayle - and your dirty washing should be delivered to him on a Monday. And in case you forget what day of the week it is there's a calendar hanging in the cabin. Well, I think that's everything. Any questions?"

"Two," Sharon said. "One: does this the wind and rain ever let up?"

"Never for any appreciable length of time."

"Right, I feared as much. And secondly: don't you feel the cold?"

In contrast to the multi-layers of clothing Sharon and Gayle had on, Brother Adrian's sole concession to the climate – and it had only been marginally warmer inside the monastery – appeared to be a pair of stout hiking boots beneath his habit. "I'll let you into a secret," he said, and lifted the hem of his habit above one of his boots to reveal an inch of dark blue material tucked into his socks, "woollen long johns."

To Sharon it still seemed like precious little.

"And faith", Gayle said.

"And faith", Brother Adrian echoed. "Oh, I almost forgot." He extracted a key from a packet and handed it to Gayle. "For the hut next to your cabin."

"I saw that, what is it?"

"Wait and see, a surprise, donated by a grateful visitor." And before he could be grilled any further, Brother Adrian went back inside the monastery and closed the door. Gayle and Sharon pulled the hoods of their parkas over their heads and made their way back to the cabin.

Howth Island was approximately two miles long by one mile at its widest point, high at the northern end, bordered by towering cliffs, gradually tapering to a shingle beach to the south. It had no natural harbours and although there were a number of inlets and beaches, they were made unreachable by a surrounding ledge of jagged submerged rocks. The only safe entrance, for a boat of any reasonable size, was on the eastern side, where the submerged rocks could be cleared at high tide to a man made jetty. The central southern end was mainly a peat bog, the remainder undulating rocky moorland, providing sufficient grass for the monastery's twenty or so sheep.

The monastery and log cabins were situated towards the northern end, in a saucer-like vale, which offered some protection from the gusting winds, and was also the site of a natural spring well. Water from the well was pumped to a holding tower, from which it was gravity fed to the monastery and the four cabins. A petrol engine powered generator provided the necessary electricity, peat from the bog fuel for the open fireplace in the monastery's main hall (the monk's cells were unheated), and the stoves in the cabins.

Sharon had found the journey from the Isle of Lewis terrifying. The ferry, which had appeared to be sizable enough in the harbour, seemed almost miniscule once upon the mountainous waves of the open Atlantic. She stayed below with her eyes closed for most of the time, not coming up onto the deck until they were safely docked - a euphemism for being tossed and bounced against a ladder the didn't seem to keep still long enough for her to get on to it – when she had to be practically manhandled on to the jetty. Then they had to walk a mile and a half to the cabins. She and Gayle were the only visitors.

"How long has the monastery been here?" Sharon asked.

"From what I've been told there's been one here from the year dot, but it had all fallen into disrepair and the monks gone sometime in the fifteenth century. The monks returned when a Victorian industrialist, reportedly suffering with a conscience, donated the present building. It was opened for use to the public as a retreat in the nineteen sixties. The cabins, electricity and running water are fairly new innovations, they certainly weren't here when I first came."

"When was that?"

"Nineteen eighty-six." Gayle didn't expand on the nature or reason for her first visit to the island.

"Were you in need of solace?" Sharon persisted.

"No, refuge."

Sharon gave up; they were going to be there for another three months, if Gayle was going to reveal the mystery surrounding her original visit she would do it in her own time.

"What denomination are the monks?"

Unexpectedly, Gayle laughed. "Do you know I've never given it a thought. Benedictine I think."

They were nearing the cabins. Gayle brandished the key Brother Adrian had given her. "Let's see what the surprise is." They walked over to the hut, and Gayle put the key in the lock and opened the door.

"What on earth!"

Sharon put her head in. "It's a sauna," she exclaimed. In fact it was more that just a sauna, it was a complete sauna suit; accompanying the four-seater sauna cabin were two reclining couches, two cane armchairs, an occasional table, a galley kitchen and a shower and toilet. "Fantastic! I love saunas."

Gayle admitted that she too wasn't adverse to them. Unfortunately the sauna was heated by an electric element, so they would have to wait until the evening, when the electricity came on, to try it out.

Allowing access to the monastery, as a retreat, had always been part of the Brotherhoods creed. The commencement of the increase of its popularity in the 1960's coincided with the decrease in the monastery's finances – bad management of the fund set up by the Victorian benefactor together with post-war inflation had seen it dwindle to insignificance. So it was decided to use this one asset as a means of filling the vacuum, and a firm of management consultants were hired to advise on the ways and means. As the income generated was only to cover the monastery's costs, it was able to attract sufficient visitors, happy to pay the modest sum charged, to meet this requirement. Initially the three visitor cells were adequate, but as the retreats popularity grew, plus an awareness that something a little less austere might be appreciated; the increased revenue was invested in the addition of the four cabins.

They were of Canadian design and manufacture, and

with the peat-burning stove provided a warm and draught-proof environment. And as visitors to a retreat are seeking quiet and solitude, they were built for single occupation. Each had a living area, bedroom, bathroom and kitchen: adequately, if sparsely, furnished. Kerosene lamps and primus cooking stoves were provided as standbys for when the electricity was off.

Initially the two women agreed that one of them would play host to the other on alternate days; but as Sharon hadn't cooked a meal, tided a room or made a bed since she married, and as Gayle's inclination was to look after Sharon, it wasn't very long before she was doing most of the chores and her cabin had become the focus of their communal activities. For her part, Sharon tended to be the instigator of what they would do for the day.

Included in each cabin were four books: Bible, encyclopaedia, dictionary, and 'The Flora and Fauna of the Western Isles'. The first three were used mainly as reference for games of scrabble and trivial pursuits. The last Sharon used as basis for their daily excursions: to try and find and log every animal and plant in the book.

A typical day would commence with Sharon rising, cleaning and lighting the stove – her only domestic chore, save a cursory weekly clean of the cabin - making and drinking a cup of coffee, showering, dressing. Around ten o'clock, she would go over to Gayle's cabin. By which time Gayle would have done something similar plus replenished each of the cabins stock of peat from the barn, collected eggs from Brother Adrian (who looked after the monastery's farm), and made breakfast for herself and Sharon. Then with packed lunches – made, of course, by Gayle – they would set off to explore the island and commune with nature. Darkness fell around four o'clock so, after once getting caught out and having to retrace their steps in total blackness, they made a rule to stop what they were doing and returning to the cabins within sufficient time to beat nightfall. Back at the cabins stoves would be replenished and kerosene lamps lit; by which each would spend the time reading and (usually Gayle) preparing the evening meal. Six-thirty, after the electricity had been on for sufficient time to heat the element, would find them in the sauna. Dinner would follow, and then chess or scrabble or trivial pursuits. Bedtime was governed by when the electricity went off at ten o'clock.

Both women became adept at sitting up in bed, adequately wrapped up, reading by torchlight.

Food was never going to be a problem; the monastery farm enabled them a certain amount of self-sufficiency in meat and dairy produce, plus they had adequate stocks of tinned and packet foodstuffs.

It was food for the intellect, in particular reading matter, that had concerned Gayle the most. She had obtained from Sharon a list of the sort of things she liked to read together with her favourite authors, to which she added her own. Then, at an

Internet café she had logged into a book supplier and ordered the books on the list. When the books were ready and packed she used the same method to contact a firm of couriers and arranged for express delivery to Castleway on the Isle of Lewis, to accompany the other supplies destined for the Howth Island monastery on the final ferry of the year. Payment was via her Spanish credit card, and she had kept her fingers crossed that the delivery schedule would be met.

There were 120 books in all. Inevitably they included some old favourites, but re-reading them was always a pleasure, and amongst each of their choices there were books they could swap. All the same they endeavoured to restrict their individual consumption to five books a week: the fear of being left with nothing to read was a fate neither wanted to contemplate.

At the commencement of their period together they had agreed that individual privacy was something that would have to be respected. In reality, perhaps because of the isolation from other people and distractions, they found that 'having space' wasn't something either particularly craved, and the majority of time was spent in one another's company. When they weren't reading, playing chess or games, luxuriating in the sauna or walking – and often when they were – they talked; especially when the weather was too severe to venture out in. Individual histories, likes, dislikes, places they had been, places they wanted to visit, people they had known and people they would be happy never to see again.

Inevitably secrets were revealed.

But not all of them.

Gayle had not discerned any reciprocation of the feelings she had towards Sharon, and fear of rebuttal or, even worse, derision, prevented her from declaring to Sharon that she was in love with her.

By the end of November it had been six weeks since Sharon's encounter in the hotel room: the longest period she had gone without sex in the past fifteen years. It wasn't like an itch that had to be scratched, she wasn't a nymphomaniac; more it was something she missed, and would rather not be missing it. Masturbation she had found an unfulfilling substitute and, unfortunately for Gayle, she gave no consideration towards a homosexual alternative. When attempts to flirt with Brothers Adrian and Neil – the only monks she came into any contact with – proved unreceptive, Sharon rationalised that she had no alterative other than to emulate them.

It came as a surprise to Gayle to discover that Sharon missed Jonathan. The son, Leon, she could understand, but to pine for a husband with whom she was regularly unfaithful seemed like a contradiction.

"Sex doesn't play as an important part in his life as it does in mine," Sharon explained. "But it's only part of a marriage, and we have an understanding to cover that. In all other aspects we are totally compatible. We're best friends, we love one another. I never think of myself as being unfaithful, I would never have an affair or leave him."

This last sentence shook Gayle, and further increased her resolve not to reveal the feeling she felt towards Sharon.

As November slipped into December and the spectre of Christmas appeared on the horizon she realised that it could be a time that Sharon would particularly miss her family. She chided herself; it was something that she had completely overlooked, although in all fairness, in the limited time she had had at her disposal, there had been little time to give it any consideration. Should she give it any now?

She decided to face Sharon directly with the dilemma. "It'll be Christmas soon, are you going to go all weepy on me?"

"Probably."

"So do we ignore it, or do I ask Brother Neil to kill one of his chickens and cook something special, and then produce the bottle of scotch I brought along in case of emergencies?"

Sharon gave it a moment of thought then said, "Seeing as I'm going to cry my eyes out in any case we might as well make the best of it. Eat too much and get pissed."

"Go the whole horrible hog and put up decorations?"

"Yuk. I think I saw some scraggy pines that might do as a Christmas tree."

"Double yuk."

They laughed, and Gayle was glad she had brought up the matter.

Later in the morning Sharon said, "I think I'll go and see if I can find one of those scraggy pines that will do as a Christmas tree; then we'll have to borrow a saw off Brother Neil to cut it down." She put on her parka. "You coming along?"

"Nah, I've a few things to do. You go, I'll come and inspect it later. Have fun."

The small copse of trees lay to the south west of the island, bordering the peat bog; a distance of less than a mile as the crow flies but a walk of just over that. Sharon had her binoculars and book of flora fauna with her, just in case; but the disappointing truth was that it was the wrong time of the year to see much: most of the birds had flown south, and everything else was keeping its head down. Still the walk was bracing and, for once, it wasn't raining.

Stepping out a good pace she covered the distance in half an hour. Mounting a rise she saw the trees below her: a sorry bunch, not one of them upright, the constant, buffeting wind causing them to grow at an angle. She picked out three that might suffice, and descended to inspect them.

One had definite possibilities. They would have to use a bucket as a pot to put it in. She knelt down and gauged how far up it would have to be cut, calculating the height of the room and size the bucket would accommodate. About there, she thought and made an imaginary cut mark with her hand. Satisfied, she stood up and stretched her back.

Suddenly, from behind, she felt an arm go around her

neck, and then, before she could utter a sound, a hand placed over her mouth.

Chapter Fourteen

It was a day of firsts for Andy Latimer: a new car, first day of his promotion from Detective Sergeant, and his first case as a Detective Inspector. A murder.

The name of the victim seemed familiar; reading the address he remembered where from: Jonathan Greaves, the Manor House, Ulmeford. The husband of the woman he had interviewed in the hospital, the woman who had had the zipless fuck before she was half strangled. Immediately DI Latimer wondered if there was a connection.

A number of reporters were gathered at the gates of the Manor House, many of whom he knew, and they moved as he swung the car into the entrance. The uniformed officer manning the gates saw who he was and opened them. As he drove through one of the reporters shouted, "Congratulations, Detective Inspector."

There was a cluster of vehicles at the end of the drive: two police Rovers, the pathologist's Saab, and the van that brought the team of Scene Of Crime Officers. Latimer parked behind the van and DS Dean Hammond approached as he got out of the car.

"Morning, sir," he said.

Last week, when they were fellow detective sergeants, it had been Andy, and he was aware of the resentment his promotion might have engendered. Latimer nodded and said, "Who found the body, and where?"

"The housekeeper, in the library," Hammond answered.

"Sounds like something out of an Agatha Christie novel; if there's a butler we'll know who did it.

Hammond didn't smile. "No butler," he said, "only a gardener, David, husband of the housekeeper, Mrs Sally Boldry."

"You've taken statements from them?"

"Yes, neither saw or heard anything. Mrs Boldry found the body at about eight o'clock this morning."

"How about Mrs Greaves?"

"She's not here. According to Mrs Boldry she hasn't been around for some time." Hammond consulted his notebook. "Not since the 28th of October. She says it's not unusual for Mrs Greaves to be away, but not normally for such a long time."

Latimer was pretty sure that the 28th of October was the date Sharon Greaves spent with her zipless, near homicidal lover. He made a mental note to check his report. Together with Hammond he made his way to the library, where the pathologist, clad in white overalls and with plastic covers over his shoes, was completing his examination of the body. "Okay to come in?" Latimer asked from the doorway.

"Well I've just about finished for now," the pathologist said, "I don't know about the others."

Latimer looked over to the chief of the SOCOs:

"Yes, it's okay to come in," he said.

Jonathan Greaves was sitting in a swivel chair by a desk; rigor mortis maintaining the body in an upright position, with his head slumped on his chest.

"Cause and time of death?" Latimer asked.

"Strangulation I would guess," the pathologist replied and he pointed at the bruising visible each side of the victim's throat, "somewhere between ten o'clock and midnight."

Latimer requested that a detailed set of photographs of the bruises accompany the pathologist's report.

They arrived a week later. The report confirmed death by strangulation, adding that the size and positioning of the bruising suggested that the perpetrator was a man, and that only one hand, the right, had been used. In the pathologist's opinion the man would need to possess immense strength – which added a sliver of confusion into Latimer's suspicion that the man who had killed Jonathan Greaves was the same man who had almost strangled Sharon Greaves. The previous day he had spoken with the doctor who had treated Sharon Greaves. Consulting his notes, and comparing them with the pathologists report, he said the bruising around Sharon's throat had been different, in that less pressure had been applied and, as the bruising on the right hand side was higher on her neck than that on the left hand side, the indication was that two hands had been used. If he could strangle a man with one hand, Latimer wondered, why, with his immense strength, had he been unable to throttle a woman with two?

Latimer reviewed the rest of the information that he had to date, eight days after the murder of Jonathan Greaves.

The whereabouts of Sharon Greaves was still unknown. According to Mrs Boldry none of Mrs Greaves' suitcases were missing and, as far as she was aware, nor where any of her clothes. An address book was in the desk and the names and addresses in it were being checked to see if she was at any one of them. As standard procedure her name and description had been issued to police divisions and hospitals nationwide.

It appeared that Jonathan Greaves' killer had gained entry through a pantry window. He had left no fingerprints on the window, or anywhere else. There was no trace of an imprint from his shoes – from which a maker might be obtained (in the hope that there was something special about the shoe) and to give an indication of the man's size and weight. Nor was there any trace of skin, hair or saliva to provide a DNA sample. Nothing of value had been taken, and Jonathan Greaves' wallet - containing £120 in cash and two credit cards - was still in his jacket pocket. It all pointed to a contract killing by a methodical professional.

But why strangulation?

It wasn't the usual modus operandi of a professional hitman: a pistol, knife or garrotte was quicker and less trouble. Okay, it was understandable in the case of Sharon Greaves, if she had also been an intended victim, to make it look as if she was the victim of a sex crime, but in Jonathan's case it would only be plausible if it had been made to look as if he had disturbed a burglar. And, if he had entered the house with the sole intention of murdering Jonathan, why had he used only one hand to strangle his victim and not two? It didn't add up.

Latimer called Hammond on an internal line and asked him to check on any criminal known to use strangulation and the national database for similar reported incidents.

The scene of crime investigators had removed personal items from Jonathan Greaves' body, together with the contents of his pockets, for further examination. No clues had been uncovered from them, and they were now in a box in Latimer's office, waiting to be returned to the Greaves estate.

He opened the box and laid the contents out on his desk: plain gold ring, gold and steel wristwatch on a leather strap, leather wallet, leather bound diary, fountain pen, electronic car key, handkerchief.

As well as the money and credit cards the wallet contained four of Jonathan's own business cards in one compartment and three other in an adjacent slot.

Latimer took them out: two were for overseas-based executives (New York and Hong Kong) and one for a London lawyer.

He dialled the London number, a receptionist answered; Latimer gave his name and rank and asked to speak with Ms Leigh Murray.

"Good morning, Detective Inspector. Would your call be in connection with the murder of Jonathan Greaves?"

"It would."

"Then I think we should meet."

People, complete strangers, can sometimes meet and immediately strike up a rapport, experience a mutual harmony, empathy; but with Andy Latimer and Leigh Murray the exact opposite was the case. They disliked one another from the word go. Neither would be able to put their finger on exactly what it was about the other that engendered this animosity – some mannerism perhaps that triggered a childhood experience or embarrassment – and each was too professional to let it interfere with the matter in hand. All the same, it was there and it was something of which they were both aware.

Nor had it escaped the notice of Graham Foreman, who was also present at the meeting.

"How do you mean, you know who Sharon Greaves is with but you don't know where? Could you be a little bit more specific, Ms Murray?"

"As I said, after the hotel incident we thought it was imperative for Sharon to disappear until the case comes up for trial. Gayle Meredith was hired to arrange this; and she convinced us that it should be to somewhere that was completely isolated. A place that was known only to her."

"So how do you keep in touch with them?"

"We don't," Leigh Murray answered.

Graham Foreman said, "No one can, not us, not Lucidel, not the media, that was the idea. Gayle has taken Sharon to a location that is completely cut off from any form of communication. That way she is safe: Lucidel can't get at her, directly or indirectly, and they can't use her family - in particular her son – to intimidate her because she wouldn't be aware of it."

"How would they know Sharon was somewhere where she couldn't be got at?"

Leigh Murray said, "Oh believe me, Detective Inspector, they know."

"Whether I believe you or not is incidental, Ms Murray, but I'm conducting a murder investigation and I need something a bit more concrete than your word."

Murray looked at Foreman, he shrugged and she lapsed into pensive thought.

Latimer said, "I don't have to remind you that withholding information during an investigation is an offence, Ms Murray."

The lawyer returned a contemptuous smile, and then

nodded to Graham Foreman.

"These offices were bugged and we are aware that at least one of Ms Murray's staff is being bribed."

"When did you become aware of these facts, before or after the morning Mrs Greaves met with her husband here, the morning she disappeared?"

"One of the first things I did when I was hired was to sweep this office for bugs. There were two, one under the desk and one under a picture, which I removed. But I didn't discover the others in the reception, and that the phone line was tapped, until later. The bribery didn't become apparent until I made certain checks, but it was after Sharon had left."

Latimer suspected that the checks Foreman made included hacking into the guilty party's bank account, but he chose not to pursue the matter. He also guessed that, for her own purposes, Murray had not let on to the culprit that she new about him or her.

"So," Latimer summed up, "during the half hour or so that Sharon spent speaking with her husband that morning, it can be interpreted that they spoke in absolute privacy." Murray and Foreman nodded in confirmation.

"And that Sharon told Jonathan where she was going."

Foreman said, "No, that wouldn't have been possible, because the last time Gayle had spoken to Sharon was at the clinic, when we were all there, and no mention of the destination was revealed. In addition to that, Gayle told me that she wasn't going to tell Sharon until they were almost there."

"But Lucidel knew Sharon was here that morning?"

"Oh yes, and they followed her when she left, Gayle suspected they would," Foreman said, and he then went on to detail the switch and the false trail Gayle had contrived, up and to when Ed Morrison had slowed down to let Sharon out of his car in the back street leading to Shepherds Bush.

"No chance of her being followed from there?"

"No, Gayle's far too good for that."

"So she's good, this Gayle Meredith?"

"For spiriting people away, the best."

"I take it that you've known her for some time, what's her background?"

"MI5, like myself, only non-operational. She has a degree in languages, Spanish and German, and initially she was with GHQ. She was seconded to us for some project, the outcome of which was to put someone into protective hiding. So good was she at it that she was persuaded to transfer to the department. This was back in the eighties, when we were having a certain amount of success against the IRA thanks to some of their top people choosing to give evidence rather than face long prison sentences. Super grasses were how the media dubbed them. One of the main reasons for this success was the record we had for protecting them, which was due in no small way to Gayle Meredith. She had a talent for it, she spirited them away, some of then for good, and those who have surfaced have done so under their own volition. Unfortunately, the IRA managed to place a mole in the department, and they soon learned that the one person who could tell them where their traitors could be found was Gayle. So she had to choreograph her own disappearance. I gather it was quite traumatic for her."

Sharon and Gayle, fresh from the sauna, showered and changed, were sitting in front of a blazing fire swapping life histories. It was a time for revealing past incidences that had affected their lives, and it was Gayle's turn. "You once asked why I had been here before, well the reason was that I used this place to hide a senior member of the IRA."

"What! You were with the IRA?"

"No, MI.5 He was an informer, a super grass, you remember those, back in the 1980's."

"Oh yeah. So how did you get involved with MI5?"

"I joined the army as an officer cadet, took my degree in modern languages and sort of progressed into military intelligence from there. I became involved in witness protection, and it was discovered that I was rather adept at arranging new lives for people."

"What were they like, these super grasses?"

"I was involved with eight of them, and in the main I found them rather unpleasant. When all was said and done they were basically just violent bullyboys, without a modicum of remorse for the carnage they had caused and, by that time, only

191

interested in saving their own skin. Any vestige of fighting for a cause was long gone. Plus some of them had families who were as equally unpleasant. Still, that made it easy not to become personally involved."

Gayle's voice and face had started to become animated. Sharon said, "You enjoyed the work?"

"Oh yes, I found it very exciting," Gayle replied, "and heady; having that power to shape other people's lives. A completely different environment from my genteel upbringing. Although I come from a military family, I was raised to become an officer's wife, not a serving soldier." She laughed. "When I joined up, directly from Roedean, I was practically disowned."

"What made you give it up?"

"The IRA discovered my existence. They figured that if they could get to me they'd find the whereabouts of their traitors. Of course I had no idea of this, not until one night when they tried to smash down the door of my apartment. Fortunately it was steel reinforced – a precaution I had thought to be a bit over the top until then – so I had time to phone for help. But it scared the fuck out of me, I was completely un-nerved, and when I realised that there was no way my safety could be guaranteed, I wanted out. So I had to orchestrate my own disappearance. I accepted my cowardice and knew that if the IRA found me I would tell them everything, and that once they had it they would kill me. I was in a state of absolute terror the whole time, I became paranoid, changing and rescheduling, revealing nothing to anyone, until I was certain I would never be found, that I had become an un-person. Later, when I surfaced in my new existence, I had a nervous breakdown."

"No one ever saw her again."

"So how did you find her?" Latimer asked.

"When Ms Murray asked me to hide Mrs Greaves I immediately thought of Gayle; figuring that as twenty years had gone past she was no longer in any danger. I still have some contacts in the department and I met with the present controller. He told me that she was still on salary, and although he didn't know where she was there was a method in place for contacting her. Which he did, and subsequently she made contact with me, and agreed to take the job on."

"And you have no idea where she is now?"

"None what so ever, other than as she was able to set it up in the minimal time available, I suspect it was a plan she had used before."

"Would this present controller have access to the details of her past projects?"

"May be."

"Can you give me his name and where I can find him?"

"No, I don't think I can."

"Oh come on," Latimer said, "don't go getting all spooky spook with me, this is a murder investigation not one of your cloak and dagger spy games."

But Foreman was not to be intimidated by the Inspector's derogatory tone. "I am still governed by the Official Secrets Act, besides which this may come within the realm of state secrets. The best I can do is contact the controller and ask if he will see you."

Latimer nodded his acceptance, aware that he was out of his depth with this type of thing and preferring to wait until he was better informed before pressing further. He then asked Foreman if he knew the name of Lucidel's chief of security and where he might be found?

Outside the lawyer's office Latimer called DS Dean Hammond on his mobile and asked him to have the Greaves household swept for bugs and to come back to him with the result as soon as possible. "And check all incoming and outgoing telephone calls," he asked as an after thought. He then informed Hammond that he would be staying in London overnight and gave him the name of the hotel Leigh Murray's secretary had just booked for him.

From the hotel Latimer telephoned the London office of Lucidel International, identified himself and asked if he could speak with Mr Chuck McCoskey. He was put through to the London chief of security, who informed him that Mr McCoskey was unavailable and could he help? When Latimer said that he was in London as part of his investigation into the murder of Jonathan Greaves, he stopped him there and said he would contact Mr McCoskey and come back to him.

Hammond called back later that afternoon to inform that listening devices had been found on the telephone and in the library. In return Latimer told Hammond that he expected to return to Exeter the following afternoon.

Minutes after replacing the receiver it rang again: this time it was the Lucidel London security chief to say that Mr McCoskey would be able to talk with him, in his office, at ten o'clock tomorrow morning.

He was soaking in a bath filled with a plentiful supply of the essence provided by the hotel when the Chief Superintendent telephoned. Wrapped in a copious towel Latimer brought him up to date with his investigation, while wondering what it was that had triggered the Super calling him at this late hour. He wasn't kept wondering for long; when he reached the part about requesting an interview with the controller of the office Gayle Meredith had worked in the Super said, "Ah. I've just had Whitehall on the line, seems they're not too keen to talk to you. How imperative is it, Andy?"

"It could save a lot of time in finding Sharon Greaves. We've discovered a listening device in the room where Jonathan Greaves was murdered. I'm meeting with Lucidel's chief of security tomorrow morning; if the bug is theirs he might have the necessary information. It might also save her life if her husband's murderer is after her. Otherwise this controller might be the only person who can help."

"I think you can expect Lucidel to be evasive; they're hardly likely to tell you something that could incriminate themselves. Still, see what happens, then if it's necessary to speak with this controller I'll pull the necessary strings."

"Thank you, sir."

The next morning, as he was about to leave the hotel to go to the meeting with Chuck McCoskey, a thought came to Latimer. His mobile trilled. It was Dean Hammond. Before he could speak Latimer asked him if he knew where Sharon Greaves' son was?

"In Florida, with his grandmother. Why?"

"I wondered if that's where Sharon was; you know the most obvious place being the best cover."

"I can get the local police to check, but I'm pretty sure she isn't."

Latimer caught the excitement in Hammond's voice. "Oh yes, why's that?"

"Couple of reasons. Firstly: checking on outgoing calls on the day Jonathan Greaves was killed, the last one, at nine fifty-five pm, was to directory enquiries. I managed to trace it through, and apparently he was asking about the location of a number, which turned out to be a Scottish public telephone box, on the Isle of Lewis. Secondly: I've just had a call in regard to information I requested from the national database, for similar incidents. The body of a man was discovered yesterday with bruising on his neck suggests that death was by manual strangulation. And guess where? The Isle of Lewis."

Chapter Fifteen

Chuck McCoskey played the recording of Jonathan Greaves being questioned and then throttled. When it was finished he said to the man next to him, "Do you recognise the voice?"

"Yes, I know it, it's Alan Swift," Carl Peterson said. His dark cropped hair and beard were peppered with grey. Swedish by birth, he spoke English with a transatlantic overtone.

McCoskey ejected the cassette and placed it in his attaché case. It would join the earlier recording, of Jonathan listening to his wife's message and repeating the number on the landline to directory enquiries, to be destroyed.

"Is this Alan Smith the guy you used on Sharon Greaves?"

"Swift, Alan Swift," Carl Peterson corrected. "Yes it's him."

"Can he be traced back to you?"

"If he is identified then, yes, he can. He was on the Paladin Security payroll. He won't be carrying any documentation that can identify him, he's a professional . ."

"Not any more," McCoskey cut in. "By the sound of it he's out of control; playing Sharon Greaves' recorded message over and over while he's strangling her husband."

"Yeah. When he bodged the job on the wife I thought it was due to burn-up, now, well now I don't know what he's about."

"I do, he's gone haywire." McCoskey shifted his considerable weight on the leather seat. The two men were in the back of McCoskey's Mercedes, parked on the top floor of a multi-story car park: deserted save for one other car, Carl Peterson's. "I had to fly in this morning to meet some fucking detective inspector who's investigating the murder of Jonathan Greaves."

"Do you know Mr Greaves' wife?"

"I know of her, we've never actually met."

"I believe she was once an employee of Lucidel, and is now the principle witness in a forthcoming case being brought against your company."

"That is confidential information, Detective Inspector, I think maybe I should have one of our lawyers present."

"Are you aware that Mrs Greaves was attacked and left for dead some weeks ago?"

"No, I had no idea. How is she?"

"Fully recovered, you'll be glad to hear. She was strangled, the same method used to murder her husband. We believe it could be the work of one man."

McCoskey was non-committal.

"Do you know the whereabouts of Mrs Greaves?"

"Presumably she's not at the Devon family home, or you wouldn't ask. No, I have no idea where she is."

"No? You didn't know she had gone into hiding, awaiting commencement of the forthcoming case against Lucidel?"

"Where are you coming from, Detective Inspector?"

"The morning she went into hiding she was followed. It wasn't unexpected and a pre-planned ruse was used to put the followers on the wrong trail."

"What has all this to do with the murder of Jonathan Greaves?"

"The morning Mrs Greaves went into hiding she met with her husband in the office of Ms Leigh Murray, the lawyer representing the plaintiff in the case against Lucidel. Subsequently Ms Murray had her offices checked for bugs and two listening devices were uncovered. Also there is strong evidence to suspect that one of her employees has been bribed. When we checked the Greaves house we also found listening devices. You're a professional in the world of espionage, former CIA, what does that imply to you, Mr McCoskey?"

"The implication of your question is not lost on me, Inspector, and I can only advise that you are treading down an unproductive path."

"Do you have an operative by the name of Jean Mortier active in Scotland, on the Isle of Lewis?"

"Not to my knowledge. Why?"

"Shortly before he was murdered Jonathan Greaves telephoned directory enquires to trace the origin of a telephone number. Anyone listening in on the bug planted there would have been able to discover that it was the number of a call box on the Isle of Lewis."

McCoskey rose to his feet. "I think this meeting is at an end, Detective Inspector." He held open the door for him.

Latimer got up, slowly. As he passed McCoskey he said, "The body of Jean Mortier was recently discovered on the Isle of Lewis. He had also been strangled. ."

"Fucking hell!"

"I take it Mortier is the guy you sent to Lewis to find Sharon Greaves?"

Peterson nodded. At the time he had convinced McCoskey that after his peoples dismal record of keeping track of Sharon Greaves it would be better if one of his 'professionals' was sent to Scotland. Jean was good at finding people, and despatching them if necessary.

"When did you last hear from him?"

"A few weeks ago, when he confirmed that Sharon Greaves was on Lewis, also that she was with another woman. He said there were a great number of places they could be hiding and that he would find it by a process of elimination."

"He didn't make regular reports?"

"No, he would let me know as soon as he had something positive. I trusted his judgment, he was a good man."

"Not as good as Swift."

"Would you rather it had been one of yours?"

"Point taken. Can Mortier be traced?"

"He was travelling under that name on papers I provided, he doesn't have a record so his prints won't tell them anything, nor would he have had anything on his person that could identify him."

McCoskey absorbed the information without comment.

"What do you want me to do now?" Peterson asked.

"Drop the whole thing," Luc Barr had ordered when McCoskey had spoken with him earlier. McCoskey could imagine him on the other end of the line, pacing his spartan office, absorbing the report of the police inspectors visit, considering the repercussions, and then making his decision. "We can't have a police investigation implicating us, no matter how circumstantial. Clear any people you have in Scotland out of there immediately and sever any incriminating ties. How about the mole in the lawyer's office, can the bribe be traced back to you?"

"I'll get the operative who approached her out of the country. Send him to the Brazilian office until it all blows over. The money can't be traced, it was transferred via an anonymous account."

"Good. Make sure you cover every contingency. Damage limitations. We'll have to take our chances in court. Use the time left available in digging up whatever dirt you can on Sharon Greaves, especially the sex angle."

"Okay, leave it to me."

"Don't let me down, Chuck." Barr's tone contained sufficient menace to let McCoskey know that his job was on the line. And McCoskey was as equally sure that as they spoke Barr's mind was busy thinking of ways to distance himself from the unauthorised actions of Lucidel's Security Department and it's Chief of Security; just as he was going to do with Carl Peterson.

"Well if I were you, Carl, I'd be personally making sure that Alan Swift never gets the opportunity to talk to the police, or I'd be winding up Paladin Security and heading for destinations unknown."

Neither of which filled Paterson with much enthusiasm: he had no great wish to go up against Alan Swift, and due to some recent dud investments his funds were a little too depleted to ensure a comfortable retirement.

But then, what other choice was there?

Chapter Sixteen

"Please believe me, I'm not here to hurt you." Although he had hardly been vocal during their last encounter, Sharon recognised the voice. The pressure around her throat slackened slightly. "Okay," she said.

The arm was removed from her neck. Sharon turned to face her assailant. He looked like a soldier, dressed in what she thought you would call combat fatigues.

He smiled and said, "I'm so glad to see you again. I'm here to help you."

What was this? "How did you find me?"

His face clouded. "You telephoned your husband from Lewis, the phone was bugged."

So, Gayle had been right all along. How could she have been so stupid?

"Who else knows I'm here?"

"No one as far as I'm aware, he answered, then in a detached voice he added. "There was someone, on Lewis, but he's stopped looking now."

Now what did that mean? Sharon shuddered involuntarily.

"Are you cold?"

God, he missed nothing. "A little, and a bit shaken. How on earth did you get here? We took the last ferry for three months, and it seems like it's been raining and blowing a gale ever since."

"I was trained for such things. It wasn't difficult, just a matter of getting the right equipment and waiting for a slot in the weather. Nothing would have kept me away."

Oh my God.

Her face must have reflected her concern. "I told you, I'm not here to hurt you, only help," he said.

"How do you mean, help?"

"To make sure no one ever hurts you again."

This was going nowhere. In spite of her fear, or perhaps because of it, Sharon said, "Who are you and what do you want?"

"Would you like to see where I'm living?"

"No, I don't think so." Sharon picked up her backpack and shrugged it onto her back. "I think I'm going to go back to my cabin." She turned to leave.

"I don't think I can allow that, Sharon."

Fear, numbing ice-cold fear, struck her like a blow to the kidneys. He placed his hands on her shoulders and pulled her round to face him. He was still smiling. Taking her arm he said, "Come and have a look at my bivouac."

His grip was like a vice. "You're hurting me," she said, and he relaxed the pressure, but it still remained firm and she recalled the bruising on her neck. "Come," he said, and led towards a gap between the trees.

His 'bivouac' was situated in the ruins of what she supposed had been a crofter's cottage. It was a mere hundred yards from where he had accosted her; down a grassy incline and snuggled so neatly into a hollow at one side that it would have been easy to have walked straight past without seeing it. Sharon had certainly never noticed the ruin before, and she and Gayle had walked the area many times. The rear of the cottage was built into the side of the hollow and much of the brickwork was still in place, as was part of the wall to one side and half of the front. Using these as supports he had constructed a lean-to roof using interwoven branches, with sods of peat placed on top of them.

As they approached the ruin he let go of Sharon's arm, took a couple of paces in front of her, turned, stepped to one side and made an elaborate gesture for her to enter. She looked around and saw that a tent had been set up beneath the make shift roof, that four aluminium pans, of various size, were placed by the front wall – to catch the rain, he explained – and beneath the driest part of the roof, supported on a tripod, a billycan hung over the cold embers of a fire. Stepping to the tent, he pulled back the flaps to reveal a ground sheet and sleeping bag. "It's warmer inside," he said, and knelt down and eased himself in. "Come and join me." An invitation that she knew she wouldn't be allowed to refuse. He sat cross-legged on the ground sheet and motioned her to take a similar position, considerately, on the sleeping bag.

They sat there, side by side, looking out at the bracken that surrounded the incline. The wind, which had seemed to abate as they descended the incline and entered the ruin, appeared to cease altogether once inside the tent. Neither said a word, until, without looking at her, he began to speak. Sharon later guessed that it was a speech he had rehearsed many times previously.

"I was hired to kill you, and when I took you to the hotel it was with the sole purpose of doing just that. I thought I had until I was informed that you were still alive. My immediate reaction was one of relief. When I thought back on what had gone on between us I realised that something had happened that made me, subconsciously, not want to harm you. I knew that someone else would replace me to finish the job, just as I knew that I had to protect you."

Like from the someone who was looking for me on Lewis but who isn't looking anymore, Sharon thought.

"I also wanted to see you again. What ever it was that

happened between us in the Exeter hotel has changed my life, I've never experienced feeling for someone the way I feel for you." He turned to look at her. "Is it just me, or did it do something for you as well?"

Being strangled was a new experience, Sharon thought but didn't say. Jesus! She had had guys in the past think that they were in love with her but never a homicidal maniac. "Yes it was something special," she said, choosing her words carefully. In a way it was true, on a scale of fucks from one to ten it was as near the top as she had ever got.

He placed his hand on her chin and pulled her head round to face him. The smile was there again. "Special, yes that's the word; it was very special," he said and kissed her. In spite of her better judgement she returned the kiss. Her libido was stirred, he had been the last person she had had sex with, and that was two months earlier; the longest period she had gone without sex since the birth of Leon. She slid her hand to the back of his neck as the kiss intensified. He pulled the tent flaps closed. Then she was helping him remove the layers of clothes. Her last coherent thought, before he entered her, was that she didn't know his name.

"Don't call me that," Sharon said sharply. He had addressed her as Shar. "My name is Sharon." It wasn't a name she was particularly fond of but it was the one she had been christened with, and ever since she was a child, at school, she had made it clear that she didn't answer to any shortening or misname: Shar, Shaz, Sharn.

It was two nights later and they were in her cabin, in her bed, post coital, and Alan had earned the rebuke when he said, "What are we going to do once we leave here, Shar?" She wouldn't have dreamed of calling him Al or Ally; more over she hadn't asked him his name - experience having taught her that it was usually preferable to keep things on an impersonal footing – he had volunteered it. In fact the less she knew of him the better: what she didn't know couldn't hurt her. And she had purposely kept Gayle's name out of any conversation: when Alan had asked who her companion was, Sharon had simply answered that she was an old friend, who had visited the island before, and who had agreed to accompany her on this occasion.

Sharon's tetchiness wasn't solely concerned with the Alan's use of the diminutive of her name: the nature of the question had irritated her, with its implication of a long-term relationship. Perhaps she had been wrong to let him into her cabin; except it was difficult to make excuses to Gayle in order to go to the ruin: there was only one Christmas tree she could return to cut down. Night, after the electricity was shut down and they had separated to their own cabins, was the only period the two women were apart for any length of time.

"I have a court case to attend and you will return to whatever it was you were doing before," she answered.

"I know, but after that?"

"Alan, I've no idea how long the case is going to drag on, and my only immediate concern is my son. God knows what dirt Lucidel will dig up about me while I'm here, and I'm frightened it will drive him away from me. It will be important to spend time with him, try to explain what it all really means."

Alan said, "Who's Lucy Dell, and what does she have to do with matters?"

Sharon looked at him quizzically, realised that he was serious and burst out laughing. His face clouded. She stopped laughing and gently touched his arm. "It's not a person, it's a company, Lucidel, L-U-C-I-D-E-L. They're the people I'm appearing as a witness against in the trial, they're the ones who probably hired you in the first place."

"I must seem thick to you."

"No, it's an easy mistake."

"Tell me about Lucidel and the court case?"

"Okay, but first," Sharon reached for an alarm clock and set it for six o'clock the following morning. "You'll need to be gone before anyone else is up and about."

"Does it matter?"

"Yes it does, you shouldn't be here, the island is private property and you're a trespasser. Don't be difficult."

"Okay, but," Alan took the clock and moved the alarm hand back half an hour, "I might have something else in mind before we get up. Then he shifted down into the bed and held his arm out for her.

Sharon smiled and slid down next to him, placing her head on his chest. "Now about Lucidel. Well I used to work for them, or rather a subsidiary," she commenced. The history got no further than the explanation of what her job involved, when she became aware that his breathing had regulated. A perceptible snore revealed that he was asleep.

Because of their constant close proximity on the island, Gayle couldn't help but notice the change in Sharon. Her eyes were bright, her walk jaunty, and her skin had a glow to it that Gayle couldn't altogether believe was the result, as Sharon insisted when challenged, of fresh air and exercise. It wasn't that she had been pasty or lacklustre before, simply that she seemed to have blossomed.

"You're positively glowing."

"I do feel pretty good," Sharon admitted, "and what's more I owe it all to you. The island life and stimulating company must suit me." Whereupon she embraced Gayle and gave her a kiss on the cheek.

It wasn't only her physical appearance, her personality had also undergone a change, and the hint of reserve she had maintained between them was gone. Gayle felt it was as if Sharon sought her company, rather than accepting it as part of the situation she had got herself into. She became more involved in the day-to-day necessities, helping out with the preparation of meals and the collection of eggs and farm produce from Brother

Adrian. Previously a large part of their time together, when not walking the island, had been spent playing chess or trivial pursuits, or simply settling down with their respective books. Now they talked most of the time, about everything, including subjects each hadn't thought she previously knew anything about. It was so stimulating, they sparked off one another, and Gayle felt that their relationship had entered a more lasting phase, that they had become intimates.

And she began to wonder if she could dare hope?

When they first began to use the sauna, Gayle, who's public school upbringing in an all girls establishment should have made her unconcerned about public nudity, was reserved about displaying her body (she had even brought a swimming costume in her bag). Whereas Sharon suffered from no such reservations: stripping off without any allowance towards modesty, and then going through a series of stretching and muscle tensioning exercises that displayed every aspect of her body. Gayle couldn't help noticing that she was devoid of pubic hair. Noticing her gaze Sharon said, "Wax job."

"It's lovely," Gayle said without thinking, and then hurried into the sauna cabin to hide the colour she felt rising to her cheeks.

Over the ensuing weeks, with no beauty parlour at hand, Sharon's pubic hair had returned. Then, in the sauna, coinciding with her new exuberance, Gayle saw that it was gone.

"You've shaved!" she exclaimed.

"Yeah," Sharon grinned. "Not as good as a wax, but you did say I was lovelier without it."

Gayle's heart pounded.

After the sauna, instead of ending the evening in Gayle's cabin as they usually did, Sharon begged off, saying that she was tired and that her bed was calling her. As they parted she gave Gayle's hand a squeeze.

Was it an invitation? Nothing like this had ever happened to Gayle before, she was in uncharted territory. Her only experiences were with men, and it had been them who had done all the running. Three times she started towards the door of her cabin, only to back off in a quandary of uncertainty, until she lost her temper with herself. This was ridiculous, for her own sanity's sake she had to know if her feelings would be reciprocated. Then she thought of a plausible excuse to go to Sharon's cabin; an awful nightmare, she was frightened of being alone. Then she could let matters take their course, one way or the other.

The electricity went off.

She stepped out of her door. There was a glow coming from Sharon's cabin: she must have lit some candles. In anticipation? The incessant wind blew clouds across a pale moon, and she could hear, and smell, the sea. At least it wasn't raining. Gayle began to make her way across the twenty yards that separated them, when suddenly she saw a shadow move on the far side of Sharon' cabin. She froze. A cloud obliterated what little moonlight there was. Sharon's door opened. In the pale light from the candles the shadow materialised into the unmistakable form of a man, and Gayle saw Sharon step into his arms.

Of the six men on the island Gayle knew that Sharon had only come into contact with only two: Brothers Neil and Adrian. The former was short and plump, and the man Sharon had embraced was neither. So there was only one person it could be: Brother Adrian.

Adrian Flynn.

Arranging for Adrian Flynn to go into witness protection was Gayle's first assignment after being transferred into the department. He was to be different from the others who followed in that he was giving evidence not to save himself from prison but out of repentance. In some way he was her easiest project in that he had no immediate family or attachment to take into consideration. On the minus side he was her most difficult because he didn't give a damn about his life.

He hadn't been captured by the security forces but had turned himself in.

Adrian Flynn was a bomb maker extraordinary. He had been taught in Libya, and he had been taught well. His devices were never bettered: they didn't malfunction; operatives knew they could safely transport and plant them without the mischance of them detonating while still about their persons: the timers never failed: and the bombs were of such ferocity as to maximise the number of ensuing casualties. He obtained a legionary status that was never sought. It gave him no satisfaction to kill and maim, other than its importance to the 'Cause', and he was able to appease his conscience by thinking himself as a soldier fighting in a just war. Neither he, nor the IRA, were morally responsible for the carnage, but an imperial British Government whose forces were stationed illegally in the sovereign territory of what would one day be a unified Ireland.

Disillusionment set in when he began to hear colleagues talk openly about the collusion that was going on between the IRA and their Union opposite number, the Ulster Volunteer Force (UVF), in the carving up of the various Belfast protection rackets. The realisation that the people he had dedicated his life to had degenerated from being freedom fighters into gangsters made him seriously begin to doubt his dedication to them and the cause. At about this time one of his bombs was detonated in a new, large Belfast shopping mall on a Saturday afternoon, killing and maiming hundreds of shoppers, including many children. The IRA claimed that they had given the security forces prior warning but that it had been ignored. The security forces said that they had received the warning only fifteen minutes before the explosion, that it had not pinpointed the exact location of the bomb, thus leaving insufficient time to complete their evacuation of the area. There was also a prevalent rumour that the bomb had been targeted at a departmental store that had refused to comply with a demand for protection money.

Adrian was sickened by it all. He approached a British army patrol, identified who he was and gave himself up to a bewildered young captain.

Word soon got out, and Adrian Flynn jumped to the top of the IRA's most wanted list.

After laying a false trail that led to California, and then to Vancouver, Gayle brought Adrian to Howth Island, as with Sharon, at the end of October. The plan was for him to remain on the cut off island until February, when he would then be spirited away to Australia. But when she returned to Howth to collect him she discovered that Adrian had found solace with the Brotherhood, and had decided he wanted to remain there. Raised within a devout Catholic environment, he had lost and, now, recovered his faith. "I believe that only by remaining here will I achieve any sort of peace for what I have done. My faith is all I have". With the aid of the Abbot, Father Cecil; Adrian managed to allay Gayle's scepticism and convince her that his reason for wanting to remain was genuine. Gayle doubted that the department would be overjoyed; and she wasn't so naïve as to discount the possibility that, rather than risk the chance of Adrian falling into the hands of the IRA, and the negative publicity to potential informers it would engender, the department would 'take him out' themselves. She believed in Adrian and decided to comply with his wish, but wouldn't let the department know. As far as Control would be aware she would have continued with the original plan, and Adrian Flynn would have become James Donovan: an immigrant with his parents at the age of nine, now an Australian citizen, raised in Sydney and currently seeking employment in Perth.

Adrian was cognizant of the risk she had taken. Six years later, when she sought sanctuary on the island, he was there for her, and afterwards, when he helped nurse her through the breakdown that followed her own escape.

Realisation of the misapprehension she had let herself become deluded with - that Sharon's solicitude towards her was as a result of a requited love - made Gayle feel foolish. And the believed relationship with Adrian saddened her, and gave rise to a concern regarding the eventual outcome.

For Sharon it would be a brief interlude, a means of sating her appetite until she returned to her previous existence. She loved her husband, they had an arrangement that worked, and was happy within their marriage. From what Gayle knew of Adrian, she couldn't see him being able to accept this. For him to renounce his vows would mean that he was, or thought he was, in love with Sharon. She was an intelligent woman and would probably be aware of this; and as she was also an honest woman, she would have acquainted Adrian of her life style, and her condition of non-involvement before embarking on an affair.

And he, in his infatuated naivety would have said he understood: convinced that he would be the one to show her the way to real love, with a real man. He would renounce his vows and leave the island, to go to a world he was unprepared for, only to find disappointment. Adrian had found peace on the island, would he be able to handle the reality of what awaited him on the mainland?

Or was she being unnecessarily pessimistic? Wouldn't Adrian leave the island at sometime anyway, as a matter of course? Wasn't he a grown man who had experienced disappointment before and could again? Except she couldn't help remembering that, repentant sinner or not, he was a murderer, who had killed indiscriminately, on a huge scale.

Violence frightened Gayle. She hadn't thought it would, not when she joined the army, nor when she entered Military Intelligence. But then, she never saw action: taking her degree and then going into the cloistered world of GHQ. Not until the stark reality of driving into the underground car park beneath her flat in the early hours and being confronted by three masked men as she was parking her car. When they had been unable to open the locked doors they had attempted to smash the windows. She had had the presence of mind to slam the car into reverse, race up to a higher level, take the lift up to the safety of her flat and telephone for assistance: only to have the illusion of safety shattered by the sound of sledge hammers pounding on her door.

Then she knew fear, stark brain numbing fear, as she cowered terrified in a corner waiting for help to arrive. The fear intensified when she realised what might have happened if her assailants had been successful: kidnap, torture and, when they had finally got the information they wanted, a bullet in the head. The fear remained with her, consigned to the back of her brain for most of the time, but always there; surfacing now and again in nightmares.

When she had learned that there was a possibility that the man who had half killed Sharon in a hotel room might be a professional killer, her gut instinct was to pull out of the job. It was the same when Sharon had produced her mobile phone on the train, exposing them to the danger of discovery. The problem was that she was in the grip of Sharon, had been, she realised, from the very first moment of meeting her.

The entry of Adrian into the equation was once again resurrecting her trepidations.

Gayle had to decide how she was going to handle the situation: confront Sharon or let the matter take its own course? She took the cowards way out and chose the latter. The problem Gayle anticipated regarding the type of demeanour she should present to Sharon – remote indifference or amiable, reliable friend or patient observer – turned out to be groundless. (a) Sharon was too tied up with her involvement in the situation to notice anything particular about Gayle, and (b) Gayle's natural affection for Sharon prevented her from being anything other than a concerned and loving friend.

This state of co-existence continued for almost two weeks, until early one morning Gayle was awoken by a frantic knocking on her door. She opened it to a distraught Sharon.

"Oh Gayle, I've been such a fool."

Chapter Seventeen

A detective sergeant from Glasgow CID, DS Danielle Nott, was waiting for Detective Inspector Andrew Latimer when he arrived at the airport. The reply from the Glasgow Forensic Laboratory confirmed that the bruising around Jonathan Greaves neck was consistent with that found on Jean Mortier. It also stated that traces of Mace had been found on him. During the wait for the interconnecting flight to the Isle of Lewis, at a secluded table in the cafeteria, they discussed the two murders.

"Mortier had been dead for over a week before his body was discovered, in the wreck of a car half way down a gully. The theory is that he was maced and then strangled."

"What do you know about Mortier?" Latimer asked.

"He had arrived on the island fifteen days previously. The driving licence and passport we found in his hotel room are forgeries, very good forgeries, so I think we can assume that Jean Mortier is not his real name. His fingerprints have come back negative, both on our and Interpol's records. He was between thirty and forty years of age with no distinguishing marks."

"A professional." Latimer commented.

"Killed by another professional, by the looks of it."

"Yes, but why, and who hired them?"

"Perhaps it's to do with this court case," Nott ventured. "One by the defendant to silence Sharon Greaves and the other by the litigator's counsel to protect her."

"It's an interesting theory, the lawyer acting for the litigant has already used outside agents to spirit Sharon Greaves away."

"If that were the case then Mortier would be acting for them, so with him dead does that mean that the strangler has finally got to Mrs Greaves?"

"Wherever she is."

The Highlands and Islands flight was called.

I must be getting old, Latimer thought, when policemen begin to look too young even to me. The detective constable who was waiting at Lewis for them as they alighted from the plane had bright red hair and the looks of a freshly scrubbed boy scout.

Latimer couldn't help but like DC Peter Ross; he was awfully keen and, Latimer had to admit, pretty efficient.

"I've been doing the rounds of the B&B's and guest

houses," Ross informed them once they were in his car, "there's not much goes on here that they don't know about. It seems that Mortier had been showing the photograph of a woman around, asking if anyone had seen her. A couple of days later another man was showing the same photograph and asking the same question."

Latimer said, "Did you get a description of this man?"

"Early thirties, clean shaven, fair hair and with a slight American accent."

"I'd like to meet these people," Latimer said. The description he had just been handed matched the one Sharon Greaves had given of her zipless lover.

Mary Harris was like many unwilling witnesses Latimer had encountered and he saw the familiar reflection in her eyes: cautious, resentful, and scared. They were in her guesthouse, sitting in the small parlour behind the reception desk. Latimer and Nott on a sofa, Mary Harris on a matching chintz armchair. DC Ross remained standing by the interconnecting doorway.

"Mrs Harris, we are informed that on the third of November you contacted a number of people, predominantly other guesthouse proprietors, in regard to the whereabouts of this woman."

Latimer showed her a photograph of Sharon Greaves. "Why were you trying to find her?"

Mary Harris went through a pantomime of getting to her feet and leafing back a calendar hanging on the wall. "Ah yes, the third, I remember, some man was asking after her. He showed me a photo similar to that one. I told him that she hadn't registered with me." She returned to the armchair.

"But being a helpful soul you offered to help him."

"Aye well, if you canna help a body now and again what's the use of being here in the first place?"

"Were that more were so civic minded, Mrs Harris. What were you able to tell him?"

"That she had staying at the Bernera . ." Mary Harris hesitated, and Latimer could practically hear the uncertainty going through her mind: how much did the police know? "And that she was sharing the room with another woman," she said, apparently having reached the conclusion that they probably knew this. "Her sister, I think."

"Susan and Clare Buchan."

"Aye, those were the names."

"Not the name the man gave you?"

"No."

"Didn't this strike you as suspicious?"

Mary Harris shrugged, went to say something, then thought the better of it.

"Can you describe this man?"

"Och, it was some time ago. There couldna been anything strange about him or I would have remembered. Pretty ordinary is the best I can tell you. You have to remember that there's people in and out of here all the time."

"Even at this time of the year?" Latimer let his scepticism hang in the air, then said. "Would you say he was between thirty and forty, clean shaven with fair hair?"

"Yes, I suppose that would describe him."

"Did he have an accent?"

There was only a slight hesitation. "I believe he did have a slight lilt, now you come to mention it. Irish or maybe it was American."

"There was someone else looking for the woman, a man named Jean Mortier." Latimer held Mary Harris' eyes, before she could look away. "Now think very carefully, Mrs Harris, did he enquire here?" The eyelids fluttered, she desperately wanted to deny the fact but wasn't sure if she should. "Mrs Harris, I am investigating a murder, maybe more than one, and I would be in dereliction of my duty if I didn't caution you that to withhold evidence in a capital case such as this is an indictable offence. So I will ask you again, did Jean Mortier ask after the same woman?" An almost undetectable nod was returned. "And would I be right in assuming that you mentioned this to the other man, the one with the fair hair and American accent?" Fear now dominated the eyes. Latimer leaned closer and in a soft voice said, "You are right to be frightened, Mary, this is a very dangerous man." Tears began to well. Danielle Nott reached for Mary's hand. "But you will be far safer with him under lock and key than with him roving free."

Tears coursed down Mary's cheeks. "He said he would come looking for me if I said anything." She broke down.

Nott extracted a packet of tissues from her shoulder bag, took one out and handed it, together with the packet, to the distraught woman. Meanwhile DC Ross went into the kitchen and put the kettle on. It took the entire packet of tissues for Mary Harris to regain her composure. Ross placed a cup of tea – to her requirements: milk and two spoons of sugar - on an occasional table. Then he resumed his place by the door. Danielle Nott reopened her note pad.

"After you told him about Jean Mortier," Latimer continued, "can you remember if the man said anything?"

"Well I didn't say his name, only that there had been another man asking about the woman, and he said 'Carl', but more to himself than to me."

"Carl?"

"Yes, and I said that I didn't think his accent was German, more like French, and then he said. 'Ah yes the Frenchman', and that they were all supposed to meet up here."

The three police officers looked at on another, then Latimer said, "Thank you, Mrs Harris, you've been of immense assistance."

Now that she had joined the forces of law and order, Mary was keen to know what Latimer's next step would be, her finger itching to get to the telephone, but all the Detective

Inspector would say was that their enquires were ongoing. As the three officers were about to leave Mary ventured one last enquiry regarding the fugitive. "Would there be a reward for information leading to his capture?"

That evening Latimer and Nott sat in the lounge bar of their hotel. Latimer had asked the young detective constable to join them for dinner. While they waited for Ross they chatted about this and that, covering generalities rather than the case. In reply to Latimer's courteous enquiry, Nott produced photographs of her husband and three children. Returning the courtesy, she asked Latimer if he had any children?

As a young PC, Andy had fallen in love with, and married the station Chief Inspector's secretary. The marriage hadn't worked out: mainly to do with his unsociable duty hours, his ambition and studying to get promotion, while she would have preferred him to resign and make a home: plus the small irritations that become amplified when a marriage is unhappy. They all took their toll. It was an acrimonious divorce, which engendered enmity and conflicting loyalties from the people they worked with. As a result, Andy swore that he would never again form an attachment within the force, and that he would keep his private life just that. At present he was living with a fitness instructor, some eight years his junior, who amazed him by seemingly preferring his modest looks and less than svelte figure to the honed hard bodies she was in daily contact with, and who didn't seem to mind his unsociable hours. Her existence wasn't a secret but Andy never volunteered information pertaining to their life together. On the odd occasion he was expected to attend a function, he went alone.

In answer to Donald Nott's enquiry he simply answered that he had no children. The slightly embarrassing silence that followed was alleviated by the arrival of DC Peter Ross.

Over dinner they reviewed the information gathered so far.

Ross had uncovered that Sharon Greaves and Gayle Meredith, calling themselves Susan and Clare Buchan, had arrived on Lewis on the 31st of October and, three days later, had departed from Castleway for Howth Island - a remote island containing a monastic retreat, which was cut off from Lewis for the months of November, December and January.

Jean Mortier landed on Lewis on the 1st of November, hired a car, made enquires about Sharon Greaves, was last reported leaving his hotel on the morning of the 5th, and his body was discovered on the 15th.

The zipless killer, as Latimer had designated him (and after explaining the origin to Ross, who hadn't read and was too young to remember the notoriety of Fear of Flying), or ZK, was reported as being on Lewis two days after Mortier, and had apparently been more successful than the Belgium in tracking down the two women to Castleway. He had also hired a car, using the name and driving licence of John Downs, returning it on the 6th - the last reported sighting of him; the presumption being that he had murdered Mortier the day before. He had paid all his bills with cash.

The question was, where was he now? He could have left Lewis for the mainland. There was no listing of a John Downs on any flight to the mainland, but that didn't mean that he hadn't flown out using another name. Ferries left regularly from Stornaway and Tarbet, so he could have been on any one of them. Or he could still be on Lewis. Or he could be on Howth Island.

Latimer decided that their next port of call should be literally that, Castleway harbour.

The harbour master confirmed that a man fitting the description of ZK had made enquiries about getting to Howth, a few days after the ferry had made its last trip to the island, and he told Latimer what he had told him.

Latimer couldn't believe that there was anywhere that could totally isolate itself. "Is it completely impossible for someone to get there?" he asked.

"No of course not," the harbour master said. "Brian Gray, the ferry skipper, if he were here, he would be able to take a craft to Howth, and there are others with sufficient knowledge of the coast and island to make the trip. But no one has registered with me about taking a boat to Howth, and I don't know of anyone who would be insane enough to leave for there without first informing this office."

After a pensive pause Latimer said, "Is there any possible way, if it was desperately urgent that I be on Howth, that I could get there?"

Almost in unison the harbour master and Ross said, "Coast Guard, Air Sea Rescue helicopter."

"Can you put me through to them?"

The harbour master made the necessary call, explained who Latimer was, and then handed him the receiver. Latimer gave a brief explanation for wanting to get to Howth and was informed that they would be happy to be of assistance provided the trip was absolutely necessary and that the request would have to come from the Chief Constable.

That was the rub, could he warrant the necessity? Events intimated that if ZK was on Howth it was for the sole purpose of murdering Sharon Greaves and probably, because of her involvement, Gayle Meredith as well. Or any one else who got in the way. But it was all conjecture; Latimer had no way of knowing if ZK was on Howth. In fact if one went with the harbour master's revue of the difficulties of getting there, it was more improbable than probable.

Because of their familiarity with a difficult and hostile environment, a coast guard helicopter would be preferable to a police helicopter. Either way both were extremely expensive modes of transport and the commissioning of a police helicopter would entail the same high office approval. To obtain this

Latimer would have to go through his immediate superior, and imagining the question and answer conversation with the Chief Superintendent, Latimer couldn't see the Super backing him at this juncture.

Latimer thanked the coast guard, said he would get in contact with them if their services were required, and replaced the receiver.

Once they were back in Ross's Land Rover, Latimer related his misgivings to his two colleagues, and that he had decided, therefore, to investigate all other avenues first. As a result, Nott was to arrange the compilation of an e-fit picture of ZK with the aid of descriptions from the various people who had come in contact with him, before she returned to Glasgow. Copies of the e-fit were to be distributed throughout Lewis and the surrounding islands and mainland, and Ross was to continue keeping his ear to the ground and report any developments and anything else pertaining to the possible whereabouts of ZK.

Latimer then returned to Exeter.

A backlog of paperwork took up most of his first morning back; including the sending of e-mails to Nott and Ross's respective senior officers, praising their efficiency and initiative. A session with Dean Hammond followed: discussing the Jonathan Greaves murder and the two other cases they were concurrently investigating – a robbery and a possible fraud. After lunch he put a call through to New Scotland Yard, explained who he was and that he wanted to speak with someone with knowledge of professional assassins. A pause followed while he was being transferred – and, Latimer suspected, having his credentials checked – before he was put through to an inspector with the Special Crimes Squad.

"How can I help you, Detective Inspector?"

Latimer returned a brief outline of the Greaves case and the description of ZK. "Everything points to the killer being a professional, and also his third victim, the man calling himself Jean Mortier. We don't get many hit men in Devon, so I was wondering if you could tell me something about them?"

The inspector gave a short laugh. "How long is a piece of string. Well, as a generalisation they come in two classes, those who come up through the ranks of organised crime – Mafia, Triads, etc. – and ex armed service personnel, mercenaries. The world is awash with both at the moment. From the background of your case I would tend to go with the latter, ex mercenary. Is there anything else you can tell me about him?"

"He kills with his hands, strangles."

"That's fairly unusual."

"When he was told of another man looking for Sharon Greaves, before the name Jean Mortier was mentioned, he was heard to say to himself the name, Carl."

"That all you have?"

"Afraid so."

"Okay, let's see what we've got. White male, fair hair, around six feet, in good shape, 30 to 40 , slight American accent, kills with his hands. That all?"

"That's about it. Oh, we're trying to get an e-fit together, I can send you a copy when I have it."

"That could help. Okay, leave it with me."

Latimer received a call from the SCS Inspector three days later, quicker than he had expected. "There's an outfit called Paladin Security which provides highly trained professional military experts, i.e. ex-services personnel, i.e. mercenaries. Initially Paladin specialised in providing men for training and running the armed forces of emerging nations, but as that market has diminished it is now mainly involved in providing private security. Everything from looking after the rich and famous and their families to nightclub bouncers, and, so rumour has it, supplying hit men. Paladin is run by a Swede named Carl Peterson. Interested?"

"Very."

"Would you like us to look into him further?"

"It would be of tremendous help."

"Do you have an e-fit yet?"

"Just arrived, I'll have copies transferred to you."

As so often happens with a case, when it seems to have gained momentum, it just as suddenly slips into the doldrums. Young DC Ross sent contentious periodic reports to say that there were no developments, and DS Hammond received confirmation from the Miami police that Sharon Greaves was not there with her mother-in-law and son. In frustration Hammond even swallowed his pride and telephoned the despised Leigh Murray – No, she hadn't heard, nor expected to hear from Gayle Meredith, and didn't expect to see Sharon Greaves until the commencement of the court case. If she were contacted by them she would, of course, immediately inform the detective inspector. Latimer pulled a face at the receiver, before putting it down.

The only related movement came from the media, when one of the tabloids ran an article on Sharon Greaves – The Scorching Sex Life of Murdered Man's Widow. It was largely unsubstantiated and based mainly on the hearsay of one of her ex-partners, but with the insinuation of sex club orgies and the enigma of where she had gone into hiding, plus the fact that the murderer remained uncaught, there was enough to titillate the readers appetites and have them coming back for more.

Otherwise, things remained static for a couple of weeks. Until, within a period of four hours, Latimer received three calls that were enough to have him requesting an urgent meeting with the Chief Superintendent.

DC Danielle Nott reported that on the 23rd of November a man fitting ZK's description had purchased an inflatable dingy and outboard motor from a boat yard in Oban. The dingy was ex-navy and the outboard the largest it would take. The man, who hadn't volunteered a name, had paid the asking price, £800, in cash, and left in the dinghy.

DC Peter Ross advised that a team, from the tabloid newspaper that had printed the Sharon Greaves exposé, had arrived on Lewis and were asking if anyone had seen Sharon Greaves. He didn't think it would be too long before they discovered that she was on Howth Island.

Latimer had barely had time to absorb the implications of these two calls, before the SCS Inspector was also on the line.

"The man you want is named Alan Swift. Until recently he was employed as a nightclub bouncer, supplied by Paladin Security. According to another of the bouncers who worked with him he was ex SBS, and possessed awesomely strong hands: according to this guy, he once saw Swift grip and crush the hands of some drug pusher who was stupid enough to try and head butt him. We checked with military records and came up with the following. Alan Swift: American mother, British father. Raised in the USA until eighteen, when he left to join his father in England and exercise his right to UK citizenship. Enlisted in the Royal Marines and subsequently transferred to the S.B.S. and saw action. He left at the end of his term with the Marines, and joined Paladin Security

"Peterson runs Paladin from a flat in Finsbury. When we visited it there was no one about and neighbours said he hadn't been seen for a couple of weeks.

"It's all in a report to you, but I thought you'd want to

hear about Swift as soon as possible."

Latimer, who had been scribbling down the salient points, said, "Thanks, I appreciate it. Just to make sure I've jotted it down correctly: his name is Alan Swift, American connection, ex-Marines, S.A.S. ."

"No, not S.A.S., S.B.S., Special Boat Services."

"Shit!"

Latimer was granted an immediate interview with the Chief Superintendent. "He's been trained to land craft on all sorts of terrain in all conditions, and we've checked with the Met Office; the Western Isles had a relatively mild slot for a couple of days at the end of November."

"So you think he's on this Island?"

"I don't think we dare doubt the possibility, sir."

Latimer remained in the Super's Office while he spoke with the Chief Constable in Glasgow and, subsequently, the Coast Guard Air Sea Rescue Centre. After imparting the relative details, the Super handed the receiver to Latimer.

"I can be with you by tomorrow," Latimer said, "could you have a helicopter at my disposal by then?" There was a sigh at the other end of the line. "Is there a problem?"

"Gale force winds are reported 200 miles off the Western Isles. At the moment they are gusting force 7 to 8 and increasing. The indication is for the gale to hit the Western Islands in the next two days, and by that time they will have reached force 10, maybe 11."

"Is that serious?"

"It means winds of over 60 miles per hour, that is, about as bad as it gets for this part of the world."

"You mean you can't fly in it?"

"Only in the most dire emergency, and it would have to be a voluntary flight by the pilot. And in conditions like these I'm afraid distressed shipping would have priority over you."

"I understand. How long do you expect this extreme weather to last?"

"Three, four days, could be a lot longer. At this time of the year the North Atlantic tends to be rather hostile."

Chapter Eighteen

One of the quotations attributed to the legendary Hollywood actress Mae West is along the lines of 'too much of a good thing – is absolutely marvellous'. But while the sentiment is amusingly appealing, in truth too much of a good thing can spoil even the most voracious of appetites. The tingle, the surrender, the chemistry that Alan's touch had sparked in the hotel, and the wondrous, intense sex that followed, which was rekindled on the groundsheet of his tent, remained only for as long as it took Sharon to tire of it. Like a true epicure she preferred quality to quantity, and variety; the intensity, excitement and novelty of a one-night episode being sufficient until the next, new encounter. In this instance it took little more than a week for the sex to become repetitive and Alan to begin to bore her, or it could have been the other way round.

For Alan it was obviously different. He wanted to monopolise her for every second they were together, talking long into the night, following her from bedroom to bathroom to living room to kitchen. Trapped in the confines of the cabin, escape was impossible. He wasn't stupid, and any lack of education was made up by an ability to absorb information, but he lacked the ability of discussion. If Sharon brought up a subject, he would rattle off the facts and opinions his reading of the topic had encompassed, counter any argument she might have by restating the self same facts and opinions, and then broach no further exchange on the matter. If it was something he knew nothing about, he changed the subject. Descriptions of places he had been took on the form of a rambling story, that inevitably revolved around his encounters with the natives, and in which he got the better of them. He didn't tell funny stories, and managed to turn a mildly amusing incident into a protracted, inconsequential tale that lost the thread, and which he would annoyingly conclude with a bout of hearty laughter. He didn't patronise the cinema or theatre, had never been to an orchestral concert, and didn't share her sense of humour. In fact he had no sense of humour. He was the exact opposite of Jonathan. He was a bore.

There was another factor to their relationship: danger. In the beginning Sharon found that giving herself to a man who was a self-confessed assassin, who had once almost murdered her, was an intensely sensuous turn-on. As her passion waned the danger element began to change to fear. She knew that the reason Alan had not killed her that evening in the hotel was because he had realised that he was in love with her - or thought he was. The depth of his passion was made perfectly clear early on, when she tried to defuse what she feared was becoming an over intensification of the affair by saying, "You know there's an opinion held by some people that fucking doesn't have to be anything but that, just fucking."

"How sad for them then, when we know that it's more than just sex, that it is, literally, making love, part of loving another person, of being in love. You need not worry about me, I'll never leave you."

For a moment Sharon had thought he was joking, making up a mock sentence from a Victorian melodrama. She had almost laughed and put her hand over her heart and, in the same vein said, "Oh Sir Jasper, take me, I'm yours." Then she realised that he was in deadly earnest. He had completely misunderstood what she had said, thinking that she was concerned that he was merely using her, that she was questioning his motives. Emotionally he was immature and, in that context, had the mind trait of a lovesick teenager.

'I'll never leave you'. Oh my God. Learning that you are the object of a sociopathic killer's obsession is a terrifying revelation.

She had returned a smile: what else could she do?

After that the dominating subject of Alan's conversation was what they were going to do when they left the island. They would settle somewhere abroad, nowhere specific although South America seemed to come up quite often. They would get married, of course. Jonathan ceased to exist, and Leon would be able to visit them during school holidays – 'I could teach him so many things'. Such as garrotting, throat slitting and planting booby-traps, Sharon silently commented. And to the statement, 'You needn't worry about money, I can always earn enough', she didn't dare ask, 'Doing what?'

Another problem was Alan's increasing reluctance to leave the cottage at daybreak. "Why should I hide? You can say I'm here as your guest."

"You know it's not that simple, Alan. I'm only here by special invite from the Abbot, I can't very well ask friends to visit. You have to see that. Please don't be awkward, it won't be for long."

During the first few days, while she couldn't have enough of him, when she walked around with a permanent smile on her face, she used to sneak away and visit him in his hideaway. She stopped going once delusion had set in, using the excuse that she had to help her friend with chores that were part of the agreement for them being allowed to stay on the island. That Sharon never used Gayle's name appeared to pass Alan by, as if she was of no consequence. Sharon feared that if necessary he would snuff Gayle out without a moments thought.

Retaining her bonhomie with Gayle had become a strain; fortunately she seemed to be preoccupied with thoughts of her own. They still went on their afternoon walks, and as she was the one who decided where they went, Sharon kept them well away from the part of the island where Alan dwelt. All the same, that didn't stop Sharon fearing the spectre of Alan suddenly appearing, approaching Gayle with his hand outstretched saying, "Hello, I'm Alan, Sharon's boyfriend."

Sharon knew the situation couldn't continue as it was, but she didn't know what to do.

Matters dramatically deteriorated when Alan's libido suddenly deserted him. First he couldn't sustain an erection, and then he couldn't get one at all. It was nothing new to Sharon, and as she was finding it harder and harder to disguise her revulsion of being touched by him, she viewed it as a welcome respite rather than a frustration. Alan, however, saw it differently, and as a result his mental emotional age regressed further and he glared at the perverse member like an angry baffled adolescent. Sharon inadvertently made things worse when she said, "It's nothing to worry about, it happens to nearly every man now and again."

"Seen it all before have you?" he sneered. He jumped off the bed and pulled on his trousers. "Well it might have happened with the pansies you're used to going with, with your husband, but it doesn't happen to me."

She sat up in the bed. "Now you're being silly."

"Am I? Perhaps I've caught something off you, some disease."

"Don't be stupid, you can't catch impotency."

It was the wrong choice of words. "Stupid am I?" Alan

roared. "Fucking impotent. You fucking whore." Sharon never saw the blow; only felt its jarring impact, as the back of his hand smashed into the side of her face; her head recoiling and hitting against the wooden headboard "Fucking whoring bitch." She curled her body up, waiting for the next blow. In her mind's eye she saw the long bladed knife he carried in the integral sheath on his trousers, and terror joined fear. From the other rooms came the sound of mayhem. Then there was silence. Sharon held her breath. The cabin door slammed.

Sharon cautiously crept from the bed, still dizzy from the blow she felt her way in the darkness to the door, slid the bolt closed, and then did the same with all the window shutters. She made her way back to the bed and lie there, terrified, listening for any sound of him returning. Finally she slipped into a doze. Daylight, creeping in through the gaps in the shutter, woke her. She felt for the light switch, the electricity was on. She got up, went into the living room, turned on the light and inspected the damage. A table had been upturned, the legs of two chairs were broken and a table lamp was smashed. In the bathroom she saw that the mirror was splintered. Her head was throbbing. Gingerly she ran her fingers against the back of her head. Quite a bump. Still, could be worse she thought, and then caught sight of her face in what remained of the mirror. She broke down into tears, and without checking to see if Alan was loitering, ran over to Gayle's cabin.

Gayle cradled Sharon in her arms and stroked her hair. The bruise on the side of her face was going to get worse before it got better.

"I've been having an affair with somebody," Sharon said, her voice muffled as it lay against Gayle's chest. "I know it was wrong but I couldn't help myself. Then last night it all went wrong and he lost it completely. I should have known he wouldn't be able to handle it, but when he hit me it took me completely by surprise."

Funny, Gayle thought, when you considered his background, but she too had never thought of Adrian as being physically violent. She surmised that there had been some sort of confrontation, which came as no surprise, but she would have expected Adrian to retreat into an introspective silence – a precursor to a breakdown, and maybe shed some tears, rather than hit out at the cause of his frustration. Any violence would be more likely directed at himself. It still could be.

"What are we going to do?" Sharon asked.

"Without going into details, I suppose I'll have to report the incident to the Abbot. Then it'll be up to him what he does with Brother Adrian."

Sharon sat up. "Brother Adrian! I don't understand. What has it got to do with him?"

It was Gayle's turn to look surprised. "Didn't he do this to you?"

"Good God no, what on earth could have made you

think that? No, it was Alan." Sharon went on to recount the complete history of her relationship with Alan, from the encounter in the hotel room to the altercation that had preceded her arrival at Gayle's cabin door. Gayle listened in a state of increasing disillusionment; the woman she had lost her heart to was nothing more than an addict to her own lusts. A shallow vessel only interested in sating her ravenous appetite for sex, even up to the point of supplementing it with the excitement of knowing that her lover was a psychopathic murderer. At least he was in love with her, whereas love, as far as Sharon was concerned, never got a look in. Gayle didn't think of herself as a prude: she knew what lust was; she had lusted after men, she had lusted after Sharon – God help her, and God knows she had lusted after Roland, but it had been within the enclave of their love, and it shared Roland's death. One thing was certain, Sharon's predilections did not include her, and as much as she tried to despise the woman for her frailties, it didn't altogether alleviate the pain of her unrequited love.

Gayle heard herself say, "Are you always as indiscriminate with your choice of partners?" She hadn't meant it to sound as censorious as it came out.

"No, of course not," Sharon replied. "Look, I know what you're thinking, but I'm not a total whore. I know what it's like to love someone to distraction, to be his body and soul. I've been there and discovered that it's too painful. Since then I've found it easier to keep love and sex separate. I have a husband who understands and we have an arrangement that suits us both, and nobody gets hurt."

"Until now."

"If you want to be unkind."

Gayle retreated, fearful that she might reveal her own feelings she didn't want the situation to become personal. Instead she reverted to professionalism. "I think the first we need to do is get you to somewhere safe, and that means the monastery."

"And Brother Adrian," Sharon said. There was a mischievous glint in her eye. "What on earth made you think it was him?"

Gayle blushed at the memory of what she had thought, at the time, was a walk to a dared-to-hope for assignation, and the sighting of a shadowy figure. "I couldn't think of anyone else it could possibly be," she said.

"Cassock, long johns and all," Sharon said, and giggled.

Despite herself, Gayle joined in. Sharon wasn't a bad woman, she thought, just a weak one. "I don't know what we're going to tell the Abbot?"

"The truth," Sharon ventured.

"I'm not sure that would be fair to him. If we were to get you into the monastery for a couple of weeks do you think this man, Alan, will go away?" As an after thought Gayle said. "How did he get here in the first place?"

"By one of those army dinghies with a big outboard

motor, he's ex-Special Boat Service. If he'll go away, I don't know; we're not exactly talking about a rational person. And how would we know for sure that he had gone?"

Amongst the various emotions Gayle was experiencing, fear began to creep in and take dominance. S.B.S., a highly trained professional, out of control. Fucking hell! "Do you know were he keeps the boat?"

"No. Near where he camps I guess."

Gayle put her head in her hands and pondered. Lifting her face she said, "I still think the best thing, for now, is to get you into the monastery. The medical wing, we can say you've had a nasty fall."

"That won't be enough for then to keep me in," Sharon said, better add concussion: Brother Neil's not a trained doctor, I'm sure I can manage to drift in and out of consciousness for a couple of weeks without him being any the wiser."

"Devious minx," Gayle admonished. "Okay, let's do that, It'll give us some breathing space to decide what to do next. Maybe he'll have left the island by then."

Sharon's expression said that she didn't think that they should hold out a great deal of hope on that score. "What about you, where are you going to stay?"

"Here of course, where else?"

"But you could be in danger."

"I don't think so, it's you he's after, though I'm not going to try any stupid heroics. I'll volunteer to help Brother Adrian on the farm during the day and bolt myself in every night. If I feel threatened I'll come to the monastery, tell the abbot whatever I need to."

The walk to the monastery was the worse part. They had to walk slowly, with Gayle being seen to be supporting Sharon least they were spotted by one of the Brothers, all the time with the threat of a maniac on the loose and liable to pounce on them ever present.

The bruise on Sharon's face was steadily worsening, and together with the bump on the back of her head there was no problem in getting her into the medical wing. Once in she promptly passed out and was consigned to a bed for observation. Gayle went back to Sharon's cabin to collect some necessary items for her stay in the wing. While she was there she surveyed the damage. As she tided up and righted the table she thought that at least Sharon's bump and bruise would explain the broken chairs and cracked mirror, and she could always say she couldn't remember exactly what happened.

After delivering the items she returned to her own cabin and went into the bedroom. From under the bed she pulled out the large backpack she had used to bring their main essentials to the island, and from an interior, zippered compartment extracted an oilskin package. She took it into the living room, opened it out on the table and viewed the contents: an automatic pistol, box of bullets, small can of oil and, in a plastic folder, a Home

Office firearm permit. They had been issued to her when she went into hiding. She had never fired it nor, as a matter of fact, any other forearm since her initial training. While with the department she was considered non-operational and therefore hadn't been required to attend a periodic session on the firing range. She dismantled the pistol and began cleaning and oiling it, an action that required no conscious thought: as a junior officer it had been part of the training, rammed into her so that she could do it in her sleep, so that even after all the intervening years it was still an instinctive ritual.

As she worked Gayle considered her options, and reached the conclusion that there was only one. For such an intelligent woman Sharon could be unbelievably foolish, the story this Alan had given, about falling in love with her, was so much eyewash. He was a professional killer who had come to complete his contract. Aware of her liking for unconventional sex, and having tasted once already, he had decided to give it another go, and had found Sharon gullible and receptive. He had until February to kill her, so why not enjoy, what was probably extremely good sex for as long as possible. Now, or as soon as he returned to rationality, he would realise that it had all come to an end, and all that was left was to finish the job.

She started reassembling the gun.

What if she revealed what was happening to the Abbot and place Sharon's safety in his hands? It was a tempting way out, except it wouldn't work. The monastery wasn't a fortress, and it certainly wouldn't keep a man with special boat service training out, besides which it would place the lives of the monks in danger. For Gayle was under no illusion that if it meant having to eliminate her, and if necessary, everyone else on the island to achieve his objective, Sharon's would be killer would not give it a moment's hesitation. And time would be on his side, they were virtual prisoners on the island for the next two months, and with no means of summoning help.

Opening the box of bullets she loaded ten of them into the magazine and then pushed it home into the grip.

So it would be a matter of getting to him first, before he discovered where Sharon was.

An initial round was primed into the chamber and then the safety catch set.

Subconsciously she had known it was the only course of action from the moment Sharon had explained his presence. All the same, when she thought about what she was planning to do there was no way of avoiding the ludicrousness of her decision: that she, Gayle Meredith, who had never fired a shot in anger, was going to surprise and kill a highly trained professional assassin. But then what other option did she have. She made it to the lavatory with only seconds to spare.

The cold, and a light spattering of rain woke Alan. He was lying in a gully; his parka open, and shirt and jumper hanging loose from where he had thrown them on before charging out of

Sharon's cabin. Then he remembered what had happened, and groaned. The uncontrollable anger that had possessed him, and the vision of Sharon's terrified face; knowing that he had to distance himself from her, frightened of what he might do if he remained in the cabin. The rest was a blur: running and running, not knowing where he was going, through the dark, pushing his body to the point of exhaustion in an effort to purge himself of the anger, until finally stumbling and lying exhausted where he fell.

He rose from the gully, readjusted his clothes, zipping up the parka and pulling the hood over his head, then looked around, trying to locate his bearing. There was little of the island that he wasn't now familiar with. His orientation quickly returned, and he saw that he was near the eastern side of Howth, not far from the jetty.

In graphic detail, like photographic slides at a presentation, scenes from the previous night began to materialise behind his eyes, accompanied by the ensuing and recriminating questions as to the reason behind his behaviour. Why did he have to blow up in that way, loose his cool? It wasn't like him and he didn't like being out of control. What was it that triggered the anger?

As he began making his way back to the camp, skirting the bog and, automatically checking that he was unobserved, he played the scenes over in his mind. Sharon's voice saying, "Don't be stupid, you can't catch impotency." Was that it, the frustration

251

of not being able to perform? Maybe, though he couldn't help feeling that it was something more than that, something that had been playing on his mind beforehand. He cast his thoughts back, re-entering his mind as it was when he was making his way to see her. Slowly the cause of his frustration became clear: it had been the fear that he was going to lose her. The subsequent uncontrollable anger was not due entirely to temporary impotency but also from the uncertainty of her feelings towards him. She hadn't been responding to his plans for them as he had thought she would. Why? Wasn't a declaration of undying love and desire to make a life with her, the sentiments every woman was supposed to want to hear? Well clearly not Sharon. He replayed the words he used and tried to think how they must have sounded to her: and had to admit that they did come across as a bit naff, gauche, unsophisticated. Not like her husband. Then he recalled his other loss of control, and what had triggered it: Sharon's voice on the recorded message to her husband – 'I miss you, darling'. She had never spoken to him in that tone, never used an endearment, never addressed him as darling.

Then he realised that he hadn't blown it the night before, because there had been nothing to blow. Whatever plans he might have had for the future, the painful truth was that they were never going to happen. And not just because there was no way, once they were off the island, that Sharon wouldn't learn that her husband had been murdered and put two and two

252

together, but because she had never ever remotely considered him as a replacement for Jonathan.

By the time he reached the ruin this revelation, the knowledge that his love was, and always would be, unrequited decided Alan: it was over for him too. The anger was gone, he bore Sharon no hatred, but he had no wish to see her again: he might be reconciled to the inevitable but it didn't stop him from still loving her. It would be too painful. There was no point in staying on the island, so he might as well leave. He didn't think Sharon would mention his having been there, even, or perhaps especially, after learning of her husband's death – fearing that she might have been sleeping with his killer. She should be safe from the people who had wanted her dead; the body of the Frenchman would have been discovered by this time, so Carl wouldn't be sending another replacement, not now and the police were involved.

Alan was fairly confident that he was in the clear, as he had left no forensic evidence linking him with either killing. All the same he'd remove all evidence of his occupation of the ruin, and leave no trace of his ever having been on the island. He was, after all, a professional.

The wind was getting up. He sniffed the air; the weather was on the turn, and he thought that if it worsened it might not be possible for him to leave immediately. With this in mind, Alan quickened his pace: it might be a case of battening down the hatches. The rain began to intensify, and by the time he reached the hill above the ruin the wind was driving it into his face, and he wondered how secure the dingy was. He debated whether to go down to the camp and put on some dry clothes and waterproof gear before going to inspect the dinghy or head for the bay where it was beached straight away. It had to be the second option, if he lost the dinghy he was stranded.

The bay, with headlands on either side, was secluded and visible only from the sea, from where access was only possible at low tide. Getting to it by land necessitated clambering down what was practically a cliff face; and back up again. Alan had hidden the dinghy in a shallow cave above the tide line. His fear was that the dinghy might be insufficiently secured to withstand a storm driven sea should it reach the cave.

Normally clambering down the cliff face was tortuous rather than difficult but now, with the ever-increasing wind, it had become hazardous, and it took all of Alan's strength and nerve to achieve the descent. The sea was higher than normal - and he expected that it would get higher – but it hadn't reached the cave. The outboard motor, separate and wrapped in tarpaulin, attached to the dinghy's mooring rope and acting as an anchor, was at the rear of the cave. Alan pushed it as far into the rear as it would go, and as a secondary precaution banked the heaviest rocks he could find against it. Then he pushed the dinghy as far as it would go into the cave and shielded it with additional rocks. The cave had an overhanging lip beneath it, which should add some extra protection. There was nothing further Alan could do, it should withstand the storm; but he had sufficient experience of the sea to know that it should never be underestimated. In the final outcome it would be up to providence.

The ascent up the cliff was slightly less difficult but by the time he reached the top Alan was exhausted, and he needed to rest against the protection of a clump of gorse to recover. At least the wind and rain where behind him when he made his way to the camp. Changing into dry clothes and climbing into the sleeping bag was a tempting thought, but he knew it would have to wait until he had put everything undercover and fully secured the tent guys. If this weather was just a precursor of a storm to come, and he was pretty sure that it was, then it would be a big one, and the make shift roof wouldn't last a minute. Girding himself he traversed the slope that led to the ruin.

Removing the cover and stepping in he saw the fair-haired woman, Sharon's companion, sitting with her back against the wall.

She was pointing a gun at him.

Gayle assessed what advantages she might have against Alan, and came to the conclusion that she had none, save perhaps surprise. He wouldn't be expecting her to kill him. But she would have to catch him off guard, an ambush. And it would be a one-off; there would be no second chance. Two places came to mind, Sharon's cabin and his camp. The cabin would be preferable, except that although she didn't think Alan would return there until his normal rendezvous time in the evening, following his performance of the previous night there was no way of knowing this for sure. Which would entail her having to wait in ambush in the cottage the whole day, and she wasn't sure her nerve would hold for that long. Going to his camp, his lair, would have the disadvantage of being on his own ground, plus having to enter his territory undetected. No, remaining in Sharon's cabin was the logical thing to do – but then when had logic ever come into the equation: what could be more illogical than a middle aged woman taking on a younger, probably armed, better trained hit man?

Hanging around waiting for him to arrive, that was what.

Gayle put on her waterproofs.

Locating Alan's camp was never going to be easy; Sharon's description of the location – hundred yards west of what she termed the Christmas trees, quarter way down a grassy incline, snuggled into a hollow, the remains of an old cottage – still left quite an area to cover. Plus she had to do it undetected. So even approaching the bog and the 'Christmas trees' necessitated hiding in a vantage point with a pair of binoculars and surveying the area for fifteen minutes, to ensure her quarry was nowhere about, or watching her. The same went for finding the ruin: secreting herself every twenty yards, watching and listening. The wind and rain were getting stronger; and although the increase didn't help her task, it did have the converse effect of helping to cover her approach.

Surprisingly, she came upon the ruin without too much trouble: more to do with the fact that there was only one grassy slope amongst an otherwise gorse-ridden landscape, than her orienteering skills. She watched it from two locations before being fairly confident that it was empty, then, with mounting trepidation, from the side rather than the front, pistol at the ready, she cautiously entered the enemy's camp. At first glance there didn't appear to be any sign of habitation, and Gayle wondered if she was in the wrong place. Until she examined it further and saw what looked like fallen beams, overgrown with brambles, were in fact a carefully placed cover for the encampment behind them. She moved them to one side and entered.

It was what she would expect of a professional soldier, clean and orderly. His cooking utensils cleaned and stowed into the largest pot, a shaving mirror rested in a nook in the old wall, and there were neatly stacked tins of food. The tent was set up in what would be the driest and warmest part of the ruin. Through the flaps, that were pulled back to allow the tent to air, she could see a first-aid kit, backpack and sleeping bag neatly folded on the groundsheet. It bore all the signs of somewhere that was going to be returned to.

Although she had approached the ruin from one side, actual entry into the encampment was only possible from the front, so Gayle replaced the concealment beam and sat herself down against the back wall to wait. Checking that the safety catch was off, she pointed the pistol at the doorway, resting her gun hand in the palm of the other, as she had been taught, and using her drawn up knees for extra support. But when it came to it, would she be able to pull the trigger? She recalled asking her instructor the same thing, after he had congratulated her on a particularly good session on the firing range. "If you're scared enough you will," he had answered. A sudden gust of wind, that blew half the makeshift roof off, caused her to start so violently as to ensure the answer to that: she was sufficiently scared as to be near to soiling herself.

Rain now poured through the roof, rattling a tattoo against the exposed cooking utensils. The waiting seemed to be interminable, though constant referrals to her watch revealed that less that twenty minutes actually evolved, until through a gap in the beams she spied the figure of Alan on the top of the slope. As he neared Gayle could see that he was dishevelled and looked exhausted, and that he took no precautionary checks as he climbed the hollow. Her heart rate increased, she gripped the pistol tighter to steady her trembling hand. As if by instinct, she reverted to the memory of her instructors voice: get the target in your sight, take a deep breath and let it out slowly to steady yourself, and relax your grip.

Alan removed the beams and saw her.

As she slowly squeezed the trigger he automatically moved to one side. The sound of the report was deafening. The shot caught Alan on the right shoulder, its impact sending him reeling backwards from the entrance and out of view. Gayle jumped up and rushed to the doorway. She saw Alan rolling down the slope and tore after him. At the bottom he righted himself. The rain hampered her view. She took aim and fired, but he instinctively crouched, and in the mist she couldn't be sure if the bullet hit or missed him. Then she saw him set off in a zigzag pattern up the opposite slope and guessed that she had missed. He made towards the cover of some rocks at the top. Gayle ran after him, anxious to press home her advantage, knowing that his progress would be hampered by the persistent head wind, rain and failing strength. But she was wary - wounded or not he was a dangerous man, plus she had to assume that he was armed – and instead of trailing him directly, to where he had disappeared behind the rocks and could be possibly waiting in ambush, Gayle climbed the slope at a tangent to obtain a more overall view. At the top she looked around, the weather was really closing in and there was no sight of him. A wave of panic hit her and she started to run, desperate not to lose him. Finally he came into sight, heading towards the cliffs, and was surprised at the ground he had managed to cover. His strength had to be phenomenal. Then she saw him stagger and fall.

When he had stepped into the camp, Alan's immediate thought on seeing Gayle, and the way she was positioned and holding the gun, was that she had been through some type of training. Then, instinctively, as she fired he moved his body so as to present as small a target as possible. Not small enough: the bullet smashed into his shoulder and sent him spinning out of the doorway. He fell, jarring the shoulder that had been hit, tried to right himself, lost his balance and tumbled down the hill. At the bottom he looked back and saw the woman descending the hill in pursuit. As she aimed the pistol he assumed the automatic crouch position for escape under fire. There was a crack and he felt the sting as the bullet tore through the flesh of his calf: then he was swerving up the opposite slope, running for his life, until he reached the temporary safety of some rocks. The pain in his shoulder was excruciating and his leg was bleeding profusely. For a moment Alan considered laying in wait for the woman: he might not be in the best of condition, and she had a gun and he didn't, but he did have a hunting knife: until he saw that she wasn't following him directly, but skirting the rocks. There was no time to hang about, he steeled himself and set off in as near a quick jog as he could manage, needing to achieve sufficient distance from her view and give her the slip, find a place to hide while he recovered and decided what to do next.

The wind and rain were in his face, and getting stronger. Was she still there? As he stole a glance round his foot caught a rock and he fell, the wounded shoulder taking the full impact. The pain shot through him, then he must have passed out for a few moments, because when he looked up he could see the woman emerging through the rain mist. Warily, she came closer, arms extended, holding the gun with both hands. Alan struggled to his feet, half turned away and, hidden from her view reached down for the hunting knife: with his dominant arm out of action the best he could hope to achieve was an underarm throw with the left.

She fired as he turned to face her.

Gayle emptied the magazine; firing into thin air long after the force of the first three bullets had sent Alan reeling backwards and over the side of the cliff.

She had no recollection of the journey back to the cabin, assuming that it was achieved on autopilot. Without bothering to remove her waterproofs, Gayle replaced the gun in the backpack, then unearthed the bottle of 'emergency' whisky and poured herself a stiff shot. She downed it, poured and downed a second, and then threw up into the lavatory bowl. As she was washing her face there came a knocking on the cabin door.

The strength of the wind practically blew Brother Adrian through the entrance. "I've come to take you back to the monastery, the Abbot thinks it will be safer there for you, until this storm passes.

Chapter Nineteen

The storm, force eleven on the Beaufort Scale, raged for a day and a half, after which there was a brief respite of ten hours before it was followed by another, though not quite so severe, that blew for a further twenty-four hours.

As far as Gayle was concerned it might never have happened: she collapsed soon after Brother Adrian escorted her to the monastery and remained in a state of semi consciousness for the next five days. Brother Neil initially diagnosed exhaustion – it appeared Gayle mentioned to Brother Adrian that she had been caught in the deteriorating weather while out walking – then became concerned when she failed to regain full consciousness.

Sharon, as soon she was judged not to be suffering any lasting effects from her fall, looked after Gayle. Brother Adrian also looked in. Sharon not only shared the Brother's concern but was also consumed with guilt. Gayle mumbled and cried out in her sleep, and during the intervals she was half-awake talked animatedly. Sharon deduced from the incoherent rambling that she was reliving her traumatic experiences from when she had had to go into hiding from the IRA. A condition, Sharon suspected, that was exacerbated by the memories stirred due to her situation with Alan. And Sharon's concurrent concern over Alan – where he was and what he might do – made her feel doubly guilty.

So when the Coastguard helicopter landed it was the considered opinion of all that Gayle should be airlifted to a mainland hospital. All that is except Gayle, who emerged the same day from her semi hibernation, to all intents and purposes fully recovered, complaining only of being starving hungry and, when the reason for the helicopters arrival was revealed, adamantly refusing to accompany it back to the mainland. But by that time there had been a dramatic development.

Sharon watched the Abbot and Brother Adrian striding down to meet the helicopter. She would have accompanied them had it not been for Gayle's return to full consciousness. Four figures emerged from the helicopter and she supposed their visit was to do with a loss at sea and the search for possible survivors. Then she made her way to the refectory to get the biggest breakfast she could for the ravenous Gayle.

When the party entered the medical wing Sharon and Brother Neil were watching Gayle, who was now out of her bed and sitting with a tray on her lap, devouring a double helping of eggs, bacon and sausages. A large man stepped forward and said to Sharon, "Hello, Mrs Greaves, we meet again."

Sharon did a double take. "We've met before."

"Exeter hospital." The man produced his warrant card. "Detective Inspector Latimer, Detective Sergeant when we last met."

"Of course."

Turning to Gayle, Latimer said, "And you will be Ms Gayle Meredith?"

"That's correct."

Brother Adrian and two of the officers left the room. The other officer, a woman, remained with Latimer. After motioning to Brother Neil to stay, the Abbot also departed. Sharon and Gayle looked at one another.

"Mrs Greaves," Latimer continued, "I'm afraid I've some rather bad news."

"Leon? Jonathan?" Sharon intuited.

"Your husband, he's dead, he was murdered."

It was similar to having one's ears block due to a change in altitude, the words echoed in her brain and Sharon could hear other questions being put to her, only they sounded muffled and not quite clear. She could feel herself going hot, and her legs buckling. Then hands were supporting her from each side and she was aware of Gayle's presence as she was lowered on to a chair. Gayle remained at her side, one arm around her shoulders and holding her hand. Vision and mind came back into focus.

"If you are feeling up to it, Mrs Greaves, I would like to ask you a few questions," Latimer was saying. "It is rather important."

Sharon nodded her consent.

"Is this a likeness of the man who tried to throttle you in the hotel room?" Latimer handed Sharon the e-fit.

"Yes, I suppose so." She didn't want to dare guess what the connection was.

"His name is Alan Swift. He is an ex-Special Boats Service mercenary, whose attributes also include the possession of extremely strong hands. Lately he has been working for a security company; whom it is rumoured hires out assassins. Following his failed attempt on your life we believe he has throttled two other people; one, I'm sad to report, being your husband. The other man."

Sharon's stomach heaved, and the breakfast she had consumed that morning, which thankfully was nowhere near the size of Gayle's, rose too rapidly into her throat to prevent it from being spewed down the front of her sweater and onto the floor. Gayle immediately gathered her up and rushed her into the adjacent bathroom; kicking the door closed behind them to discourage any attempt of assistance from either the policewomen or father Neil. She helped Sharon, who was shaking uncontrollably, to remove the soiled sweater, and the one beneath, then sat her on the lavatory seat lid.

"I can't get it out of my mind," Sharon said, almost in a whisper, "he had murdered Jonathan, all the time he was with me, in my bed."

Gayle said, "You realise, don't you, that the policeman is going to ask us if he's here?"

"Oh my God! We can't tell him. Please, Gayle. How would I explain it?"

"It's all right, I won't say anything."

"Thank you. Oh no, I've just thought of something; what if they search the island and find Alan: he'll tell them what we've been doing, I just know he will. Then it'll become public knowledge; how on earth will I explain it to Leon?"

Gayle took hold of Sharon's arms. "Calm yourself. It wouldn't matter what he says, it would be the word of a demented killer against yours. Anyhow, I think he left the island. I found the ruined cottage where you said - it had to be the one, there are no others in that area — and it was empty, no trace of ever being occupied."

Sharon's eyes widened. "You went there, on your own!"

Gayle let go of Sharon's arms. "I know, I can't believe that I did, I go hot and cold just thinking about it. I guess at the time it just seemed better to know where he was than waiting for him to turn up."

Sharon imagined what Gayle must have been going through, the fear, the mental torture. No wonder the poor woman had collapsed. She stood up and opened her arms. "Oh,

Gayle, I really don't deserve you."

Half-laughing, half-crying, the two women embraced.

There was a tap on the door and the policewoman's voice saying, "Are you all right, Mrs Greaves?"

"Yes, just a couple of moments more, tell the Inspector that we'll be right out."

Sharon washed her face and put on the unsoiled sweater. "Okay," she nodded to Gayle.

Together they rejoined the detective inspector, sitting side by side on the edge of one of the beds. There was a smell of disinfectant from where Brother Neil had cleaned the floor.

"I don't like having to press you further at this time," Latimer said, "but if you are able to continue it would be of great help to us."

Sharon said, "However I can help." She reached for Gayle's hand and held it.

Latimer said, "Our theory is that after his failed attempt on your life Swift was sacked."

"By Lucidel," Sharon said.

"By the agency that employed Swift, Paladin Security. As to the identity of Paladin's client, Lucidel might have the motive but there is no concrete evidence to prove such an accusation," Latimer said.

"But surely there's sufficient circumstantial evidence. Who else would want me dead?"

"Lucidel might well counter that it's one of your ex-lovers –disgruntled, jealous or otherwise – and of whom, by your own admission, there have been many."

Sharon coloured. "Thank you," she said, acidly.

"I'm sorry, Mrs Greaves, but it's an accusation you are going to have to get used to. One of the dailies has already printed an article casting aspersions, based on the revelations of one of your previous partners."

"Oh God! Leon."

"As I was saying," Latimer continued, "Swift was sacked and in an effort to placate his wounded professional pride he decided to complete the contract. In many aspects our case against Swift is circumstantial, because he's a professional killer and leaves no incriminating evidence. We know he was on Lewis looking for you and that he traced your movements up to taking the last ferry to here. There was also another man on Lewis looking for you, probably Swift's replacement, whom we believe he murdered. Swift left Lewis and was last reported purchasing a high-powered dinghy in Oban, which we can only assume was for the purpose of making for here. The Abbot and the Brothers say they have not seen him, and I take it neither have either of you?"

Sharon and Gayle shook their heads.

"So that leaves me with three possibilities, (a) he was killed trying to get here, (b) he tried to get here but failed and turned back, and (c) he was injured in getting here and has been lying low and recuperating until fit enough to be able to complete his contract and get back to the mainland. Until we have located his body or have Swift in custody we must assume that your life is still in danger, Mrs Greaves."

"Oh!" Sharon exclaimed; it was a possibility she hadn't considered up to then. Alan had said that he wasn't there to harm her, only protect her, and she believed that was true. But what about now? She couldn't be sure.

In her heart she wanted him dead.

"Over the next couple of days my men and I, aided by any able-bodied monks who volunteer, will make a thorough search of the island. In the meantime Detective Sergeant Nott," Latimer gestured in the direction of the policewoman, "will remain with you."

The policewoman said, "Danielle Nott, I'll try not to be too intrusive."

Sharon returned a smile. She felt Gayle stiffen.

For the sake of convenience it was decided that Sharon and Gayle, together with Danielle Nott, would remain in the medical wing. Latimer stayed in Sharon's cabin, the young detective constable and the uniformed officer in Gayle's. When she went to get a change of clothes and a few items, Gayle put them in the large backpack. Somehow she felt better having the gun with her rather than a couple of feet from the two policemen.

Brothers Adrian, Neil and Colin volunteered to assist the police. As the monks were familiar with the island, Latimer put each with an officer and the three teams divided the search areas up equally.

True to her word Danielle Nott kept her presence as unobtrusive as possible. When she removed her coat an automatic pistol was visible on her waist, and Gayle noticed that when Danielle undressed to take the bed nearest the door she placed the holstered gun on the bedside table next to her. Sharon and Gayle were not confined to the monastery, but neither were they encouraged to roam. As Sharon was the prime reason for her presence Danielle remained mainly within her vicinity: discreetly, allowing her the privacy to mourn her loss.

Latimer gave Sharon his mobile to phone Leon. He was still with his grandmother in Florida. It is difficult to put feelings into words when all you want to do is hold one another. Sharon and her son exchanged platitudes, each cognizant of the others pain. It was Leon, with the advantage of having already gone through the shock and agony of his father's demise, and displaying a maturity beyond his years, who took the initiative. He allowed his mother the cushion to break down and weep and then, when she had regained her composure, to gently guide the conversation towards what the immediate future held for them. Gratefully, Sharon used this opening to explain the general situation, and that she would be remaining on the island until she gave evidence at the trial in the beginning of February – which she expected to take a couple of weeks, say a month. She went on to say that after this telephone conversation she would be reverting to being incommunicado.

"Lucidel will wage a smear campaign, not only to discredit my credibility but also as a means at getting to me through you. By being isolated I become inviolable, and because of that so do you. Do you understand, darling?"

"I think so. You might retract your evidence if you thought I was being persecuted by the media, but if you're somewhere that is isolated from the outside world it would be a wasted exercise."

"Clever boy. But they're still going to try and smear me. What I ask is that you don't accept what they say at face value, and that until you hear my side of the facts that you are not judgemental. Can you promise me that?"

"Of course. I'm not a child, mother, I don't expect you to have been an angel."

Sharon couldn't help but laugh. "Well thank you, darling, I'll take that as a vote of confidence."

Leon laughed along with her, then they both fell silent. "Mum," Leon said, "are Lucidel behind dad's death?"

"That's what I believe, darling, but there's no evidence to support it."

"But your evidence in court will do them a great deal of harm."

"Probably."

"Good, fucking crucify the bastards."

Sharon didn't have the heart to admonish her distraught son's language. Besides she shared the sentiment. "I aim to do just that," she said. Another, reflective, silence followed. "Are you missing school?" she asked.

"No, not really, they've given me an exeat for as long as necessary, but in the meantime Gran's got me into the local high school."

"How do you like it there?"

"Great, nowhere near as stuffy." There was a muffled sound, then Leon said, "Gran would like a word."

"Okay, darling. I don't have to tell you that I love and miss you."

"Yeah, me to. Here's Gran."

"Hello, Celia, how are you bearing up?"

"Sharon. As well as can be expected. And you?"

"Well you know, coping. Thank you for looking after Leon. I hear he's enjoying the local school."

"I think that might have something to do with the number of nubile young things who are forever calling round. He's a great boy, Sharon, you and Jonathan have done well by him. It's a joy having him here. So, tell me, what's happening?" Sharon gave her mother-in-law an abridged account. Celia said, "There was some man from a British newspaper, with a photographer, out here asking questions. I told him nothing, and I had a word with the sheriff's office. Sheriffs up for re-election and a generous donation to his campaign fund has made sure Leon's been left alone."

Sharon thought that she should be appalled by this manipulation of the police force and curtailment of press freedom, but she wasn't, just grateful, one less problem to worry about. "I'll be out to collect Leon when it's all over," she said.

After two days of intensive searching, Latimer concluded that Alan Swift was not on Howth Island. He didn't think there was much chance now of Swift landing on the island, but it couldn't altogether be ruled out.

As a result of this, the Abbot asked if he could have a quiet word with Gayle. "Had you known about this man when you arranged to come here?"

"No, of course not" Gayle replied; which when she contacted the agency, who handled Howth Island Retreat bookings, from Spain had been partly true – all Graham Foreman had said was that there might have been an attempt on Sharon's life. She was able to hold the Abbot's scrutinising gaze.

"I'm sorry, Gayle, but I can't help being concerned about the possible repercussions should this killer land on the island. Perhaps it might be better for all concerned if you and your friend accompany the police when they leave."

It's not going to happen, she wanted to tell him, Alan Swift is dead; but of course she couldn't.

Sharon had been horrified, especially when Gayle

admitted that although she had always had a contingency plan –
there had been no way of knowing, during the delay while the
ferry relayed the agency's booking, if her unusual three month
stay would be accepted by the Abbot before she left Spain – it
would be awkward to implement at this juncture.

What Gayle omitted was that there were also some
unknown factors she would prefer to clear up before leaving the
island.

Nor, it seemed, did Latimer relish the prospect of
Sharon's departure: he would far prefer Sharon to remain
isolated on Howth, where it was far easier, and cheaper, to keep
her isolated and safe than having to supply around the clock
protection on the mainland. At his instigation he accompanied
Gayle and Sharon to meet with Father Cecil. Sharon related a
brief outline of the court case and the necessity for her to remain
incommunicado, while Latimer re-stated the unlikelihood of
Swift still being alive.

The Abbot wavered.

A far bigger problem, Latimer added, would be keeping
the press and media at bay, a nuisance he had already gone some
way in curtailing by putting Howth – private property - out of
bounds. The police and coastguard would be patrolling the area
to ensure the island's privacy would be maintained.

The Abbot relented.

"Off the record," Latimer said to Sharon, "I'm of the

same frame of mind as yourself, that it was Lucidel who were Paladin's client. Unfortunately Paladin Security has closed down and the guy who runs it, a Mr Carl Peterson, has disappeared. If we had the opportunity to question him and/or Swift there might be the slim possibility of establishing a link between them and Lucidel. Or rather Lucidel's chief of security, an American, Chuck McCoskey."

"Yes, I know of him. He takes his orders directly from Luc Barr, Lucidel's Chief Executive Officer."

"Who, of course, would completely disown McCoskey should a link between him and Peterson be traced."

"But you think it's a slim chance anyway?"

"McCoskey is ex CIA and too much of a pro to leave any trail that would lead back to him. Besides, I would guess that Peterson is living in luxurious anonymity somewhere in South America, and that Swift is dead, lost at sea, and that at sometime his body or debris from his craft will be washed ashore."

Relief was Gayle's overwhelming emotion as she watched the helicopter, carrying the four police officers, finally take off. Throughout the whole of their two-day sojourn she had been in a state of anxiety: would they discover Alan's body? Or his camp for that matter, though that wasn't so vital; there were a number of theories that could have explained its presence, and he would not have left anything among the articles that could identify him. Yet they missed the encampment within the ruin: easily enough done under normal circumstances, except in this instance they were supposed to be carrying out a thorough search. As for Alan's body, all she could think was that it was either hidden among the rock at the bottom of the cliff, or it had been swept out to sea in the storm.

She would have to see for herself.

The day of the helicopter's departure, the two women spent moving back into their respective cabins. In the evening Sharon, as before, drifted over to Gayle's cabin, and spent most of the time talking about her son and their telephone conversation. After she left Gayle retrieved the gun from the backpack. She dismantled, cleaned and reloaded the automatic pistol, all the time debating whether she should dispose of it. But exactly where gave rise to its own problems: the surrounding soil was thin so an animal might well dig it up, the bog could give it up when the monks cut out the peat, and throwing it off the cliffs gave no insurance of not being discovered. If it was discovered and handed to the police it might be traced back to her: for even though the service kept its details secret the gun was registered in her name, and in this instance they might be persuaded to reveal the fact. Off the side of the ferry on the return to Lewis was probably going to be the best place. So why was she cleaning and reloading the gun?

Habit she guessed.

Early the next morning, at daybreak, Gayle made her way to the cliff top. She wasn't comfortable with heights and cautiously leaned over and peered down. The tide was out, but as far as she could see there was no sign of a body. Next she lay on her stomach and looked over the edge for a more detailed search. Still nothing. The temptation was to conclude that Alan had been swept out to sea, but unless she actually went down to the base of the cliffs she would never be sure. Skirting around the top and peering down and across she could make out a rudimentary track leading to the base. Mustering her courage and putting her vertigo on hold, she commenced the descent. Twenty nerve racking minutes later she reached the bottom, and spent a further thirty minutes scrambling over the rocks, until she was positive that they did not contain the body of Alan Swift. What she did fine was a length of rope trapped in a shallow cave: was this where he had moored his boat? If so where was it now? Had it also been swept out to sea? Would it be found, floating empty or washed up on some distant shore? Would Alan's body eventually get washed up somewhere? Every question seemed to lead to another.

Stop it!

It doesn't matter; Alan's dead, it doesn't matter if they find his bullet-riddled body, not if she had thoroughly disposed of the gun. That at least was one vacillation decided, the gun had to be permanently lost.

Gayle found the climb back easier than the decent; although when she checked her watch she saw it had taken about the same amount of time. She would have to hurry if she was going to clear the ruin of Alan's belongings before Sharon was up and about. As she retraced her footsteps of the chase of seven days earlier, Gayle thought of how she would dispose of the tent, cooking utensils, et cetera, and decided to wrap everything in the tent and throw the package off a cliff at high tide. Then she remembered the knife. The one Alan was holding when she emptied the gun into him. Did he take it over the edge with him? There had been no sign of it below, but it could have been swept out with the body. So if it was still on the island it would have to be at the cliff top. Recalling the incident jogged her memory further, the spent cartridge cases: when an automatic pistol is fired the used cartridge case is ejected before a new bullet enters the chamber. There had been at least six bullets fired on the cliff top. She could understand the search party missing the knife if it had gone over the cliff with Alan, but how had they failed to notice the spent cases? There was nothing else for it, it wasn't far, she would have to go back and check.

But when she got there, and conducted a thorough search, there was no sign of the knife or cartridge cases. Confused she resumed the walk to the ruin.

Only when she reached it, it was to discover that all traces of Alan's habitation had been cleared away: tent, ground sheet, cooking utensils, shaving mirror: the whole caboodle, gone. Like the boat, knife, cartridge cases and body, there was no indication that they had ever existed. If she hadn't found the single cartridge case by the wall – from her first shot – she might have been inclined to think that the whole affair had been a figment of her imagination.

Chapter Twenty

The press and media contingent had grown by the time Latimer returned to Lewis. They were waiting by the landing pad, and surrounded the party as soon as the helicopter's blades ceased turning. Latimer refused to be drawn into answering their questions, but was left with little option than to promise that he would be issuing a formal statement. After conferring with his Chief Superintendent Latimer called a press conference. The hotel he was staying at provided an ante-room. He spoke with the aid of notes.

"The man we are seeking, in connection with the murders of Jonathan Greaves and Jean Mortier, and the attempted murder of Sharon Greaves, is named Alan Swift. He was reported to be on Lewis trying to trace Mrs Greaves, and learned that she had taken the last ferry to Howth Island. Howth, as you know, is cut off for the months of November, December and January, without any means of communication. Swift was last seen in Oban, purchasing a dinghy and outboard motor. He is an ex-Royal Marine who has served in the Special

Boat Service. Suspecting that he was on Howth my team and I went there and made a thorough search. No trace of Swift was found. Our present opinion is that he either perished at sea or is still at large. He should be regarded as extremely dangerous, and if seen should not be approached but reported to the police.

"Swift was last reported as being employed by a company called Paladin Security, who specialise in supplying security and protection personnel. We are also trying to establish the whereabouts of the head of Paladin Security, a Mr Carl Peterson.

"A formal statement, together with descriptions and E-fit likenesses of both men, will be distributed to you."

Latimer then took questions.

"Can you say what motive was behind the two murders and attempted murder?"

"We are investigating various possibilities. We do not believe Swift's motive was personal."

"Are you saying he is a hired hit man?"

Latimer neither confirmed nor denied this deduction.

"Is Sharon Greaves still on Howth?"

"Yes."

"How long is she expected to stay there?"

"I believe she intends to remain on Howth until the first ferry at the beginning of February."

"Was the attempt on Sharon's life and her decision to stay on Howth in anyway connected with the recent revelations made about her?"

"As I have already stated, we are still investigating the possible motive. With regard to her stay on the island, I am informed that her reason was to obtain unobtrusive asylum prior to a forthcoming civil court case in which she will be giving evidence."

"Can you give any information regarding this court case?"

"No, I'm not in a position to reveal any details."

Sharon Greaves achieved international celebrity status.

Leigh Murray was delighted with the information divulged in the press conference. No details, but sufficient to stir the pot, and put a shot across Lucidel's bows. She had been considering mounting her own slur campaign against the so-called ex-lover and his revelations, but now there was no need to. The public's curiosity was aroused, journalists would dig and discover Sharon's background, and all paths would lead to Fatale, and hence to Lucidel. Then people could assume whatever conclusions they wanted.

A point not lost on Luc Barr. The ex-lover's revelations were turning out to have no foundation - more likely of his own invention - and with no other ex-partners taking the bait and coming forward, the whole slur campaign was in danger of backfiring.

He instructed Otto Klee to form a task force dedicated to either disproving Sharon Greaves' findings, or accumulating sufficient evidence to cast doubt on her accusation that Fatale was the cause of the reported deaths.

Chuck McCoskey was contacted. "Put the smear campaign on hold and concentrate on delving into Sharon's professional background," Barr said, "see if there was anything there that could be used to cast aspersions on her technical ability."

"I wouldn't hold out too much hope," McCoskey said at the other end of the line, "we've already been down that road, and other than astonishing everyone and only scraping through on her degree – attributed to an emotional problem rather than inability – we found nothing else."

"Couldn't we capitalise on that, cast doubts on her mental state, hint that her findings were emotionally motivated rather than scientifically? Gather as much information as you can surrounding that incident of her life."

"Okay, if you say so," McCoskey drawled, his tone implying that he thought it was clutching at straws.

Barr said, "Just do it, McCoskey, it could be that our jobs might depend on it. It's looking as if this business is going to be decided in court, and it could all come down to casting doubts on that fucking woman's capability. That or she turns up dead before the trial begins."

"Miracles have been known to happen."

"Divine intervention."

"Amen to that."

Chapter Twenty-one

During the days following her discovery, Gayle became convinced that Alan was still alive. There could be no other explanation. With the failing light, the visibility must had been bad enough for her to have missed, or only wounded Alan, when she fired at him. Wounded would be more likely, otherwise he would have finished her off with his knife. Plus he was already wounded in the shoulder and leg. In her highly charged state of fear and anxiety she had imagined that the shots had been fatal and their impact driven him over the cliff. Whereas in fact he had only dropped, wounded, into the gorse. Somehow – she remembered how far he had managed to run with the bleeding leg, his amazing strength – he had staggered way back to his camp, dressed his wounds and hunkered down in his tent until the storm abated. Then, during the ten-hour lull between the two storms, while she was drifting between consciousness and sleep, he must have cleared away all evidence of ever being on the island, including her spent cartridge cases – easy to see how he missed the one by the wall, the storm had caused wide spread havoc – loaded them into the dinghy and left the island.

The question now was, did he perish at sea or did he reach safety, and if he did, where was he now? And would he be back? Unless advised otherwise, Gayle had to conclude that he was alive, and set on revenge?

The police were gone, and they were cut off until the arrival of the first ferry, over a month away. She suddenly felt frightened and alone.

All thoughts of discarding the gun were postponed, and she took to permanently carrying it on her person. She also took to keeping all doors and windows locked, though when Sharon was present she did it as surreptitiously as possible, in order not to unduly alarm her. It was an advantage that the only means of keeping the door to the sauna hut closed, against the persistent wind, was turning the key in the lock. And because the search parties hadn't actually found Alan's body and Latimer was taking the cautious approach that he could still be alive, helped Gayle in persuading Sharon to take elementary precautions.

None of which did anything to alleviate the ever-increasing terror that became Gayle's permanent companion. The brief interval of their skirmish was sufficient for her to conclude that Alan Swift was the most dangerous man she had ever known. An acquaintanceship that included some of the IRA's most ruthless killers. She had witnessed his incredible strength and fortitude. She had faced him, in adversity, when the advantage had been all hers, and still experienced his naked aggression. Even when at her mercy on the cliff's edge, she could see that his whole being was concentrated in an effort to kill her before she could pull the trigger. And in blind terror she had emptied the gun at him. With the passing of time her fevered imagination fed on the illusion of his invulnerability, until in her mind he began to acquire a Schwarzenegger Terminator-like persona.

Concurrent with this paranoia was an equally strong determination to keep her gnawing trepidation a secret from Sharon. There would be nothing to be gained by having them both worrying.

Christmas arrived and passed uncelebrated. Neither woman was religious. Sharon, still in mourning for Jonathan and missing Leon, was in no mood to make anything of the occasion, and Gayle, who had done her best to ignore the whole business for the past twenty years, had only suggested making something of it for Sharon's sake. The Christmas tree lay where Sharon had left it, outside her hut; shedding what little foliage it had, and finally sawn up to accompany the turfs of peat in their respective stoves.

Ignoring the day didn't stop each of them privately recalling past Christmases; though Sharon's, with invocations of the decorated manor house and a young Leon opening his presents, were more pleasant than Gayle's. Her recollection was of the last Christmas spent with her widowed mother: increasingly imperious with age, demanding to be continuously waited on, and demanding that Gayle resign her commission – she had reached the rank of captain – to look after her. By the following Christmas Gayle was in hiding, and she had never seen her mother again; only a letter from a solicitor, informing of her death and the fact that Gayle was the beneficiary of a comfortable inheritance. Subsequently, left with an older Brother whom she barely knew, and a few cousins who she didn't want to know, Gayle had cut all family ties. Roland had positively hated Christmas, and they had always escaped the December misery to some remote sunny beach.

In contrast, and as an antidote to their Christmas blues, they did celebrate New Year's Eve, emptying the medicinal scotch bottle and getting, as Gayle eloquently put it, mildly shit-faced.

January was bitterly cold but devoid of any substantial rain, what little there was consisting mainly of morning and evening drizzle and the odd shower. This resulted in enabling Sharon and Gayle to resume their fauna and flora discovering walks: a two-edged sword as far as Gayle was concerned, glad of the opportunity to maintain a vigilant look out for Alan Swift, while terrified of his sudden reappearance.

As a gesture of gratitude the two women offered their services to the Abbot: Gayle to help Brother Adrian on the farm, and Sharon to give Brother Neil the benefit of her professional knowledge in sorting and cataloguing his present stock of medicines and drugs, and suggestions for future upgrades and replacements. An offer that was gracefully accepted. It didn't involve a great deal of time, a couple of hours every other day or so, but it constituted an absorbing addition to their usual routine. The two Brothers seemed to appreciate the help; Neil, whose knowledge of drugs was sketchy, perhaps more than Adrian. To each woman's great relief neither monk questioned them about what had happened. Adrian, true to his Celtic roots, liked to talk but kept the conversation to farming matters and anecdotes about the monastery and its inhabitants, while Neil didn't appear to have a loquacious bone in his body and spoke only when spoken to. Sharon made a mental note to endow the monastery with a comprehensive medicine chest – of the type used by mobile medical units – when she returned to the mainland.

Following the evening sauna, chess evolved as the chief preoccupation of the evenings. Sharon, a chess club member and regular combatant, was the better player, but Gayle, using the matches as a means of temporarily obliterating the constant threat of Alan and concentrating her mind on something different, was able to raise her game and present Sharon with something of a challenge.

The weeks passed.

Gayle continued to maintain her vigilance, but with no indication of Alan's return it began to slip into the realms of routine. She was aware of this and the inherent danger of becoming complacent; all the same, with each passing day the likelihood of him having perished at sea was becoming more and more feasible. The rain might have abated but not the wind, it continued to howl around the force 7 to 8 mark (according to Brother Adrian), and to Gayle's eyes the waves looked more mountainous than ever; thus diminishing the chance of anyone, no matter how well trained and experienced, being able to land a boat onto the island.

As February approached they began to talk about the future, what they would do on return to normality. For Sharon it meant being reunited with Leon, though she accepted that she would be required to put Jonathan's affairs in order before going to Florida. Latimer had informed her that Jonathan, in accordance with his will, was buried in their local churchyard. It was a low-key affair, with only the vicar and warden in attendance, and Sharon thought she might arrange some sort of remembrance service, with all his friends present, when she returned from America with Leon. A holiday in some exotic location with her son was a tempting prospect, but Sharon guessed that it would be more appreciated by her than Leon. He seemed to be enjoying himself where he was, so the chances were that it would have to be a compromise, and she'd have to settle for a Florida vacation at her mother-in-law's. Then it would be a matter of sorting out what she was going to do – go back to work, or not: sell the manor house, or not: stay in England, or not, et cetera, et cetera - and getting on with her life. (And your promiscuous sexual encounters, Gayle couldn't help but think.)

Gayle missed her music. It hadn't occurred to her to bring her CD's and a CD player, because on her previous visit to Howth there hadn't been any electricity, and the installation of the generator had come as a surprise.

It didn't bother Sharon – she liked music and had fairly catholic tastes, but when she wanted music she turned on Radio three, went to concerts, and bopped to the thudding beat at the fitness centre as she went through her exercise routine. She admitted to Gayle that although there were three CD players in the manor house – drawing room, Jonathan's study and Leon's bedroom – the CD's were all theirs and she herself didn't actually own any.

In contrast Gayle needed her daily fix of blues, jazz and rock and roll. Cranking up the CD player the moment she entered her house was as automatic to her as putting the kettle on or feeding the cat was to others. Her first priority, once she was back in Spain, would be getting back to playing base guitar with the band. And hit the beach; she hated the wet and cold of Scotland, and was suffering from sun withdrawal symptoms. Once her system was back to normal she thought she might travel, a sort of musical odyssey: the Montreux Jazz Festival, head for the States: New York, Chicago, places where she knew they still played her kind of music, raw and unadulterated. That was what Gayle told Sharon, leaving unsaid an overwhelming desire that she would receive an invite to the manor house, or that Sharon would come to stay in her converted Spanish farmhouse. What she dreaded was a life completely without Sharon.

Brother Adrian mentioned to Gayle that it wasn't completely unknown for seals to be seen on a small barren rock, a skerry he called it, just off the south-western end of the island. "They like to dive for fish from it," he said.

"We have to go and see them," Sharon responded when Gayle told her.

"He didn't say they would definitely be there."

"Don't be so negative. We'll make an expedition of it, take the binoculars and sandwiches. That is unless you can think of something better to do?"

Gayle admitted that she hadn't and, with a condescending smile, agreed to accompany Sharon on the 'expedition'. The sandwich making would, of course, be left to her, but then what was new? She would have followed Sharon to Timbuktu on a Rollerblade if asked.

They set off the following morning. The route took them in the proximity of the derelict cottage, as there was no way they could avoid passing the cliff top where Gayle had emptied her gun into Alan. In an unspoken mutuality they passed by these landmarks as quickly as the terrain would enable them. When they reached the point Brother Adrian had described, it was to discover that he had omitted to mention that there were actually three small skerries. Did the seals dive off all three or only one? And if the latter, which one?

They clambered down to a niche, settled in it, and for over an hour sat and closely observed each of the off-shore formations, passing the binoculars backwards and forwards to each other, without seeing a whisker of a seal. "Looks to me as if Brother Adrian gave us a bum steer," Gayle said.

"Yeah," Sharon agreed. Then she suddenly stiffened. "No, I think I can see one. Quick, give me the glasses." Gayle passed the binoculars across. Sharon eagerly focused them. "Yes, I was right there's one, two, three, more. Oh look." Sharon handed back the glasses to Gayle.

"Where? I still can't see them."

Sharon then knelt behind Gayle, placed her hands over Gayle's and directed her view to where the seals were emerging from the sea.

"Oh yes."

They remained in their niche for a further two hours, watching the seals, eating their sandwiches and smiling to one another at the simple wonderment of the scene. In the midst of anguish and trepidation, and perhaps, to some extent, due to it, Gayle experienced one of those out-of-time intervals when she was truly happy.

As suddenly as they had appeared the seals vanished, and it was time to head for home.

Gayle said, "There's still a couple of hours of daylight left, instead of going straight back, why don't we walk to the other side of the island and make our way from there?" She was loath to relinquish the moment.

"Great idea."

They decided on a route that took them towards the south of the island, skirting that side of the peat bog, then up the east coast, which in hindsight turned out to be a mistake, as the going was harder than anticipated. The southern, flatter, extremity of Howth was an area they seldom visited, simply because its stony terrain was devoid of flora and of minimal interest. It was also difficult to walk on, requiring constant vigilance to avoid catching a foot on one of the stones and tripping over. Once negotiated, the terrain became more interesting but steeper, the ground suddenly rising to encompass the cliffs that surrounded the sheltered bay where the jetty was located. By the time they reached the path that led upwards the 'couple of hours of daylight' were quickly beginning to diminish. There was nothing else for it than to press on. At the crest they rested to catch their breath.

"Wow!" Sharon exclaimed, looking back down the track they had just ascended. "Have we just climbed that?"

"We must be fitter than we realised," Gayle said. "Some view, ay?" She pointed to the bay that lay beneath.

"Oh my God!" Sharon grabbed Gayle's arm and pointed downwards. There below, where the path from the jetty merged on to an incline that led to the track they had just taken, was the figure of a man. The combat fatigues, backpack, fair hair, and movement – half run, half walk - engendered from years of clandestine engagements, were all too familiar.

Alan Swift.

Chapter Twenty-two

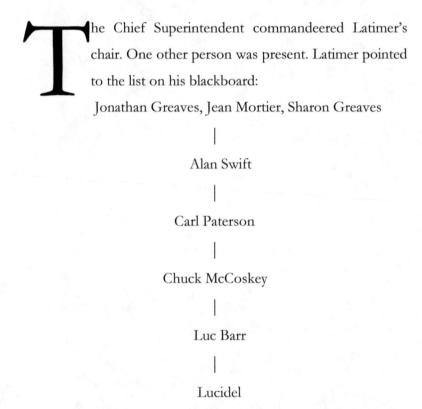

The Chief Superintendent commandeered Latimer's chair. One other person was present. Latimer pointed to the list on his blackboard:

Jonathan Greaves, Jean Mortier, Sharon Greaves

|

Alan Swift

|

Carl Paterson

|

Chuck McCoskey

|

Luc Barr

|

Lucidel

"Apart from the murders of Jonathan Greaves and Jean Mortier, and the attempted murder of Sharon Greaves, where there is fairly conclusive circumstantial evidence linking them to

Alan Swift, the rest of the link is purely hypothetical, there is no conclusive proof. Even if they were to be found, and Swift fingered Paterson, and Paterson fingered McCoskey, it would still be the word of two mercenaries against that of the chief of security of a multi-national company. But there is one common denominator: money. Swift and Paterson don't come cheap; this isn't a case of a few pound notes in a plain envelope. Money has to be transferred. There has to be a trail. That's why I've requested Helen's assistance."

"Do you think you can trace this money trail?" the Super asked the neat well-groomed young woman, Inspector Helen Skinner of the divisional fraud squad.

"I don't think it's beyond the realms of possibility, sir. Post 9/11 it has become much more difficult for money to be transferred undetected. But it's not something that can be done overnight. Initially I will need to get a look at Swift and Paterson's private papers, which will entail entrance into their homes and offices. They are London based, so we'll require the assistance of the Met. As the trail gets nearer to Lucidel, providing of course that there is one, they will become aware that someone is probing and it won't take them long to discover who is investigating them. If they've anything to hide they'll set about dissimulating and severing links."

"Inextricably?"

"Not necessarily, sir, no matter how well hidden, the money still has to originate from somewhere. But the further up the tree we get the greater the amount of flack we will have to expect. Lucidel is a mega concern with, I should imagine, friends in high places."

"So, Andy, let me get this right. What you require from me, in the furtherance of your investigation, is permission to involve fraud squad resources, the arrangement of inter-divisional cooperation, provision of necessary search warrants, and protection from political interference?"

"That's about it, sir," Latimer said.

The Chief Superintendent was pensive. The two officers had obtained their rank from opposite ends of the spectrum: Andy through the ranks: Helen, ten years his junior, fast-tracked from university: yet, from what he had heard and observed, there was no rancour from either. This had to be the way ahead. He was as ambitious as they were, if the investigation was successful he would get the kudos for imaginative management of resources. It was worth taking the chance for.

"Okay."

Andy and Helen looked at one another; they hadn't expected it to be that easy. Andy said, "You mean go ahead as we've just discussed?"

"That's right. I will expect to be constantly kept abreast of developments, regular reports and forewarned of any possible political ambushes. Helen, for reasons of expediency and not due to any chain of command, I'd prefer the reports to come through Andy. Although at the end of the day I would expect to see your joint signatures on the final report. Would you have any problem with that?"

"None at all, sir."

"Good. And I have to warn you, that if I think it is becoming apparent that the investigation is going nowhere, I will pull the plug on it. Is that understood?"

"Yes sir."

"Goes without saying, sir."

Latimer put a call through to DS Danielle Nott, to let her know what was happening, and ask how things were going her end.

"Lots of reports of sightings of Swift and Paterson since I did the television thing."

"I thought you were very good on it," Latimer said. "A star is born."

"Flattery and bullshit will get you everywhere."

"Anything interesting from the sightings?"

"A couple that could possibly interface, I'll let you know when we finished interviewing. I spoke with young DC Ross, he tells me that the coastguard is getting pissed off chasing away reporters."

"They still there?"

"The organised media has left but there's still lots of paparazzi about, and they've got money to tempt hard-up fishermen with empty boats."

"Ah well, it's only for a couple of more weeks."

Armed with the necessary warrant, Inspector Helen Skinner accompanied two members of the Metropolitan Police Force on a search of Carl Patterson's flat cum office.

All it revealed was that the owner had gone to great trouble to remove every item of evidence that would prove his very existence. The flat was dusted for fingerprints as a matter of routine.

They had more luck with Alan Swift's flat.

The address had been obtained via some diligent questioning of the staff of Mandy's nightclub. One of the barmen had once given Alan a lift home. As with Carl Peterson's flat entrance had to be forced. Unlike Peterson, Swift had left sufficient information to give Helen Skinner a foothold on the ladder to the money trail: the name and address of his landlord.

Mr Pandit Rana, concerned that a search of his bank account by Inspector Skinner might reveal more than he would like, reluctantly divulged that Alan Swift paid his monthly rent by direct debit. From there it was easy for Skinner to follow the trail from Rana's bank to his tenant's bank and hence obtain details of Alan Swift's account. A fairly recent cheque, made out to Inland Revenue, led to the revelation of Swift's National Insurance number and the fact that Paladin Security employed him.

There were regular payments into Swift's account from

Paladin Security - which enabled Skinner to obtain Paladin's banking details – and a recent transfer, dated 29th October, of £5,000, from a Cayman Island numbered account. On the debit side there was a cash withdrawal on the 30th October of £5,000 – according to the sceptical assistant bank manager, when he questioned Swift he was informed that it was for an antique buying trip, where cash was often an advantage.

Paladin's computer trail led directly to a Jersey account. From there it separated into three other offshore accounts.

Now Skinner and her team had to start digging.

The first thing Thomas McBride, the proprietor and sole employee of McBride Property Letting, did on his return to Lewis from his annual Christmas vacation with his wife– this year it had been South Africa – was to replay the video cassette he had set on the timer to record his favourite television programme.

In response to the telephone call he received from Mr McBride, DC Peter Ross contacted DS Danielle Nott. When she had given a description of Alan Swift and shown the e-fit likeness during her appearance on the television Crime Watch programme, in regard to the murder of Jean Mortier, McBride heard bells ringing. Apparently a man answering to Swift's description had rented a remote shoreline cottage, on the west of the island, from him in mid December. McBride described the man as being fit looking, clean-shaven, with fair hair and a slight accent, which could have been American. He couldn't recall the name the man had given him, and the signature on the agreement was undecipherable, but at the time McBride hadn't been worried about formalities for an unexpected three-month let, paid in advance, in cash.

Knott, recently returned from a fruitless visit to Fort William, as a follow up to what had sounded like two likely, and corresponding leads, was tempted to tell Ross to go and check on it himself. The journey to Lewis necessitated taking a plane flight, and she wasn't too sure if she would get budget clearance. Except Swift was a very dangerous man and any approach like this should be with an Armed Response Team, something the Isle of Lewis constabulary didn't run to. After discussing the situation with her superior officer, she accompanied an ART unit in a police helicopter to Lewis.

The cottage McBride had let was located on the side of an inlet, and included a mooring jetty. Access to it was down a forest track. The ART unit infiltrated through the forest until they had the cottage surrounded. An intensive watch was maintained for half an hour, then two officers forced an entry and the unit moved in. The cottage was uninhabited, but the clothes and supplies left in it indicated that the occupant expected to return there.

Around the clock surveillance was organised.

The Metropolitan police, moving on a parallel path to

Helen Skinner's investigation, extracted from Pandit Rana the address of the lock-up garage he also rented to Alan Swift. Parked in the garage was a Ford Scorpio. In the glove compartment they found a dossier describing Sharon Greaves, her habits and routines, with times and addresses. Only the photograph, mentioned in the itinerary, was missing.

Dmitry Balakireff sat the opposite side of the desk in Luc Barr's inner sanctum, where there was no chance of them being overheard. As usual Barr paced the office.

Balakireff said, "Someone, with official sanction, is checking on our external banking arrangements."

"Do you know who?" Barr asked.

"Not exactly, but from the sort of clearance they have I would suspect it's either a government office or police."

"How far have they got?"

"They are closing in on McCoskey."

"I see. Can you shut down and erase everything leading from us to him?"

"A programme is in place, it just requires your go ahead."

Barr did not hesitate. "Do it," he said. Recent meetings with Klee and Nadleson had indicated that if Sharon Greaves appeared for her, the odds were on the plaintiff, Wendy Lister, winning the case. It was time for him to look to his own survival from the repercussions that were sure to follow.

If Sharon Greaves appeared.

"How is our battle fund?"

"Still extensive," Balakireff answered, "It's barely been touched.

"If necessary, could you arrange for an untraceable one-off payment?"

"Just let me know how much and where and when."

Once Balakireff had left the office Barr rang down to McCoskey and asked him to come up. McCoskey arrived ten minutes later. As soon as the door was closed Barr told him what Balakireff had reported.

"I'm afraid I will have to ask for your resignation. You'll be amply recompensed but after that you'll be on your own."

"Sacrificial Lamb. Even if Sharon Greaves were to be retired before she gives evidence? Swift's not been found, he might still be out there and finish the job."

"Too late in the day, this investigation into our funding arrangements is too far down the line. I expect your complete disappearance, McCoskey. Balakireff is setting up a handshake of a million euros to ensure it."

"Should help me disappear into a comfortable retirement."

Latimer laid his report on the Super's desk. He was motioned to take a seat. "Take me through the main points, Andy."

Latimer cleared his throat, gathered his thoughts, and

then began. "Swift's flat had been located. A dossier on Sharon Greaves, giving details of her life style and habits, was found in his car. Incriminating evidence that she was the mark he was hired to kill. We know that he drew £5,000, in cash from his bank the day after he killed Jonathan Greaves. Swift has been traced to a cottage on Lewis. On investigation the cottage was found to be empty, and there was nothing to indicate when Swift vacated the property, but sufficient items were left in the bathroom and bedroom to suggest that he expected to return. Hair, from a comb and hairbrush, for possible DNA analysis have been collected and fingerprints are being checked against those found in Swift's car and flat. And a 24-hour surveillance is being maintained.

"Swift's banking details led to Carl Paterson's. He has a London banking account and three offshore accounts. It appears that up to recently his finances were none too buoyant – he had been playing the stock market with pretty disastrous results. Then in mid December one of his offshore accounts received a transfer of 25,000 euros, of which 5,000 was transferred to his London bank, and which he drew out the same day in cash – seems this was not unusual as casual nightclub bouncers prefer to be paid in cash. Two weeks ago a further 100,000 euros was transferred into another of his offshore accounts. Both transfers into Paterson's accounts come via a tortuous route of shell companies, which Helen Skinner has managed to trace to an import/export company: one of whose directors happens to be a

Mr Charles McCoskey, the other his wife. Charles 'Chuck' McCoskey is Lucidel's Chief of Security."

"Positive proof connecting Lucidel, Andy?"

"Ah, not that simple. All records of transfers into McCoskey's company have been irredeemably erased. Two days ago Lucidel released an internal notice, leaked to the press, that McCoskey had tendered his resignation on health grounds – a misnomer for fired. My guess is that if pressed Lucidel will say that McCoskey had been appropriating funds for his own private use. Not unexpectedly, McCoskey has disappeared. Interpol has been alerted but I don't hold out much hope of them finding him. McCoskey is a spook's spook, he will have had an escape route in place for years."

"Conclusions?"

"Swift was hired to kill Sharon Greaves, and was sacked when he botched it. For reasons of professional pride he decided to finish the job. He killed Jonathan Greaves after extracting Sharon Greaves whereabouts, and then killed his replacement, Jean Mortier.

"Paterson, aware that Swift's trail would lead back to him, and on McCoskey's instigation, with a 25,000 euro sweetener, decided to do a runner. Except with his finances in such a mess 25 grand wasn't going to get him very far. My guess is that the second payment of 100,000 was to ensure his disappearance, but he's got to get his hands on it, and if he doesn't know we're watching the money's movements we probably have a good chance of catching him."

The Super's telephone rang. He snatched it up, irritably. "I thought I said I wasn't to be interrupted? – Oh, okay, put him through." The receiver was handed to Latimer. "DS Hammond for you, something about Swift."

Latimer took the phone. "What is it, Dean?"

"Swift's turned up."

From an unidentifiable location Chuck McCoskey sent a text message to a mobile number kept solely for communication between him and Luc Barr.

If a certain nuisance could still be eliminated what would it be worth?

The answer came back.

The same again.

Chapter Twenty-three

"Oh my God, its him," Sharon gasped. Gayle grabbed hold of her and pulled them both down on to the ground. Then she raised her head to glimpse over the clump of gorse they were hidden behind, at the same time extracting the gun from her pocket. The figure had reached the junction with the track they had just taken and was beginning the ascent.

"Quickly," Gayle commanded, "follow me and stay down." As she turned to face Sharon she saw her staring, open mouthed, at the gun.

"Where did that come from?"

"There's no time, I'll tell you about it later. Now, quickly, come on." It was all Gayle could do to contain the panic that threatened to overwhelm her. She grabbed hold of Sharon's hand and led her, in a crouching run, away from the cliff top and along an undulating track that afforded them cover and took them back to the cabins. Darkness was closing in, which also helped to cover their progress, and they knew the terrain.

But then, as they were fully aware, so did he.

The final spurt, across the open area where the cabins were located, would have been the worst part had not night fallen by the time they got there. But night brings its own terrors, especially if you are already frightened for your life. There was a hint of rain on the freshening wind.

They ran into Gayle's cabin and slammed and bolted the door. As an extra precaution they placed the dinning table across the entrance, then ensured all window shutters were closed and bolted. The sofa was positioned against the far wall, where there were no windows, facing the door. They collapsed into it, holding on to one another. Then Gayle began shaking, so violently that no matter how tightly Sharon held her she was unable to contain the spasms. In desperation Sharon searched in the kitchen until she unearthed the scotch bottle, with a quarter of an inch still remaining in the bottom, and poured the total amount into a mug. She brought it back to the sofa and gave it to Gayle.

"So what's with the gun?"

Gayle swallowed the last of the whisky, then pulled the weapon from the waistband of her trousers and placed it on the arm of the sofa. "I'm licensed to carry it."

"But why now?"

"I've been carrying it since just after the police left, when

I discovered that Alan might not be dead."

Gayle's monotone delivery frightened Sharon. And God knew she was frightened enough as it was. "You're not making sense. How do you mean, you discovered he might not be dead?"

Gayle's shaking was replaced by tears, that were unaccompanied by sobs, just a continuous outflow rolling down her cheeks, as if her eyes were leaking. "I thought I had killed him, then I found his camp gone and the cartridge shells had been picked up, and I knew it had to be him . ."

Sharon took hold of Gayle by the shoulders.

"Gayle, you're not making any sense. Take a deep breath and start from the beginning. Tell me what happened?"

With as much composure as she could muster Gayle began, "Just before the storm, after I had taken you to the medical wing, I decided to try and find Alan." She proceeded to relate the sequence of events that followed, up until discovering the deserted and tidied encampment. "When I shot him the visibility was poor, the wind driving misty rain into my eyes, and I suppose I missed or only wounded him. He must have dressed his wounds and sat out the storm, and made his escape during the lull. And now he's back."

The wind was now gusting and there was the sound of rain being driven against the shuttered windows.

Sharon said, "And you've been carrying all this baggage around ever since. Why on earth didn't you tell the police while they were here? You could have told them that it was self-defence – it was self- defence, he had a knife. He's a murderer, no one would have blamed you."

"But the police would have questioned us, and the Brothers, and eventually it would all have come out; that he had been on the island, and what had happened between the two of you exposed; the very thing you didn't want anyone to know about. So, unless they found him I decided to keep quiet."

"Oh Gayle!" Sharon pulled Gayle into her arms, kissed her tear- stained cheek and hugged her. "You really are the most wonderful friend I've ever had."

When she was released from the embrace Gayle gave a self-effacing grimace and said, "Anyway, at the time I thought he was dead. And besides, would the outcome have been that much different; when they left the island the police hadn't discounted that Alan was still alive, they'd still be looking for him and we'd still be here."

"They might have left us with an armed guard."

Gayle wiped away the tears with her hand. "But, darling," she said, picking up the gun, "you've got me," and she started to laugh. After a moment Sharon joined in, and their laughter, fuelled by a shared fear, intensified until it was in danger of deteriorating into hysteria.

There was a heavy thud against the door.

Suddenly they were sober. Gayle held the gun with both hands and pointed it at the door. Another thud, this time against one of the shuttered windows, and another on the next window, as if circling the cabin, followed by Gayle's pointing gun. Then a sound that could have been a voice calling.

Alan; knocking, calling, demanding entrance? Or just the wind, gusting against the door and howling around the cabin?

They remained on the sofa. The thudding against the door and windows diminished as the wind lessened: coincidence or, now that the wind was no longer howling, was Alan skulking around outside, ear to the door listening for signs of them falling into sleep?

He knew Gayle had the gun, and was prepared to use it, so he would wait until their guard was down before mounting an assault. The silence was worse than the banging, and Sharon and Gayle found they were talking in lowered voices.

"Oh this is ridiculous," Gayle said.

"I know," Sharon agreed.

But they still continued to whisper.

"We should make some sandwiches and a thermos of coffee, and take turns standing guard."

"Good idea."

Neither moved from the sofa.

The thumping of helicopter blades woke Gayle. Daylight was seeping through the shutters. A voice was calling over a loud hailer. Her head was on her arm, which was resting against the arm of the sofa. The gun had slipped onto the floor.

Sharon stirred her head from Gayle's shoulder. "What's happening?"

"Dunno, I'll have a look." Gayle retrieved the gun and slipped it into her pocket. She cracked open a shutter and peeked out, when that failed to reveal what was happening she did the same with the door.

"Stay where you are," the loud hailer commanded. Presuming that it was referring to them, Gayle opened wide the door, and saw the helicopter circling above. "Come out and show yourself," the loud hailer continued. "The captain of the boat that brought you has been arrested. You cannot get off the island. Give yourself up."

Sharon joined Gayle at the door. She asked, "Are they talking to us?"

"I'm not sure."

The helicopter descended over a point near the edge of the cabin enclave. A figure rose from a cluster of gorse, hands in the air, the draft from the helicopter rotors whipping his hair around his face.

"Alan!" Sharon exclaimed.

He remained motionless while the helicopter landed. To the surprise of both women, instead of the squad of armed police they expected the only person to emerge was the gangly figure of the young detective constable who had accompanied Latimer and Nott previously. He walked over to Alan, who lowered his hands and presented them for the handcuffs that were slipped onto his wrists. The two coastguards who manned the helicopter joined the young policeman and his prisoner.

Curiosity getting the better of them, Gayle and Sharon left the cabin and walked towards the group. Spotting the two women, DC Ross left the prisoner in the hands of the coastguards and came to meet them.

"I'm not sure if that was brave or foolhardy," Gayle said to him.

"I'm not sure I know what you mean," Ross said.

"Taking on a professional killer single handed."

"Oh," Ross said, as the understanding of what Gayle was inferring became apparent to him, "that isn't Swift, it's a member of the paparazzi, a certain Graham Bannerman. The skipper of the boat that brought him was nabbed late yesterday afternoon but rather than tackle the high winds and darkness, and as we knew he couldn't go anywhere, it was decided to wait until this morning before coming to pick him up."

"We saw him from a distance and thought he was Alan Swift," Sharon said.

"Right, I can see that the combat fatigues would give the impression of an armed assailant," Ross conceded. "I hope he didn't cause you too much distress."

"Well it was a bit disconcerting," Sharon said.

Gayle, who was suddenly marching towards the man, said, "He scared the fucking shit out of us."

Bannerman, left in the care of one of the coastguards while the other was retrieving his camera, grinned at Gayle as she approached. "Ello," he said.

"Bastard." The flat of Gayle's hand hit his face with such ferocity that his head snapped back. The coastguard was as surprised as Bannerman, and didn't manage to grab Gayle until after her second, anger fuelled, blow knocked the photographer to the ground.

Ross and Sharon ran to the scene. Gayle was crying and Sharon gently removed her from the coastguard's hold. "The stupid, stupid bastard," Gayle sobbed. "I know," Sharon whispered, cognizant of the true cause of Gayle's anger – she might well have shot the idiot and had him on her conscience.

Once helped to his feet, Bannerman became the epitome of injured indignity. "Did you see what she did to me?" he said to Ross. "I want her charged with assault."

"No you don't," Ross advised. "At the moment all you'll be charged with is trespass, which means you'll probably get away with a caution or, at most, a fine. However, if you want to take the matter further, I could add aggravated harassment, assault and resisting arrest."

"Yeah, okay," Bannerman conceded – adding, to himself, "Fascist bastard." He didn't want to get into a pissing contest with this little jumped up plod. The last minute half dozen shots he had got of Sharon Greaves, with her dyke minder, at the cabin door, gave him a head start on everyone else, and the sooner he had them on offer to the highest bidder the better.

But the 'jumped up little plod' was one step ahead of him. Taking the camera bag from the coastguard who had retrieved it from the gorse, Ross extracted the camera, opened the back, removed the film and exposed it to the light. For good measure he also removed all the rolls of film and exposed them.

"You can't do that!" Bannerman exploded.

"I thought I just did," Ross said. "Sue me." He replaced the camera in the bag and handed it to the coastguard. "Take this and Mr Bannerman on board would you. I'll join you in a moment." He walked over to where Sharon and Gayle had been observing the drama.

"Thank you," Sharon said, and Gayle added, "I'm sorry I lost it for a moment back there."

"I'm sure I speak for my two companions when I say that we entirely approved of the action.

"Now, I do have a bit of good news, what we think are the remains of Alan Swift have been washed ashore. To be more precise, a leg, foot and boot, snagged in a rope attached to part of a rubber dinghy. The letters and numbers on the remnant are the same as those registered on the dinghy sold to Swift. The remains are being sent for DNA comparison with hairs found in Swift's London flat, but it's considered just a formality, we're pretty sure they belong to Swift."

Sharon said, "That's, that's wonderful news." - she was hesitant because she wasn't sure one should celebrate the death of another human being, albeit one whom you hated – "Isn't it, Gayle?"

"Absolutely marvellous," Gayle said, and laughed with the exuberance of joy and relief. After a second Sharon joined in, and then they were hugging and laughing.

Ross smiled and said, "It's nice to be the bearer of good tidings for a change."

Releasing Gayle, Sharon said to Ross, "Thank you," and gave him a kiss on the cheek. Gayle planted one on the other cheek, that was greeted by cheers and a wolf-whistle from the helicopter.

Ross blushed, said, "Thank you, ladies," and turned to make his escape. "Oh, one other thing, the ferry is scheduled for next Thursday, DS Nott will be coming over with it to accompany you back."

Sharon said, "Danielle, oh good."

The helicopter disappeared into the clouds. Gayle volunteered to go and see the Abbot and explain the reason for its appearance. Sharon took a long shower, scrubbing her body, shampooing and conditioning her hair, needing to feel clean. Fresh clothes completed the treatment. Realising she was starving, she did what she always did when she was hungry and went over to Gayle's cabin.

Gayle was in the kitchen. She too had showered and changed, though in a quarter of the time Sharon had taken, and now, in anticipation of Sharon's arrival was preparing breakfast. "You smell nice," she said.

Sharon mentioned the name of the hair treatment, followed by its television catch phrase and then attempted a pirouette.

Gayle's smile was perfunctory.

"Something wrong?" Sharon asked. Did the Abbot give you a hard time?"

"No, he was fine." Gayle didn't expand.

"Then what?"

Gayle said. "It was just before you came in, I was thinking about that stupid idiot of a photographer and how I might well have killed him, when it suddenly hit me, that I have killed someone, Alan."

"I, for one, am pretty glad that you did. If you hadn't it's most likely that he would have killed me, and maybe you, and one or all of the Brothers, so I really wouldn't feel too bad about it."

"That's just it, I don't, and I should. I've taken a life and no matter what the reason or how bad the person I should feel some remorse. But I don't, and it worries me. It makes me just like Alan Swift and any other hired killer."

Sharon took Gayle firmly by the arms and shook her. "You are not like Alan Swift. Somewhere along the line part of his character went missing or was never developed. He was mentally deficient in whatever it is that gives one a conscience.

And in the field of human relationships he was immature. You have just been through a horrible period and you are still in shock. Plus I suspect, like the sole survivor of some disaster, you are in regression for feeling relieved that it's him who is dead and not you, which is perfectly natural. You've got to allow yourself a little time to get back to normality."

"Like being a middle-aged woman playing electric base in a rock and roll band," Sharon added, to lighten the atmosphere.

"Right on," Gayle said, and gave Sharon's hand a squeeze.

The days that followed were, for Gayle, some of the happiest. Free from the threat that had hung over them she and Sharon were now like children let out of school. They were light-hearted, often running instead of walking, and there was a lot of laughter.

When Gayle revealed her ploy for fooling the media circus, which they had been told awaited their arrival back on Lewis, Sharon fell about laughing. Scenarios, that became more and more bizarre by the minute, were developed until they were helpless with fits of the giggles.

Plans were made: Gayle would come to visit in Devon and Sharon holiday in Gayle's Spanish cottage. "Whatever happens," Sharon said, more than once, "we will always be friends."

In the midst of this euphoria Gayle came to know

Sharon, as intimately as it was possible without becoming lovers, and learned not to be blinded by these declarations of solidarity. Rather to accept them for what they were, statements made in the climate of the moment; which were not necessarily a true reflection of Sharon's intentions or meant to be misunderstood as binding commitments. Except when they concerned Sharon personally, and then there was no ambiguity. Asked if she would be returning to her previous sexual habits, Sharon had shrugged and said, "At the moment I'm right off men, but I guess when the urge returns I'll be back to using them again. You know how it is, you can't tell me you've remained celibate since your husband died." Gayle had just smiled, enigmatically - but in fact she had remained chaste, and sadly reflected that the only person who she might want to awaken her libido was never likely to requite her feelings. Just as when Sharon tearfully stated, "I don't know how I'm going to manage without Jonathan, his death has left an awful void," It was said with the possibility of Gayle filling it never being a consideration.

Sharon would survive her husband's death because, Gayle realised, Sharon's world revolved around Sharon, and apart from Leon she had no need for anyone else. Even her love for Jonathan had been a long- term development, borne from the discovery of a deep and mutual affection, and which suited the life style she had chosen. When Sharon said, "You must come and stay with me," she meant it, at that precise moment, but Gayle had come to accept that when Sharon was back in her own world the entreaty would be placed in the realm of a half forgotten promise, only resurrected with a Christmas card, put off until finally it ceased to be an issue. Not because Sharon was an uncaring, cold woman; rather that other events and interests would displace Gayle, and the promises made to her.

Accepting Sharon's failings did not stop Gayle loving her, or hoping that her analysis was mistaken. But in her heart of hearts she knew that these few days of blissful happiness were as good as it was going to get.

DS Danielle Nott was surprised to find that neither of the two women was there to greet her when she disembarked from the ferry. She was the only passenger; no other seeker of peace and tranquillity, real (of which there were none) or false (of which there were myriads) being allowed on the island until the departure of Sharon Greaves. Supplies, that three of Howth's monastic community were assisting the ferry's crew to unload, had taken up the majority of space on the small ferry.

"They'll be packing for the departure," Danielle explained their absence to herself, and proceeded to follow the track that one of the monks informed her led to the cabins.

"An easy walk," he said. Like hell, she was aching and breathing heavily by the time they came into sight. She must start going to the gym more often. Automatically, she made for Gayle's cabin and knocked on the door.

"Come in, it's open."

"Hi," Danielle said as she entered. Gayle and Sharon were sitting on the sofa facing the door, except it wasn't them but two women who might have born a close resemblance, only somehow they didn't.

Seeing the confused look on Danielle's face the two women burst into laughter and removed the wigs they were wearing. Sharon's long hair was severely pinned flat to accommodate a wig of short fair hair, while Gayle's hair had been easily concealed beneath a wig of long black hair. "Now you see us," Sharon said, then replaced her wig, "And now you don't."

"Something I brought along in case it became necessary to confuse our appearances, Gayle said. She put her wig back on. "What do you think, just the job for giving members of the media the run-around?"

"It could . ." "I think . ." Danielle mulled the suggestion over in her mind, trying to imagine all the repercussions that might arise from such a deception. It seemed inspired.

"It's bloody marvellous," she declared.

"But I'll have to run it past DI Latimer first, and if he gives the okay, let Peter Ross know what's happening."

During the ferry's return journey, Gayle disengaged herself from Sharon and Danielle and slipped unobserved towards the bow of the boat. She took a package containing the automatic pistol and remaining ammunition from a pocket in her parka and held it over the side. In her mind she imagined a wounded Alan Swift dragging himself to his encampment, dressing his wounds from the first-aid kit, waiting for the weather to clear, removing all evidence of his habitation in case she reported the incident, painfully lugging it down the cliff and loading the dinghy, launching it on to the becalmed sea, thinking he had escaped, only to be caught by the second storm and drowned.

Gayle dropped the package into the sea.

Why would he have collected up the used cartridge cases, she wondered? Then realised that there would have been very little chance of the light copper cases being able to withstand the force of the storm, and that they had probably been scattered over the cliff and swept out to sea, and were now with what was left of Alan Swift beneath the waves.

Good riddance.

Chapter Twenty-four

"Sharon Greaves, is she the one with the black hair? Do you know, Steve?"

Steve, that was the name by which the paparazzi knew him. They accepted him as one of their own, and all he had had to do was carry a camera and case, and mention some of the places he had been. All of them had copies of the e-fit likeness but none suspected: amazing what a change of hair colour and simple alteration to the face can achieve.

"Yep, that's her," he said.

"Who are the other two, policewomen?"

"Probably." Within minutes it would be the accepted truth, facts and rumour spread like wildfire. A week earlier it had been the reported finding of the remains of Alan Swift, which caused him to smile to himself: now the heat would be off. Reportedly, Sharon was to be taken to a hotel in Stornoway, where she would spend the night before flying to London.

Along with the rest of the paparazzi he was watching the

three women disembark from the ferry, but his concentration was on Sharon, and the job to be finished. Beneath the hooded parka he was wearing a suit, with a silenced automatic pistol in the rear waistband of his trousers. He would have liked to use his hands but he didn't have the strength.

Mrs Agnes McBride was a suspicious woman; twenty years of marriage to Thomas – Tomcat – McBride had given her good reason to be.

He hadn't come home for lunch, there was no reply to the office phone and his mobile was switched off. She had waited until two-thirty then gone to his office, only to find he wasn't there. Neither was Nicky, the sixteen-year-old who was supposedly working her half-term break with McBride Property Letting as 'work experience'. As far as Agnes was concerned Nicky looked experienced enough, with the short t-shirts and low rise jeans that revealed her thong underpants every time she sat down or bent over – and somehow she was always bending over. The type of letting Nicky was most liable to do once she left school would have nothing to do with property.

Agnes inspected the board that held the keys, and saw that only one set was missing. Trust him to choose the most deserted spot. Sixteen, the dirty old sod.

She saw his car by the gated path that led to the property and parked her own across it to impair his escape. At least approaching the cottage on foot meant she wouldn't be heard.

The front door wasn't locked, neither was the one to the bedroom. Agnes found them in there. The bedclothes were ruffled but Tommy and Nicky weren't in the bed, they were at the foot, both still fully dressed, each with a bullet hole in the forehead.

The severed lower half of the leg that had been found washed up near Dunvegan Head, on the Isle of Skye, was sent to the forensic laboratory in Glasgow. Hair found in the Lewis cottage was also sent there for DNA analysis and comparison.

Fingerprints found in the cottage were forwarded to the Metropolitan Police Force headquarters in London, for comparison with those found during their searches when assisting Inspector Helen Skinner. In return, hair they had collected was sent to the Glasgow laboratory.

DI Andy Latimer considered the case all but closed, there being sufficient circumstantial evidence to link Alan Swift with the murder of Jonathan Greaves. All that was required to put the seal on it was the DNA comparison to confirm that the leg was Swift's and that he was presumed dead. He left the final coordination of evidence with DS Dean Hammond.

DS Danielle Nott was in a similar position in regard to the murder of the man known as Jean Mortier. In the meantime she had to get Sharon Greaves safely to London, unmolested by the members of the media.

The media circus, en masse, in convoy, followed the car taking Sharon Greaves to her hotel. On arrival the police herded them into the car park to await a photo-call and press conference with the lady. Those who could, checked into the hotel.

The security, for a man trained and experienced in penetrating the most heavily guarded compounds, was pathetic. Disuniting himself from the crowd by slipping under an ornamental hedge, Steve disappeared in name and substance. He reconnoitred the terrain and chose his point of entry: the kitchen. The parka placed beneath a tree, ready to be donned again, with the alias, when the hit was completed.

There had to be no mistakes.

DC Peter Ross was sitting in a chair, in the corridor, outside the room designated for Sharon Greaves, when he received the news of the discovery of the two bodies in the cottage, expertly killed by single shots to the forehead. He immediately contacted DS Danielle Nott on her mobile. She was at Stornoway Ferry Port, about to board and accompany a blonde wigged Sharon Greaves to the mainland, and hence to London. She quickly absorbed the news; it's possible repercussions and the permutation of options open to her: police manpower on the Isle of Lewis was limited: Alan Swift might be anywhere: she should remain with Sharon: Peter Ross required her assistance.

"Should I go to the cottage and investigate?" Ross asked.

Moving out of Sharon's earshot Danielle said, "Are you still armed?" Ross replied that he was. "Then tell them to put a cordon round the cottage and stay where you are I'll be with you as soon as possible."

"Problems?" Sharon asked.

"Change of plans." Danielle led Sharon to the Harbourmasters office, identified herself and asked for Mrs Greaves to be afforded sanctuary there until further notice. It was the best she could do in the circumstances.

"Are you going to tell me what is going on?" Sharon asked.

"There's been an incident, the police force here is stretched and I'm going to stand in for Peter Ross while he sorts it out. It shouldn't take long. I should be back before the ferry leaves, but if I'm not we can easily take the next one."

"Why can't I go on my own?"

"Because I've been ordered to escort you to London. Please, Sharon, a few more hours isn't going to make that much difference."

"You're right. Okay I'll wait until you get back."

Going back to the cottage had been a mistake. He had left it when he saw the police interest – they really were such amateurs, did they expect him to just walk back in there, one would have thought, knowing he was a professional, that he would always reconnoitre a base on returning – and camped out in the hills above, keeping tabs on the police surveillance through his binoculars. Their departure coincided with the discovery of the body remains, and the next day, lured by the sheer audacity of the act, he decided to chance moving back in to take a shower and change into the suit, shirt and tie. It was stupid, unprofessional vanity. He hadn't expected McBride and the girl, and it could have been far worse, the police. He was drying his hair from the shower when he heard them at the front door, and barely had time to locate and extract the gun from under the clothes on the bed and screw on the silencer before they entered the bedroom. The two clean shots to the heads was the only salvation to his professional pride.

There must be no such slip-ups this time.

He waited until one of the male kitchen staff appeared, alone, for a quick smoke. The man was rendered unconscious by a blow to the back of the neck, divested of his white coat and cap and hidden behind a stack of empty beer kegs. With full reservations for dinner, the kitchen was in turmoil and everyone was far too busy to notice one of their number pass through and into the passage leading to the hotel reception area. The coat and cap were discarded into a linen cupboard, and a lounge suited figure emerged into the busy hotel foyer, quickly ascending the stairs. The first floor was clear, but at the top of the stairs to the second floor a uniformed constable stood on guard.

"I'm sorry, sir, you can't come up here." They were the constable's last words as two body shots – chest and heart – sent him crumpling backwards.

"Jamie," a voice called, and a redheaded detective came running down the second floor corridor, endeavouring to find the unused-to pistol in the holster beneath his coat. He didn't stand a chance.

DS Dean Hammond received an e-mail from the Glasgow forensic laboratory. The initial DNA analysis result revealed that the hair found in the cottage did not match the leg. They were counter checking with the specimens sent by the Met and would send findings as soon as they were available. Hammond immediately reported the news to his boss: that the washed up leg did not belong to Alan Swift.

Latimer called Nott on her mobile and passed on the information. Danielle told him about the double cottage murders, that she was on her way to assist Ross, and that she had placed Sharon in the care of the harbourmaster – as there were insufficient police available she thought Sharon would be as safe there as anywhere. Latimer concurred and they both agreed that, until known otherwise, it had to be assumed Swift wasn't dead and that he had to be the prime suspect for the cottage murders.

Latimer said that he would contact her superior officer and put him in the picture, and suggest that the Armed Response Unit be returned to Lewis.

Stepping over the body of the red-haired detective he made his way down the corridor to where the chair parked outside indicated Sharon's room. There was no time for delay; he had got to know the newshounds only too well, always on the look out for a gap in security, one of them could appear at any moment. There was the muffled sound of a mobile telephone trilling somewhere. Was there another armed copper in the room?

He listened at the door. All was quiet. He gave it a tap.

"One moment, Peter," a woman's voice called out.

A lavatory flushed and a few moments later the door was opened.

Danielle could get no reply from Peter Ross's mobile. She pulled up outside the hotel's main entrance, flashing her warrant card to the constable on guard as she got out of the, unrecognised, hire car.

"Come with me," she said to him.

At the reception desk, again displaying her warrant card, she asked the clerk for the hotel telephone and Mrs Greaves' room number. She dialled it and heard it ring once then go dead. "Follow me," she ordered the constable.

The two e-mails arrived almost simultaneously: the findings of the second DNA analysis from the Glasgow forensic laboratory: followed by the discovery of the fingerprint checks made by the Metropolitan police.

Hammond rushed them into Latimer's office.

The woman staggered back as the door violently slammed into her. He saw her catch her leg on the edge of the bed and fall to the floor. She looked up at him and gasped. He looked at her in wonderment; the black wig had fallen off with the impact of the fall. There was a momentary hiatus, as both looked at one another in uncertainty, then he put two bullets into her body: chest and heart.

The bedside telephone rang. He pulled the cable out of the wall before it could ring again. Was Sharon hiding? He rushed into the bathroom and wrenched open the shower curtain, and then looked in the wardrobe and under the bed. Then the truth dawned in his confused brain: there had been a switch. Fuck!

Danielle saw the body of the dead constable and motioned the PC behind her to stay where he was. She pulled her pistol from its holster and peeked round the corner into the corridor, and saw Peter Ross's lifeless form.

Oh no!

Further along the corridor a chair stood beside an open door. Assuming the textbook position: a half crouch, arms outstretched with one hand supporting the gun hand, she moved into the corridor.

A fair-haired man exited from the open door. Her appearance surprised him and he crashed into the chair, loosing his balance.

"Stop! Police!" Danielle shouted, but it was obvious from the man's body language that he had no intention of obeying the command. He was righting himself and raising the long barrelled, silenced pistol when she squeezed the trigger. The bullet hit him where she had been taught to aim: the upper torso. He staggered backwards, once again falling foul of the chair and crashing to the floor, his gun spinning from his hand. As Danielle closed in she saw him stretching for the pistol. Keeping her pistol trained on his head she reached it before him and kicked it away. He closed his eyes. Danielle picked up the fallen pistol.

"Ma'am," the constable called enquiringly from the top of the stairway.

"Ring for an ambulance, as many as possible, this one's still alive." She peered through the open doorway and saw Gayle Meredith's sightless eye looking out at her. "But he's the only one." she said to herself.

Her mobile rang. It was Andy Latimer.

"Bit of confusion I'm afraid, Danielle. It now appears

that the leg does belong to Alan Swift, a DNA test using hair found in his flat and car confirm it. The hair in the cottage is that of Carl Peterson, the fingerprints taken from there match those retrieved from his London flat."

Danielle looked down at the unconscious face on the floor; mentally she changed the clean-shaven face and fair, longer hair for the short dark haired bearded face of the e-fit likeness.

"I think I've just found him," she said.

The Armed Response Unit arrived in time to help marshal the media corps who were besieging the hotel.

Carl Peterson was rushed by helicopter to a hospital on the mainland.

DS Danielle Nott was taken to the local infirmary. On the way she used her mobile to report to her boss. He said he was leaving for Lewis as they were speaking. She told the doctor who examined her that she felt fine. He said that her blood pressure was up. He gave her some sleeping pills and tranquillisers: "You may feel all right now," he said, "but you may well not when all that has happened finally hits you."

Her boss phoned to inform that the Chief Constable was also on his way to Lewis, and that he would be giving a press conference once he had assessed the situation. She was to inform the media of this but make no other statement.

"What about Sharon Greaves, should I continue as planned and escort her to London?" Danielle asked.

"Does she know what has happened?"

"Not yet, as far as I know."

"Then you had better put her up in some hotel, as discreetly as possible, and we'll decide how to get her to London tomorrow. Somehow I can't see it being done quietly now."

"No sir."

Then he enquired after her health.

Half a dozen reporters had followed Danielle to the infirmary and they surrounded her as soon as she stepped outside, where she told them what she had been instructed to say. "How's Sharon Greaves?" one of them asked. Danielle repeated her statement, and then said that she had to go back inside for some further tests.

Through the waiting room window, while dialling the Harbourmaster's office she watched the reporters leave. "Hello, this is Detective Sergeant Nott, can I speak with Mrs Greaves please."

"Mrs Greaves boarded the ferry shortly after you left her. It sailed an hour ago."

Chapter Twenty-five

Sharon Greaves entered the courtroom. There was a buzz from the public and press galleries; this was what they had been waiting for. She had not been seen during the two weeks preceding the trial, and had been conspicuously absent from the Isle of Lewis for the funerals of Detective Constable Peter Ross – a full dress uniform affair - and Gayle Meredith – far more muted with, the media outnumbering her brother, a cousin and one of the monks from the Howth monastery.

She was pale and dressed entirely in black, a simple linen sheath dress and jacket, with her hair – recently, and expensively, cut - hanging simply to her shoulders. An expert had applied the minimalist make-up earlier that morning.

The world knew that Sharon Greaves was the widow of the murdered Jonathan Greaves, with details of the murders and the shoot-out on the Isle of Lewis having filled the newspapers and news media- nationally and internationally for the preceding weeks. Interest was further stimulated by two other events. The verdict from the inquest into the death of Jonathan Greaves: that he had been murdered by Alan Swift (believed dead), as a result of Swift endeavouring to discover the whereabouts of Sharon Greaves, whom he had been hired to kill: and during the indictment of Carl Peterson for the unlawful killing of Gayle Meredith, when it was revealed that she had been killed in mistake for Sharon Greaves.

Speculation as to who had hired Swift and Peterson was galvanized when it becoming public knowledge that Wendy Lister was suing Lucidel for negligence, and that Sharon Greaves, previously Chief Chemist for CVC Ltd - the manufacturer of Fatale - was their leading expert witness. Conclusions were inevitable drawn and Lucidel shares dropped an alarming number of points.

The trial had opened two days previously, and the details of Lister versus Lucidel publicly aired, when Sharon Greaves entered the witness box and took the oath.

Council for the plaintiff's opened. After requesting her to repeat her name and profession – "Sharon Greaves, I have a degree in Chemistry," in a clear, precise voice - he handed her a thick bound folder and said, "Can you confirm that this is a statement of your involvement with the beverage that is sold under the trade name of Fatale?" She opened the folder, turned to various pages and examined them, then stated that it was.

Council addressed the bench. "It is a duplicate of the copies supplied to your lordship and my learned friend." Returning his attention to the witness he said, "Could you please summarise he contents of your statement, Mrs Greaves."

Sharon proceeded, without recourse to the folder in front of her, to give a concise history of her relationship with Fatale: from its concept, through the development, the successful marketing, her continued monitoring, trepidations, experiments, detailed reports of her conclusions to Lucidel and their refusal to withdraw Fatale from sale, the confiscation of her work on the matter, and her final dismissal. It was a performance that had been carefully rehearsed, modified and polished, by Sharon and Leigh Murray. Although précised, and omitting detailed scientific evidence, it took almost an hour to present, and was received by a silent, rapt courtroom.

"To reiterate, Mrs Greaves, did you present your findings and theory to Lucidel?"

"Yes, I sent them to the Head of Research, Otto Klee, with the recommendation that Fatale be withdrawn from sale."

Council presented her with a headed and dated typed letter. "Is this a copy of the letter that accompanied your findings?"

"It is."

"Your Lordship will note that it was dated a year prior to the plaintiff's unfortunate accident."

Council left it at that, and said that he had no further

questions for the moment, but that he would be recalling Mrs Greaves. Council for the Defence said the same. The court was adjourned.

Outside the courthouse Sharon posed for the cameras but refused to answer questions. Leigh Murray read a statement, within which was stated Mrs Greaves confidence in being able to answer any counter arguments from the defence, scientific or otherwise, to the court's satisfaction.

The next morning council for the plaintiff called three eminent scientists, each of whom stated that they had read and studied Mrs Greaves findings. Before the first of these had been able to speak, council for the defence had objected: Mrs Greaves had done this work while she was an employee of Lucidel and that it was therefore the property of Lucidel and being used illegally. The judge overruled the objection on the grounds that the information was in the public interest. The witness then went on to say and that he concurred with the findings, and Mrs Greaves theory on the detrimental damage to the nervous system. An opinion shared by the other two witnesses called. Video recordings of the experiments on the rats were shown to further argue the conclusions of the findings. Could the videos have been tampered to give a false impression, council for the plaintiff asked? The unanimous answer was no, that Mrs Greaves had scrupulously used counter checks and supportive, detailed notes to disprove such an accusation should it be made.

After lunch Council for the defence presented another three, equally eminent scientists, who's counter argument was that the findings were open to interpretation – they gave examples – that the conclusions were marred by bias, and that Mrs Greaves' theory of the damage to the nervous system was very far from proven.

At the end of the day an independent assessor would have said that honours were even.

Sharon was recalled the next day and council for the plaintiff reiterated the accusations put forward by the defence's witness of the previous day. Would she care to comment? In reply Sharon went over the points raised, one by one. She gave examples of the way results could be misinterpreted, and then demonstrating how she had allowed for this by approaching the issues from different directions, so as to counter any false impression, and support the initial finding. With regard to the claim that her theory of damage to the nervous system was inconclusive, she said that it was a logical conclusion on the information available, and as yet there had been no other theory presented. In fact Lucidel had had possession of her work up until the present moment, and for over a year preceding Ms Lister's accident, and during that time had been unable to reach an alternative theory.

In the afternoon council for the defendant cross-examined.

"How did you feel when your department at UVC was

closed and you were made redundant, Mrs Greaves?"

"I was upset for my staff, but I appreciated the reasoning behind the decision."

"Which was?"

"That the parent company, Lucidel, preferred to monitor quality control of the manufacture of Fatale from within their own laboratories, and as such my department was redundant to requirements."

"Wouldn't it be more accurate to say that your department was closed because you had been using it primarily for the purpose of conducting unauthorised experimentation?"

"Your words not mine. Lucidel were fully aware of the nature and content of my work, which was fully documented and included within my monthly reports to them."

"Your work and results would have been fed into the department computer?"

"Yes."

"And copies made?"

"Of course, it's standard; a safety procedure."

"When Lucidel decided to continue your departments work from their own laboratories the computer records, and the copies, would have been made available to them?"

"That is correct."

"But not all the copies, you kept one set for yourself."

"Yes."

"Illegally?"

"Yes."

"What was your reason for doing this?"

"Insurance."

"Were you aware that Lucidel continued with your line of research and to analyse the results?"

"I hoped they would but I had no way of knowing."

"But they didn't follow your recommendation?"

"To withdraw Fatale, no."

"To recap: you had used your department to conduct experimental work, contrary to standard procedure, which was subsequently taken out of your control, thus separating you from the product you had created, not to mention a lucrative salary. Lucidel subsequently discovered that you were not only redundant to requirement, but when your unauthorised work was analysed it was found to be based on an unfounded premise, and that the results are inconclusive and open – as we have heard expert witnesses testify – to conjecture. When your experiments and theory were dismissed as unfounded your reaction was one of anger and injured ego, and you sought revenge. Is it not true that as a result you have cajoled a distressed person into believing that the loss of her loved ones was as a result of my clients negligence, and that you are using the case as a means of conducting a personal vendetta?"

"That is completely untrue."

"I have no further questions, my Lord"

Council for the plaintiff took over. "Mrs Greaves, would

I be correct in saying that when UVC Ltd was acquired by Lucidel, as a major shareholder you received a settlement that was in the tens of millions?"

"That would be correct."

"And that your salary as Chief Chemist when you were made redundant would be in excess of £30,000 per annum."

"Well in excess."

"Which would represent, if my sums are correct, less than one months interest from your settlement invested at a modest return?"

"That would not be an unreasonable assumption."

"Not, I would venture, one of the contributing reasons, as my learned friend suggests, for conducting a vendetta."

"Personal gain, material or social, has never been my motivation in baring witness for Ms Lister. From the very outset of producing Fatale the inclusion of factor Y had given me cause for caution. Before allowing Fatale to go on sale we conducted extensive tests – which were presented to the Health and Safety Executive – until it was considered, as far as could be ascertained, safe for human consumption. Even then I continued to carry out tests and monitor the results. Tests that Lucidel were informed of and which were included in my monthly reports. When, as I have already stated, results began to give reason for concern I brought them to Lucidel's attention. After they declined to follow my advice and withdraw Fatale from sale, and following my dismissal I endeavoured to publish my findings in a scientific journal. Lucidel's reaction was to take out a high court injunction to prevent publication. I believe that my work confirmed there was a contributory link between Fatale and the symptoms that led to one untimely death, regretfully it wasn't until after Ms Lister's accident, and the deaths resulting from it, that I have been able to bring my conviction to public attention."

"Thank you, Mrs Greaves. No further questions, my Lord.

The court was adjourned for the weekend.

General opinion was that the advantage lay with Sharon Greaves and the case for the plaintiff.

"It's not going well," was how Ruben Nadleson summed up, after relating the days events in his nightly telephone report to Luc Barr.

"Then use the sex angle."

"I wouldn't advise it."

"It's all we have left. Isn't it said that the British public and judiciary might be ready to forgive murder, rape and robbery but never sexual indiscretion?"

"The British public might enjoy a bit of titillation but I think you'll find that these days, with so much hanky-panky from politicians and alike, that they're no longer scandalised. Besides, there's no jury involved, and judges tend not to be as censorious as the entertainment industry would have one believe. The stereotyped bumbling old fart is a thing of the past, if he ever existed in the first place."

"How about public opinion? Politicians still resign from office after they've been found shafting their secretary on the quiet," Barr retaliated.

"True," Nadleson conceded, "but it's more to do with it putting the security or integrity of the public office they occupy in jeopardy than sexual scandal."

"Can't you use that angle?"

"You mean insinuate that Sharon Greave's sexual proclivity adversely effected her scientific judgement."

"Being fucked out of her brain, fucked up her brain," Barr surmised, less eloquently. "Or perhaps one should say, impaired her integrity, her ability to impartially interpret the results of her experiments."

"Emm, I'm not sure, difficult to prove. Remember how the slur campaign fell apart when we were unable to obtain corroborative evidence."

"But it planted the seed. All that might be required now is implied conjecture, insinuation, sufficient to provide a margin for doubt." Barr warmed to the idea. "You've got the report McCoskey compiled, go through it and see what you can come up with."

"I'm not so sure . ."

"It's what you're paid for," Barr interrupted, "and results," he reminded the vacillating lawyer, before abruptly terminating the call.

Nadleson sighed. He extracted the dog-eared file that comprised McCoskey's report from his desk drawer. It was going to be a long night, and probably a cancelled weekend.

The following Monday Sharon Greaves was once again called to the witness box. Council for the defendant cross-examined. "Is it not true, Mrs Greaves, that you conducted a vigorous, surreptitious, extramarital, sex life throughout the duration of your marriage?"

"If, by surreptitious, you mean without the knowledge of my husband, then no, it is not true."

"Perhaps I should say private?"

"Discreet."

"But with the full knowledge of your husband?"

"Yes. Although he had little interest in the physical side of our marriage he was needful that I did."

"You had a regular series of casual partners, what would be termed as one-night stands, as well as belonging to a private sex club?"

Council for the plaintiff jumped to his feet. "Objection, my Lord, I fail to see the relevance of this line of questions."

The judge also aired his doubts, adding that the witness's private life had already been aired in the tabloid press. Defence council asked if he might, together with his learned friend, approach the bench. The judge nodded his assent. A muffled conversation ensued; then the judge proclaimed to the court that he would, provisionally, allow the questioning to continue, but that his patience was not to be tried.

Defence council repeated his last question to Sharon Greaves and she answered with a simple, "Yes." He then asked her if she was continuing with this life style during the period she was conducting her experiments. Again she answered to the affirmative. Was Professor Adam Taylor one of her partners during this period? He stated a date?

"Yes he was."

"Think carefully before you answer my next question, for I am prepared to subpoena Professor Adams if necessary, did you discuss your research and results with him?"

In the visitors gallery Ruben Nadleson watched Sharon Greaves closely. He saw her glance at her council, noticed him return an almost imperceptible nod, and felt a pang of anxiety. Could it be that Professor Adams' testimony was not unexpected, and that Sharon Greaves had been coached in anticipation? Was it just a nod of support, or one of confirmation for her to answer as rehearsed? Nadleson feared it might be the latter.

Adams' name had come up when he had cross-referenced the list McCoskey's team had compiled of Sharon Greaves possible sexual partners, with the names included in the plaintiff's submitted list of supportive witnesses. He then arranged to meet with Adams, on the excuse of re-checking certain facts, and had come away with what he thought could be submitted as sufficient reason to cast reasonable doubt on Sharon Greaves testimony. The impression Adams had given Nadleson was of an ambitious man, convinced of his own infallibility, but who's surroundings and demeanour suggested that it was an ambition that may not have been fully achieved. He had also come across as a man who would not bear a slight gracefully. Not ideal but the best he could come up with at such short notice. The defence had also considered using Adams but the controversy surrounding his work had decided them against calling him; and it had been presumed that it was for the same reason that the plaintiff's council had excluded him as a candidate to corroborate Sharon Greaves' conclusions to her experiments. Now, after Adams had readily revealed the nature of his entanglement with Sharon Greaves to Nadleson, it was obvious that it was not the only reason.

Adams had provided him with the ammunition he had been seeking, but the exchange of eye contact between Sharon Greaves and her council gave rise to a nagging doubt.

"Professor Adams is a neurologist, I sought his opinion," Sharon Greaves answered.

"What was his reaction?"

"As it touched on a line of research he was presently engaged in he was extremely interested."

"Was his opinion supportive?"

"He propounded a possible connection between the chemical composition of Factor Y and its effect on the muscular nervous system?"

"A possible connection that was subsequently eluded to in a highly controversial paper he published on the subject of muscular disorder."

"That is correct."

"Briefly, and in layman's terms, how would you describe this controversy?"

"The basis of Professor Adams paper was that certain types of muscular disorder result from the background and lifestyle of the sufferer, but the general consensus was that it was an ambiguous and contentious proposition, and that his findings were insufficiently researched, and that they were interpreted to suit the theory.

"But a theory, none the less, that was basically concurrent with your own?"

"Loosely, yes."

"Mrs Greaves, it has already been established that, even by today's lenient standards, you lead an amoral personal life. Could it not be construed that you used the same standards when it came to personal ambition? That, due to the nature of your relationship with Professor Adams, and because it suited your purpose, you chose to disregard the controversy surrounding his theories. That flattered by the romantic and supportive interest of a renowned academic you chose to go against the general consensus and let his opinion sway your judgement. A reasonable doubt, Mrs Greaves, that you elected to ignore in pursuit of your own interests?"

Sharon Greaves declined to comment.

"A case of ambition and infatuation clouding reasoned thought?" defence council persisted.

"Your words not mine."

"Thank you, Mrs Greaves. I have no further questions for this witness, my Lord."

A murmur swelled and reverberated around the courtroom, until silenced by the Clerk of the Court. The judge's head was bent over his notes as he busily added to them. In the public gallery an exuberant Ruben Nadleson, trepidations dispersed, mentally punched the air and silently shouted, "Yes!" A seed of doubt had been planted.

Council for the plaintiff rose to his feet and walked to the witness box. "Mrs Greaves, how long did the liaison between yourself and Professor Adams last?"

"Just the one night."

"Was this a mutual agreement?"

"No, Professor Adams was keen to continue."

"But you were not?"

"No."

"Did Professor Adams ask you for copies of the data from your experiments?"

"Yes."

"Did you comply?"

"No."

"Why was that?"

"I was still formulating the results of my work and had not reached any absolute conclusions. I was concerned that Professor Adams would use my data for his own purposes and compromise my results."

"How did he react to this double rejection?"

"He threatened that if I did not comply with his wishes he would inform my husband of our liaison. When I told him that I already had he became very angry. Following two further aggressive confrontations, I had my solicitor send him a letter, rejecting his personal and academic advances, and stating that unless he discontinued his harassment I would be forced to take legal recourse."

Council produced a document and presented it to the witness. "Is this a copy of that letter?" Sharon Greaves briefly studied it and said that it was. The dated letter, on the headed paper of a firm of solicitors, was then given to the Clerk of the Court, who showed it to the judge for his perusal, and then the defence council.

"Did Professor Adams then cease his demands?" Council continued.

"Yes he did."

"But he still used your work in his paper?"

"Obliquely."

"To echo my learned friend, a case of ambition and infatuation clouding reasoned thought."

Sharon Greave's face displayed no emotion. She said, "I suppose you could say that."

"You chose not to pursue Professor Adams' unethical use of your work?"

"No, as I said it was only used obliquely, besides which I had reached the conclusion that his theories were unsound, and that my findings would stand on their own merit."

During the thirty-minute recess he had requested, defence council consulted with Ruben Nadleson. "Do you want me to call Professor Adams?" he asked.

"Good God no, enough harm has been done already without having that egocentric idiot compound it further. I should have guessed his motive was self-promotional, whichever way the verdict goes he'll maintain that it proves his theory."

"Then there's nothing further I can do. We might have sewn the seed of possible doubt in the Judge's mind."

"Maybe," Nadleson said, without conviction.

He decided not to bother returning to the public gallery, having come to the conclusion that it was a lost cause, or to his office. And he was in two minds whether or not to telephone Luc Barr that evening. In reflection the whole business left him with two regrets: not unloading his Lucidel stock when he had the chance: and that one of the two attempts on Sharon Greave's life hadn't been successful.

Chapter Twenty-six

Following the award of £2.25.million to Wendy Lister, plus costs, an extra-ordinary meeting of Lucidel shareholders was called. The three motions tabled received an overwhelming vote in favour. They were (a) that Fatale be immediately withdrawn from sale, (b) that a fund of 50 million euros be set aside in anticipation of further law suits, and (c) that Luc Barr be immediately removed from the position of Chief Executive Officer.

The last motion, which came as no surprise to Luc Barr, was softened by the redundancy package of five years salary, equal to 7.5 million euro, that he had negotiated as part of his employment package when first appointed as CEO. After a career of being at the centre of multi-national commerce, and having no family or close friends, he feared that it would leave a large hole in his life. He relocated to southern Spain, a move he considered as semi-retirement, while he decided what his next career move might be, but he was barely settled there when he received the first of three offers – all for chief executive posts.

He is at present CEO for a company that sells and hires executive jet aircraft. Under his leadership sales and profits have trebled, as has his remuneration and bonuses.

Carl Peterson was tried and found guilty of the murders of Detective Police Constable Peter Ross, Gayle Meredith and Thomas McBride. He was sentenced to thirty years imprisonment on each charge, to be served concurrently.

A new entry is included in Chambers Medical Encyclopaedia.

Greaves Syndrome: a disorder to the muscular nervous system believed to be the result of a chemical imbalance caused by the reaction of a compound of tetranydronaphthalene with Artemisia absinthium, cider and various herbs. Discovered by Sharon Greaves BSc while Chief Chemist with CVC ltd., manufacturers of a beverage marketed under the brand name of Fatale (discontinued) that contained the above constituents.

Shortly after the remembrance service for Jonathan, attended by most of the village, and swelled by friends and members of the golfing fraternity – amateur and professional, with the proceeds from her husband's estate (bolstered by the timely sale of his Lucidel shares), after tax and the settlement of outstanding debts, Sharon purchased UVC from Lucidel.

Reverting to the original name of Ulme Valley Cider Ltd, she holds 95% of the shares, with her mother-in-law having the other 5 %. On his eighteenth birthday, together with the trust fund set up by his father from the sale of his Lucidel shares, Leon will be awarded a 40% holding. Sharon re-employed as many of the laid-off labour force as could be viably accommodated, and by purchasing apples and additives from accredited suppliers, acquired the necessary credentials to make Ulme Valley Cider an accredited producer of a range of organic ciders.

A general manager was appointed and Sharon resumed her role of chief chemist. Her duties were not exacting and allowed time for extensive visits to America, where Leon had elected to remain and attend high school, later graduating to university.

In addition, as a silent partner with the four musicians that formed the group Gayle has played with, she put up the money to purchase the bar where they performed, which was transformed into a rock and blues club, and called, after the name they knew her by, Della's. Ironically, and completely unknown to either of them, situated in a Spanish resort town only a dozen or so miles from where Luc Barr had initially retired.

The Howth Island monastery received a sizable donation.

The tragic waste of Gayle's life saddened Sharon more

than she would have previously thought possible. Apart from Jonathan she eschewed personal relationships and had never had a close woman friend, but during the three months they had spent together she had developed a deep platonic love for Gayle. She was cognizant that it was a friendship forged by the peculiar circumstances of their enforced coexistence on the island, and that its intensity would have been dissipated with the return to normality, but she liked to think that it would have been a lasting friendship.

In her own way she grieved for Gayle.

She grieved for Jonathan.

But life had to go on. Sharon continued to reside in Calderham Manor and, outside of her work schedule, returned to the pursuits of her previous life: chess, bridge, working out at the health centre, making solitary excursions to the Picture House, and sex. During the year following the events of the island her libido seemed to go into limbo. On it's re-emergence she was wary of casual pick-ups and in their place cultivated a selection of partners - to accompany her to concerts, theatre, functions, etc., as well as bed. But missing the spontaneity of the one-off encounter, she continued to attend the clandestine sex club regularly.

It was generally considered that Sharon Greaves had survived the trauma of the previous year amazingly well. But then they didn't know her as Jonathan and Gayle had, and they weren't to realise that the overwhelming emotion that dictated Sharon Greaves' existence was the pursuit of her own desires.

Sharon never completely accepted that Alan Swift was dead, but she rarely thought about him. In all but buried memory he had ceased to exist: except for the odd occasion when, on a busy street or in a crowded throng, or walking from the cinema to where the car was parked, out of the corner of her eye, she thought she saw his figure limping towards her, and her heart skipped a beat.

Alan Swift's body was never found. He is described as being missing, believed dead, but remains on the wanted list.

Chapter Twenty-seven

Adrian Flynn, Brother Adrian, sat on a cliff top on Howth Island whittling a piece of wood and thinking about Gayle Meredith. Her death hung on his conscience. Had he done the right thing? It was on this spot, all those months ago, he had seen her shoot the man he now knew to be Alan Swift.

The deteriorating weather had given him cause for concern and he mentioned his fears of a storm to the Abbot. Father Cecil agreed that it would be safer for Gayle to shelter in the monastery until the weather turned for the better. She wasn't in either of the cabins, so he carried on to check on the few sheep the farm possessed - to ensure none was likely to be in a spot where it would be unable to shelter from the storm.

It was as he neared the western side of the island that he heard the pistol shot; and of all the inhabitants on Howth Island none was better experienced to recognise the sound of a small calibre pistol being discharged that Adrian Flynn – being witness to a few disciplinary executions had ensured that. Cautiously he ran in a crouch towards the direction of the shot, and reached the incline in time to see a man roll down it, with Gayle, standing outside the ruined cottage, firing a second shot. The wounded, limping man then scurried for the shelter of some rocks and Gayle ran down the incline after him. Adrian followed them as the weather closed in: he saw the pursuit to the cliff top, Gayle empty the magazine of the pistol, and the man fall backwards and out of sight.

Adrian was stunned, didn't know what to do. He saw Gayle turn away from the cliff edge and watched as like some sort of automaton, she walked back in the general direction of the cabins. Was the man still alive? Adrian reached the cliff edge and peered over: the wind driven rain stung his eyes, on a rocky ledge, some hundred or so feet below, he could make out the form of a spread-eagled body. He thought it unlikely that the man would have survived the bullets and the fall, and in this weather it would be futile to risk his own life to make sure.

Gayle was entering her cabin by the time he caught sight of her again. She was in a dazed state when she opened the door to him, and collapsed when they reached the monastery. Brother Neil took her into the infirmary and put her in a bed next to the tranquillised Sharon. The storm raged. During the night Adrian sat by Gayle's bed and listened as, drifting in and out of consciousness, unaware of his presence, she spoke of having to save Sharon's life.

When the storm abated the next day he knew what he had to do. There was no choice; Gayle had once put her life on the line to save him. There wouldn't be much time, sea birds were still flying towards the mainland and all the signs indicated that a second storm was following on the coat tails of its predecessor. He went back to the cliff top, and looking down he saw that the rocky outcrop had somehow held the body, presumably because it was situated sufficiently high to be out of reach of even the highest sea. He surveyed the climb, down and back, and decided the he wouldn't want to have to do it more than once. If he was going to get rid of the body it meant that all traces of the man would also have to go, so before doing anything else he needed to go and check out the ruined cottage, where the man had obviously been staying, before making the perilous decent.

Cooking utensils and tins of food were scattered about the ruined cottage as well as a collapsed tent. Righting the tent he found a haversack, first aid kit and sleeping bag on top of a ground sheet. Adrian dismantled the tent and rolled it up with the ground sheet. He collected up the scattered articles, opened the commodious backpack and put them into it. The first aid kit had a familiar look, he opened it and seeing the way the articles were packed remembered where he had seen something similar before: a captured British undercover soldier. Adrian emptied the box and found the secret compartment at the bottom. It held a lightweight automatic pistol with attachments for turning it into a sniper's rifle, plastic explosive, detonators and timing device. The man was a professional. Gayle had been very brave or very foolish.

Picking up the spent nine spent cartridges, before attempting the climb down the cliff, he guessed from the excess shots – the first two had probably done the job – that Gayle must have also been very frightened.

The descent was as bad as he had anticipated, made more difficult with the shouldered backpack. With the tide now out Adrian was able to see beneath the ledge, that held the broken body, there was a cave, within which was an inflatable dingy with an outboard motor wrapped in a tarpaulin. Adrian had a mental picture of a blazing Viking funeral ship.

Adrian looked out to sea and remembered. It had only required a small piece of the plastic explosive; the outboard's petrol tank had done the rest. A ball of fire. For an ex bomb maker setting the explosive, detonator and time had been the easy part. Far more difficult had been getting the craft and its cargo out there: manhandling the dinghy from the cave and into the sea, loading the body and backpack into it, securing the outboard tiller, starting the motor and then having to dive into the freezing water once the boat was headed straight out to sea.

Later, when the police arrived, he had learned who the man was and why he was there. It was while helping them in their search that he found and secreted the hunting knife.

If he hadn't done anything, and the body had been discovered, would Gayle have been safely in a cell, on remand for a crime she would more than likely have been acquitted, instead of in a hotel being murdered by mistake?

Adrian shrugged, he would never know. He got to his feet, tossed the piece of wood over the cliff and sheathed the knife. He headed back to the monastery, to try and seek a peace of mind he doubted he would ever find.

Footnote

In the pre-qualifying trials for the United States Winter Olympics ice skating team, half way through her presentation, fourteen-year old Sallyanne Cook suddenly lost control of her limbs and collapsed on the ice.

She was taken to hospital, where her mother told the duty doctor that it was the second time that this had occurred. After examining her, the doctor summoned the hospital's neurologist. Sallyanne was subjected to further tests and, subsequent to obtaining second and third opinions, and consultation via the Internet, she was diagnosed to be displaying Greaves Syndrome.

Sallyanne and her parents were teetotal Mormons from Salt Lake City, Utah, where Fatale had never officially been on sale. Daughter and parents categorically stated that they had never drunk Fatale.

Sallyanne had never even heard of it.

When it was withdrawn from worldwide sale she had been nine years old.

Made in the USA